Fire Maidens: London

Billionaires & Bodyguards
Book 2

by Anna Lowe

Twin Moon Press

Editing by Lisa A. Hollett

Covert art by Kim Killion

Contents

Other books in this series

Fire Maidens - Billionaires & Bodyguards

Fire Maidens: Paris (Book 1)

Fire Maidens: London (Book 2)

Fire Maidens: Rome (Book 3)

Fire Maidens: Portugal (Book 4)

Fire Maidens: Ireland (Book 5)

visit www.annalowebooks.com

Free Books

Get your free e-books now!

Sign up for my newsletter at *annalowebooks.com* to get three free books!

- *Desert Wolf*: Friend or Foe (Book 1.1 in the Twin Moon Ranch series)

- *Off the Charts* (the prequel to the Serendipity Adventure series)

- *Perfection* (the prequel to the Blue Moon Saloon series)

Chapter One

Gemma clutched the overhead railing as the subway car rattled around a curve. It was just a normal afternoon in London, and yet the hair on the back of her neck prickled. The minute she'd left her floating home — a barge in Regent's Canal — she'd had the sensation of something afoot. As if someone had left an unsigned note that said, *I'm coming for you, sweetheart. Ready or not, here I come.*

Which would have been paranoid — except for one thing. She had moved to London in a hurry, fleeing a creepy man who had been stalking her in Boston. Petro was his name, and he'd claimed she belonged to him. *Belonged*, like a goddamn pet.

You, Maiden. You are mine, and I shall have you.

A shiver went down her spine, and she reminded herself how careful she'd been to leave Boston without a trace. She'd flown via New York, changed airports and airlines, and paid in cash. So, technically, she had little to fear.

Still, those internal sirens refused to stop wailing, keeping her on edge.

She scanned the subway for the tenth time. Most of the other passengers had that checked-out look typical of commuters on the London Underground. Other than a tourist couple murmuring to each other while pointing out stops along the Northern line, everyone was silently scrolling through their phones. People of all nations, religions, languages, and cultures — something Gemma loved about London, one of the most multicultural cities in the world.

Still, that edgy, *I'm being followed* feeling didn't let up. But surely, London was far enough — and big enough — to shake off the man who'd been so obsessed with her back home?

1

Gemma turned her bracelets nervously. What if she hadn't been careful enough? She traveled to London regularly to visit her father, so how hard could it be to track her down?

"On your way to Hyde Park, love?" someone asked.

Gemma nearly jumped out of her skin, even when she turned to find an older woman with a friendly smile.

"How did you know?"

The woman motioned to the *Say No to Racism* sign Gemma held. "My granddaughter told me about the rally."

Gemma exhaled and gave her sign a little wave. "Yes, I'm going. Are you?"

The woman shook her head. "Not today, sadly. But I did sign the petition."

Gemma nodded. It was a start, she supposed. But if people really wanted to see significant change, they had to work for it, and that meant informing themselves, attending rallies, and voting to make their voices heard.

Still, the change she most wished for was to shake that ominous feeling she'd had all day.

"The next stop is King's Cross St. Pancras," a recorded announcement blared. "Change for the Victoria, Piccadilly, Metropolitan, and Circle Lines."

The subway rattled into the station, and Gemma stepped out, trying not to worry. Still, she kept throwing glances over her shoulder and peering into the mirrors set up at blind corners of the twisting underground walkways. When she reached the Piccadilly line platform, she paced. The next train would arrive in only three minutes, but that felt like an eternity, and her heart hammered. The sense of looming danger intensified, as if someone were chasing her and getting nearer all the time. Why?

Finally, the train rolled in, and she scanned the passengers quickly and boarded.

"This train is ready to depart. Please stand clear of the doors," the announcement said.

"So, go already," Gemma muttered.

Doors all along the train slid shut, but one in the next car bounced open when a last-minute passenger rushed in. As the

2

train rolled into motion, the man turned, peering down the length of the subway. When he spotted Gemma, he grinned.

Gemma's blood ran cold. That wasn't Petro, the man who'd been stalking her at home, but they looked a lot alike. Hell, they acted alike, right down to that weird sniffing action, as if they were part dog. And the faces... The resemblance was close enough to make that man and Petro brothers.

Gemma's mouth opened in a silent cry as the train rolled into motion. She backed up slowly, praying she was imagining things. Still, she dug out her keys and anchored the longest, sharpest one between two fingers as she'd learned in self-defense class.

Help, she wanted to cry out. *I think that man is after me.*

Petro had never physically threatened her, but it had started to feel as if he might. And this man was even scarier. Voldemort-scary, even if his face wasn't disfigured by anything more than a cruel frown. He shoved through the set of connecting doors and entered her car, still grinning. Not a friendly, *fancy seeing you here* grin. If anything, his expression was cruel and triumphant, like that of a man about to crush a bird under his boot. And his eyes... God, they were glowing, just like Petro's had.

Got you, those eyes said. *Now where will you go?*

Gemma eyed the emergency brake. *Emergency* was right, but halting the subway between two stations wouldn't help. She gripped her rally poster harder. The cardboard stapled to the top — *Say No to Racism!* — wouldn't be much use as a weapon, but the wooden handle might help.

Step by step, she backed up to the last door in the car. And step by step, Petro's look-alike approached.

"The next stop is Leicester Square," an announcement said.

Every muscle in her body tensed. Should she jump out at the next station and run?

The man raised an eyebrow, and his cocky smile said, *Sure, run. I can run too, Maiden.*

Her hand trembled. The man hadn't uttered a sound, yet Petro's words had echoed through her mind. *Maiden.* What did it mean?

3

She'd met Petro at a rally on Boston Common — *Stop cruelty to animals* — and though he'd come on strong, she hadn't thought much of the encounter, especially once she'd shaken him in the crowd. But he had turned up at a PETA meeting a week later without showing the slightest interest in the cause. He just stared at her the whole time. Next, he had appeared on her bus ride to work. When she'd stormed over to demand what the hell he wanted, he had flashed that *I know something you don't know* grin and uttered, *You, Maiden. You are mine, and I shall have you.*

Which was creepy as hell. What kind of person came out and uttered something like that? And what was with the *Maiden* part?

She stared at the man in the subway. Like Petro, he was a tall, twentysomething with short dark hair. She might even call him handsome if it weren't for the cruel glint in his eyes. His designer slacks and black silk shirt gave him the look of a young stock trader who'd left his jacket in his corner office. No tie, but his sleeves were anchored by shiny cufflinks. All in all, he had the same look as her stalker. If he spoke, would he sound like Petro too? Petro had a trace of an accent, like the son of a wealthy Italian banker who'd topped off a private school education with four years in the Ivy League.

And, geez. Why would a guy like that stalk a girl like her? She was pretty enough in a girl-next-door way, but hardly the type to drive a man to extremes.

I want you, Maiden. And soon, I will have you, the man in the subway car mouthed, just as Petro once had.

Gemma raised her chin and made sure her eyes telegraphed defiance, not fear. No man would bully her into anything.

But, dammit. The man's eyes sparkled in amusement, as if that was all part of the fun.

There were three sets of doors in that subway car, and as the train decelerated toward the station, Voldemort paused by the first set, ready to follow if she made a break for the platform. Gemma stepped to the third and last set of doors, leaving one exit between her and him. If she were lucky, there

4

would be enough of a crowd to mask her movements, and she could decide whether to rush out or to remain on the train.

The train stopped, but the door didn't open. She thumped on it. "Dammit..."

"Mind the gap," the announcement said as every door on the train opened except hers.

Only then did she spot the notice taped to the doors. *Out of order. Please use next exit.*

She could have screamed. Now what? Passengers stepped on and off, using the door between her and the stalker. But when she took a step toward that exit, Voldemort advanced, ogling her through the crowd.

Got you, sweetheart.

One last passenger boarded the car, stepping between her and him. The doors closed, and the train slowly got under way.

At first, Gemma tried peering around the newcomer to keep an eye on Voldemort. But once she registered the new arrival, it was impossible to look at anyone else. Her spinning mind coasted for a moment, giving her time to take in the details. Enjoy them, almost.

Unruly golden-brown hair wound around the newcomer's ears, and wide shoulders tapered to the waist of his jeans. His head brushed the ceiling, he was that tall. His skin had the healthy, bronzed tint of a man who spent time in the sun. Definitely not a banker, lawyer, or marketing type. His eyes were distant, as if he were thinking about the rugby game he was scheduled to star in, how much weight to dead-lift, or how things at his construction job were coming along. At least, that's what Gemma imagined, because he could easily have been any of those things.

Then his eyes met hers, and a warm, genuine smile spread over his face. His eyes lit up, and for a moment, Gemma wondered if she knew him and even fumbled for his name. Richard? Michael? Will?

Lancelot, a corner of her mind decided. *A knight in shining armor.*

Then she remembered the stalker, and her smile faded. Voldemort was at the far set of doors, she was at the near set, and Lancelot was at the exit in the middle of the car.

Please, she wanted to whisper to Lancelot. *Help me. Please.*

Behind him, Petro's look-alike leaned into view, and Gemma froze. Her alarm must have shown, because Lancelot's smile vanished, and his nostrils flared as he spun to face the stalker. Everything about his stance bristled with power.

The stalker's expression changed too, and he and Lancelot stood facing off like a couple of gorillas. They didn't actually rage and beat their chests, but they did give off serious vibes. Vibes packed with testosterone, anger, and...something she couldn't quite define. A raw, elemental force that made the air around their shoulders shimmer.

They were so still, it was frightening. The orange-red hue of the stalker's eyes intensified, and he balled his hands into fists.

"The next stop is Piccadilly Circus," an announcement declared. "Change for the Bakerloo line."

Voldemort's eyes shifted to her, then snapped back to Lancelot, and Gemma swore she heard a mafioso's voice in her mind.

She's mine. Mine, I tell you.

I'm nobody's, she wanted to yell, though the other passengers would have thought her nuts. Was no one else aware of the energy crackling between those two men?

The train screeched into the next station, and Gemma held her breath. With the nearest exit out of order, all she could do was wait or rush for the middle door. If she did, would the stalker grab her, or would Lancelot stop him, giving her the chance to flee?

The doors slid open. The stalker's eyes became those of a cobra aiming its venom, but Lancelot didn't budge.

"This train is ready to depart," the announcement said. "Please stand clear of the closing doors."

Lancelot leaned toward the stalker as if to say, *Yeah, asshole. Time for you to depart.*

Gemma held her breath. Lancelot's shoulders stiffened in one final warning, and—

The stalker shot Gemma one last, lethal look, then stomped out. The doors closed, locking him out. As the train chugged away, he stood on the platform, eyes blazing, lips moving with one parting message.

You are mine, Maiden. And soon, I will have you.

Gemma shook inside, but on the outside, she bared her teeth. *Try me, asshole.*

Then, *zoom!* The train accelerated around a corner. Lancelot watched her stalker disappear, then stepped over to Gemma.

"Everything all right?"

His voice was smooth as golden honey, his eyes concerned.

Gemma nodded and tossed her hair. "Fine." Which she was, now that Voldemort was gone and she got to gaze into Lancelot's eyes.

And, wow. She'd never seen eyes quite as deep or sparkly as his. Sweet, gold-green eyes that could draw a girl in and tempt her with all kinds of things.

"Truly all right?" he asked.

She gave herself a little shake. She'd never been the swoon-over-a-man-at-first-sight type, but she could barely get a word out. "Yes, thanks."

He motioned over his shoulder. "You know him?"

"No. Do you?" She could have sworn there'd been a glint of recognition in the stalker's eyes.

Lancelot shook his head, though she wasn't convinced.

She tilted her head. "Do I know you?"

It felt like she ought to, though she was sure she didn't. It was more like they'd met in a previous life or had a mutual friend who'd told her all about the wonderful guy she simply had to meet.

He cracked into a grin, and just like that, his relaxed, easy-going side returned, though the sense of coiled power remained. For some reason, she imagined him as a lion — roaring away his foes one moment, and the next, snoozing peacefully in the sun.

"You know me now. Liam Bennett. Pleasure to meet you."

The moment his hand covered hers, heat rushed through her veins, and she swayed. But that was just the motion of the subway, right?

"Gemma," she said. First name only, in case Lancelot turned out to be a creep.

The train lurched around a tight corner, and she all but stumbled into his arms. She nearly stayed there too, it felt that good.

She cleared her throat and forced herself away. "Sorry."

His eyes twinkled. "All good."

Someone shuffled by, and she and Lancelot — er, Liam — were forced to inch closer again. And, wow. The London Underground had been modernized over the years, but Gemma would have sworn sparks crackled in the air. Even Liam seemed to hold his breath.

"The next stop is Green Park," the PA announced. "Change for the Victoria and Jubilee lines."

Gemma took a deep breath and gave Liam a little space. He motioned to her sign — the one she'd managed not to thump into his groin, thank God — and raised an eyebrow.

"Say No to Racism?"

She raised the sign higher. What a pity it would be if Lancelot turned out to be a prick. "You don't think it's a cause worth rallying for?"

Liam stuck up his hands. "It's a great cause. It's just that your accent made me think you were a tourist."

"Not a tourist," she growled. "My father is English."

He raised his hands higher. "Sorry. Not implying anything. I'm only half English myself."

She waited, fully expecting to hear about Viking lineage. But instead, Liam said, "My father was Welsh."

She burst into laughter, and Liam grinned.

"You're the first Yank — beg your pardon, half Yank — I've met who knows the difference between the two."

She grinned. "Oh, I know the difference, all right. My dad took me walking in Wales lots of times. I love the Brecon Beacons."

Liam's face took on a soft, sentimental look, and he murmured, "I haven't been there in years."

And, dang. There were those sparks, charging the air around her again. But then the next announcement blared out, and they both looked up.

"The next stop is Hyde Park Corner. Change for the Victoria and Jubilee lines."

Gemma pursed her lips. She really had to get herself together.

"Well, this is me," she said at exactly the same time Liam did.

They looked at each other in surprise. Then Liam chuckled. "Fancy that."

Every time he smiled, she couldn't help doing the same. "So, you're going to the rally after all?"

And, hey. That didn't count as flirting, right? She was just rallying supporters for an important cause.

Liam smiled. "I was heading home, but—"

His phone rang just then, and he dug it out of his pocket with an annoyed look. "Hello?"

Gemma looked away, cursing the damn thing.

"Yes?" Liam listened to whoever was on the line. Probably a gorgeous supermodel asking him for a date.

The train stopped at the next station, and they both exited. Gemma headed for the Hyde Park exit, and when Liam followed, her hopes rose.

But his voice dropped as he strode along at her side. "Now? Right now?" He paused. "They can't wait?"

Gemma forced herself to look away. That was none of her business, right?

"I was going to a rally," he said into the phone. "Say No to Racism. It's *important*," he emphasized, making her grin. But after a pause to listen, he sighed. "Dammit, Sergio..." He listened for a moment, glowering the whole time. "Fine. I'll be right there." Then he hung up with an angry jab.

"Demanding boss?" she joked, telling herself she wasn't disappointed.

Liam's eyes clouded. "Something like that."

9

Still, he remained at her side all the way up the stairs and into the park. When she'd entered the Tube earlier, the sky had been dark and foreboding. Now, the sun was shining in one of those mercurial changes in English weather. Pedestrians streamed in all directions, and a voice blared through a megaphone in the distance. The rally was getting started.

"Well, I ought to go. Thank you again."

Gemma meant it, and yet, she found herself rooted in place.

Liam's honey eyes darkened a shade, and his lips moved wordlessly before he finally spoke. "Why don't I give you my number? Just in case."

"In case what?"

Liam motioned back to the subway station. "In case dragon man there shows up again."

She chuckled. Dragon man — that was fitting. The man sure had been intense. But the more she thought about it, the more ridiculous her fear seemed. Nightmares of Petro had plagued her the previous night, so she could have been projecting that on to an innocent stranger. Maybe he hadn't been a relative of Petro's at all.

Still, she couldn't help feeling disappointed that Lancelot — er, Liam — wasn't offering his number for friendship's sake. Quickly, efficiently, she typed his number into her phone and stored it under L. Liam. God, she loved that name. Then she looked up into those amazing, honey-green eyes one more time and forced a chipper, "Thanks. Bye."

"Anytime."

His voice was low and mournful, a sound that went with those *Please don't leave* puppy-dog eyes. Like her, he stood quietly, not making a move.

Ask him, her heart begged. *Ask him if he wants to meet sometime.*

She rolled to the balls of her feet, and Liam leaned closer.

Asking doesn't hurt, she told herself.

Butterflies danced in her belly as she opened her mouth to speak. But Liam's phone beeped first, and he scowled. At the same time, a cheer went out from the direction of the rally.

"I'd better go," she sighed as his phone beeped and beeped.

10

He nodded wearily. "Me too." Then he flashed a sad smile. "A pleasure to meet you, Gemma."

God, was he sweet. And, oops. Was she blushing?

"Pleasure to meet you."

She turned away, intending to hurry off. But three steps later, her feet shuffled to a stop, and she found herself turning.

Liam was still there, looking at her like he didn't want her to go. And, heck. She didn't want to go either.

"Call me if you need anything," he said over the incessant beeping of his phone. "I promise to answer faster than I answer this bloody call."

He was so earnest, she could picture him in chain mail with his hand on a sword, making a solemn vow. But it was impossible to dwell in her fantasyland with his phone bleating like that. So she waved a second time, clutching her rally sign tightly.

"Thank you. Goodbye."

That time, she forced herself to turn, get real, and walk away. She'd been brought up to believe in civil action, not love at first sight. And if her heart ached as she went, well, she would survive.

Chapter Two

"Answer that, for God's sake," someone snapped.

Liam blinked. For a few moments, he'd been an island in a stream of humankind, and time had slowed down as he watched Gemma go. Now, the world rushed by again, and his phone made an earsplitting sound.

He fumbled with it. "Yes?" Then he frowned. "I'm coming."

"You are not coming," Sergio said in his rat-a-tat-tat, Italian accent. "You are standing in the corner of the park. *Mannaggia.* Never mind. I'm already here."

A limousine pulled up at the curb, and the door swung open. "Get in," Sergio grumbled.

Liam didn't budge. He was still staring in the direction Gemma had gone. One minute, she'd been there with that beguiling smile and long, silky hair that was somewhere between black and brown — and the next, she was lost in the crowd.

"The Guardians are waiting," Sergio said.

Liam didn't care who was waiting. Not with his inner lion growling the impossible in his mind.

Mate. Don't let her go!

His heart felt like it had doubled in size, squeezing against his lungs. His throat was dry, and little birds sang in his ears. Bloody hell. What was wrong with him?

Love, his lion insisted.

Love, an even deeper voice echoed in his mind.

"We're already late for the meeting," Sergio warned. "*Andiamo.*"

Liam slid into the vehicle, then cursed himself. Had a decade in the military made him that quick to follow orders without questioning them?

"Wait," he tried, reaching for the door.

But it was too late. The limousine pulled into traffic and was on its way. Past the row of luxury apartments where he lived, past the crowds of people milling toward the rally. Right past his own destiny, it felt like.

"What's wrong with you?" Sergio demanded.

I just found — and lost — my mate, his lion said.

Liam frowned. That couldn't be. Maybe it was just a little lust — something every normal, functioning lion experienced from time to time. And no wonder, given the way Gemma's trim body had fit so comfortably against his when they'd bumped in the subway.

Except, he'd felt lust before, and this was not the same. Lust was when the body yearned for physical release. This time, his soul was yearning too.

He twisted in the seat, looking back. Sergio twisted as well. "What?"

Liam wasn't sure. Could that really have been his mate? His destiny?

He forced himself to face forward. Man oh man. He'd been spending too much time around shifter species who believed in that kind of thing. Wolves crooned on and on about love, fate, and forever, believing with childish certainty that somewhere out there was a single, predestined partner just for them. Dragons were even more enamored of the concept of love, as if it wasn't just another fleeting emotion but an entire force in itself. Bears were fairly laid-back about the whole fable — until they met Miss Right. Then a perfectly grounded, reliable grizzly would go loopy with love, ready to drop everything and make a fool of himself for the woman he adored.

Lions, on the other hand, were far more reasonable when it came to matters of the heart. Love was fun. Flirty. And above all, fleeting. It never lasted. Lions formed attachments, dissolved them, and moved on. Any self-respecting male waited until his golden years to settle down. Only then would he find a suitable mate — a pretty young female who could be counted on to take care of him as the years went by. Oh, and to make sure he left a few heirs. So really, the only aspect of fate lions heeded were their expiration dates.

Love wasn't written in the stars or whispered on the wind. It came and went, like day and night, the seasons, or an ocean tide.

And yet, there he was, barely moving, barely breathing.

Gemma, his inner lion cried.

Who was she? Where was she from? Her accent said American, but her porcelain-perfect face had a hint of Asia mixed into predominantly Anglo roots. Her father was English, she'd said. But that barely scratched the surface, and he knew it. One look into the depths of her dark, East-meets-West eyes and he'd known she was something else.

In the subway, she'd looked spooked yet ferocious, as if that stubby stick in her hand could function as a sword. And, hell. She looked like she could — and would — use it.

"There was a woman..." he started.

Sergio put his face in his hands. *"Mamma mia."*

Liam shook his head. "Someone was after her."

Sergio's brow knotted. "Who?"

"I'm not sure."

The man in the subway had been a shifter of some kind, though Liam hadn't been able to identify which — not from that distance, and not with all the interfering scents of the Underground. A dragon? A wolf? Just about the only thing Liam could rule out was feline. Whoever that shifter was, he'd frightened Gemma badly.

She's mine, the ass had declared, as if he had the God-given right to claim any woman he fancied.

She's mine, Liam's lion growled in his mind.

But, wait. Did that make him just as bad?

Sergio threw up his hands. "Is that significant? I doubt the Guardians will think so."

It was significant, and Liam knew it, though he couldn't explain why. He burned to run after Gemma. To protect her. To get to know her.

ANNA LOWE

He looked back again. She was going to a rally. Well, he could rally. *Say No to Racism?* That was a good cause.

But the Guardians had their own causes, and they would never understand.

"Not even three weeks in London, and you're already working on losing your job," Sergio warned. "My job, too. Did the Legion teach you nothing about responsibility?"

Liam snapped around at that echo of all the warnings he'd received throughout his life.

Lions are responsible. Dutiful. Make sure you remember that, lad.

We live to serve. To protect. To maintain our pride's power.

Remember who you are, boy. A lion from the mighty Blackwood pride.

He stuck out his jaw as the gates of Buckingham Palace flashed by. Ten years ago, he'd signed up for the Foreign Legion, determined to forget who he was — a half-breed, the product of forbidden love. But somewhere along the line, his roots had started calling to him like never before, and here he was — back in London, ready to serve a greater cause alongside the members of his illustrious pride.

So, get on with it, he told himself. Duty wasn't about chasing after women. It was following orders for the common good.

He shot one last look in Gemma's direction. His mother and father might have felt that kind of irrepressible pull toward one another, but look where it had gotten them.

But— his lion tried.

The limousine driver beeped at a tourist who'd strayed into the oncoming lane. Liam's eyes drifted to the figures surrounding the statue of Queen Victoria. Four men and women in bronze, each with a snarling lion alongside. If that wasn't a reminder of duty, what was? Lions had protected the kingdom from the very beginning.

Liam closed his eyes wearily, but all he saw was Gemma. When he opened them again, he spotted Sergio flicking a speck of dust off his sleeve.

16

"I was on my way home," Liam muttered, trying to focus on something other than Gemma.

"I was already home." Sergio sighed. "Or as at home as possible two thousand kilometers from Rome."

If Liam had been his usual, lighthearted self, he would have poked fun at his friend. The man was as dark, broody, and impeccably dressed as ever. Who dressed like that to relax at home? In the Legion, Sergio had even managed to make fatigues look stylish. When their all-shifter unit had retired from the service, they'd all headed to a bar to celebrate — except Sergio, who'd only joined them after a visit to a tailor. Now, he looked like he'd stepped straight from the pages of a men's style magazine.

Liam raked his fingernails over his jeans, imagining the looks he'd get when he walked into the Council meeting. And when he pictured the matriarch who presided over it all. . .

He winced and slumped in his seat.

Sergio, on the other hand, peered out the window with interest. He was new to London and to the city's Guardians, so he didn't know what awaited them. Liam, on the other hand, knew all too well.

The limousine passed St. James Palace, swung around a few corners, and coasted down a side street. One that didn't look like much from the outside, but inside. . .

The driver rolled down the windows for the security guards, and Liam flashed a robotic smile. Then they drove through a huge gate that opened on to a courtyard and came to a halt.

"Not bad," Sergio murmured. "Not bad."

Liam scowled, determined not to be impressed by Lionsgate Hall — headquarters to the Guardians of London. But the place oozed with history, and power just about hummed from between the cobblestones. Centuries-old Tudor buildings stood around an immaculately trimmed yard lined with statues and fountains.

"They make it damn clear who's in charge here," Sergio noted as they stepped out of the vehicle.

Liam snorted. There were lion images everywhere, from proud statues of great Guardians to aloof profiles carved into

17

shields. Lion muzzles growled from every door knocker of every building. There was even a frieze of lowly humans, prostrating themselves at the feet of lions.

Liam sighed and set out for the Great Hall. Sergio followed, looking around.

"It's very... royal."

Liam snorted. "It's London. What do you expect?"

"Changing of the Guard?"

Liam pointed to the line of uniformed men staring into the distance at one side of the courtyard, just like they did at Buckingham Palace. "Watch what you wish for. If we're not out of here in forty-five minutes, we'll have to endure the whole goddamn show."

He led Sergio through an arched doorway, up a flight of marble stairs, and then to a set of massive oak doors guarded by two huge men who crossed — no joke — giant axes, blocking the entrance.

"Who wishes to enter this grand hall?" a bossy footman demanded from behind the guards.

Liam rolled his eyes. The Guardians had called him and Sergio in, which meant the guards knew perfectly well who they were. But tradition was everything to the lions of London, and he'd learned to play along, no matter how much it got on his nerves.

"Liam Bennett asks permission to enter the Great Hall." He jerked a thumb at himself, then at Sergio. "Sergio Monser-ratti as well."

Officially, the line was supposed to be, *Liam Bennett begs permission to enter yon Great Hall,* but Liam wasn't begging anyone for anything.

The footman scowled and made a show of checking his tablet. That, at least, showed that some aspects of the twenty-first century had slipped into the staid lion world.

"You may enter," the footman announced glumly.

The guards moved aside in two stomping steps. The minute Liam and Sergio were through, the bears stomped back and banged their axes into position.

Sergio winced, looking back. "Have we been called to a meeting or to a prison?"

Liam sighed, looking into the Great Hall. "You'll see."

Chapter Three

Liam led Sergio into the Great Hall, keeping his chin high despite the fact that everything about the place was engineered to make a guy feel small. The soaring cathedral ceilings... The colorful flags hung from the rafters in neat rows... The light streaming through ancient windows made of dozens of circular glass panes. Raised platforms lined each side of the oak-paneled hall, and the shifters gathered there gazed down at him, aloof.

Liam headed for the middle platform on the right side, trying not to gnash his teeth. The council was run with the same strict hierarchy as everything in the lion world, and everyone had their place. At least he'd worked his way up from the back left corner where he used to stand before he left London. That was a plus.

"Now what?" Sergio whispered.

"We wait for them to call us."

For a time, they stood quietly, getting their bearings. The bigwigs were all clustered at the head of the room, arguing over some point in their agenda.

"The father, it seems, comes from weaker stock. But the mother's side of the family includes some exceptional bloodlines." One of the elders went on at length about someone Liam couldn't care less about. "Strong pedigree. Not just from the Aquitaine side, but the Qi Ping dynasty as well."

Liam made a face. Bloodlines were everything to lions. That had been his problem from the start.

"How can you be sure?" someone asked.

"She homed right in on the treasure we set out to attract her — a piece from an ancient dragon hoard."

Sergio raised his eyebrows in a question. *Attract whom?*

Liam had no idea. He didn't care either, not with his mind drifting back to Gemma.

"No human would recognize that treasure," another of the elders said. "Only someone with shifter blood."

Sergio sniffed the air and whispered, "Not just lions here."

Liam shook his head. "Whatever they're discussing must be serious. They've called in leaders from all over the UK." He pointed to one shifter after another, taking Sergio through a who's who of the Council of Elders, following the waiter going around with drinks.

"The core of the Guardians are all lions." *The ones drinking gin*, he might as well have added. "See the one who looks like Churchill? That's Augustus Llewis-Jones. The man pacing to his right is Frederick Ainsworth. And the woman with silver hair sitting over there like a queen is Electra Huxley."

Sergio perked up. "*The* Electra?"

Liam sighed. "The one and only. Just wait till she speaks up. Or should I say, starts ordering everyone around. Picture Judi Dench crossed with Margaret Thatcher. You definitely want to stay on her good side."

Liam decided to leave out how closely he and Electra were related on his mother's side. Instead, he went on.

"The others represent different parts of the UK. Welsh dragons..." He pointed to a delegation of short, stout men with deeply creased faces being served frothy ales. "They get blustery, but they don't meddle with politics much. Mostly, they just want to be left alone."

Sergio nodded slowly. "Relations of your father?"

Liam made a face. "He comes from a different dragon clan. None of which lions consider good enough to mix with their regal blood." He tried keeping the bitterness out of his voice but didn't really succeed.

Sergio studied him closely but let it go, and Liam was more than happy to change the subject. "That's Fergus MacGregor — the head of Scotland's unicorns."

Sergio's eyes went wide. "Aren't unicorns extinct?"

22

Liam shook his head. "There are a few left." He pointed out the handful in attendance, most of them sipping wine spritzers. "They make a show of being independent, but when push comes to shove, they always side with the lions."

"Who is that colossus?" Sergio pointed to a man standing a head above the rest.

"Eamonn Barley of Northern Ireland. One of the last of the giant deer."

"Giant what?"

Liam splayed his fingers over his head like antlers. "The animal species went extinct when mammoths did, but a few shifters survived. They're loyal to the lions — blindly loyal, some say. You know — the enemies of our enemies must be our friends. That kind of thing."

He watched as Eamonn accepted a double whiskey and downed it like water.

"I wouldn't like to cross him," Sergio observed.

"Neither would I. Anyway, the problem is, there are too many factions, and they bicker endlessly. It's worse than Parliament sometimes."

Indeed, as he spoke, the council broke into an ever-louder exchange.

"I knew our treasure would reel her in," one of the lions said smugly.

"Our treasure? It was stolen from Wales," a dragon thundered, turning red.

"It was won in a fair fight," Augustus Lewis-Jones pointed out, sticking his nose higher. "Have you forgotten the Battle of Llangwellyn in 1262?"

"No, we haven't," Cian Talog, the leader of the Welsh dragons, growled.

"Can't you just let that go?" one of the unicorns sighed.

"We'll let it go when you stop going on about the Treaty of Aberfiddy," one of the dragons shot back.

A dangerous gleam appeared in the unicorns' eyes, and they tossed their heads in agitation.

Several dragons growled in response, and the bear guards stepped closer. Lions bristled, and Eamonn, the giant deer, lowered his head as if ready to shift and charge. Shouts broke out as the various factions voiced their outrage, and—

"Gentlemen, please. Quiet. I said quiet!" the grand old dame of the lion council, Electra Huxley, barked.

And just like that, the whole assembly went still.

Liam shot Sergio a look. *Told you to watch out for her.*

"Allow me to bring us back to the matter at hand." Electra's low, dangerous tone said, *I command you to return to the matter at hand*, and every man in the room stood at attention. "The key point is that we have located a Fire Maiden at last."

Liam whipped his head around.

Sergio caught his eye and mouthed, *Fire Maiden?*

Liam nodded slowly. Until recently, he'd thought that was just a legend, but there really were powerful ancestors of the mighty dragon Queen Liviana. Their royal blood was capable of reviving ancient spells that protected the great cities of Europe. However, their power attracted both good and evil factions, as he'd witnessed in Paris.

"When the shifter world is at peace, the human world tends to follow," Electra said. "And as we all know, Britain needs that badly."

Everyone nodded earnestly — even Liam. But, wow. Another Fire Maiden? Who was she? Where had they found her?

His inner lion scowled. *Who cares about a woman with royal bloodlines? I just want Gemma.*

"Now that we have identified our Fire Maiden, we must act quickly," Electra went on. "We have received reports that members of the Lombardi clan may be on the move in London."

Liam narrowed his eyes. Could that have been the shifter he'd seen on the Tube? Then again, hundreds of shifters passed through the city, so who knew?

"Again, the Lombardis." Sergio cursed under his breath.

Liam mulled it over. The Lombardis were a clan of ruthless dragons who had been exiled from Europe decades earlier. But they had recently returned in a renewed attempt to seize power. They'd tried and failed in Paris. Had they shifted their sights to London now?

"We cannot allow those filthy dragons to get to the Fire Maiden before we do," Augustus declared.

"Filthy dragons?" Cian Talog bellowed.

Augustus rolled his eyes. "I don't mean all dragons. Just those no-good Italians."

When Sergio's canines extended into a wolf grimace, Liam elbowed him in the ribs.

"It's said that Lorenzo Lombardi — one of the younger, more dangerous members of the clan — has become involved with that Parisian outcast. Another dragon." Electra snapped her fingers, trying to recall the name.

"Jacqueline?" Liam blurted.

Dozens of pairs of eyes turned to him, and Electra spoke in a low, menacing hum.

"Ah, Mr. Bennett. So good to see you in attendance." Her tone was so flat, it was impossible to read.

"Good to be here, ma'am," Liam said, working hard to keep his voice as even as hers.

When she scowled in one of those *Children should be seen but not heard* expressions, Liam stood straighter. He might be a mixed breed in Electra's eyes, but he wasn't a child any more. He was a warrior, and a damn good one, hired by the lions of London to protect the city. Let Electra remember that.

She turned away, snapping her fingers at an assistant. The nerdy owl shifter pressed a remote control, and a screen lowered from the ceiling.

Liam snorted and whispered to Sergio. "They let the twenty-first century in to the same degree that they admit dragons. A little at a time, and only when they find it convenient."

The Welsh dragons looked on, unimpressed, and someone pushed a gawking Eamonn Barley out of the way before the screen tangled in his antlers. Then the lights dimmed, and Electra spoke, clearly relishing the sense of mystery.

"Allow me to introduce you to our Fire Maiden."

A picture appeared on the screen, and Liam squinted at the image of a crowd around a juggler in Covent Garden.

"Which one is she?" Sergio whispered.

25

Liam shrugged. It beat him.

Then the slide show clicked to another image — one of a young woman with long, dark hair, a dancer's trim figure, and gorgeous, teardrop eyes.

Liam's jaw dropped. Gemma?

Her name must have slipped out, because Sergio jerked around. "You know her?"

Liam couldn't answer; he was that dumbstruck.

The photo showed Gemma strolling along a crowded street lined with pastel-colored houses, her face set in an expression that said she had no clue she was being watched. She wore jeans, a T-shirt printed with something about hedgehog habitats, and had her hair in a pair of cute schoolgirl braids.

"A Miss Gemma Archer," Electra continued.

Another photo went up, that one with Gemma gazing at a parchment of some kind. A woman who was smart, sassy, and had seen the world.

Liam's mind went into overdrive, and his stomach knotted with a sense of impending doom. Somehow, he knew this wouldn't be good.

"A young woman of mixed heritage," Electra said. "Anglo-Norman dragon lines, Welsh, and even Chinese dragons on her mother's side. Now, you may think, as I initially did, that that type of interbreeding would produce inferior bloodlines..."

Electra didn't gesture toward Liam and say, *Exhibit A*, but he could sense everyone making the connection. His mother was a lioness from a noble family, and his father, a roguish dragon. The two had eloped, setting off a scandal, and when they'd returned with a baby boy — him — everyone had shaken their heads. Liam knew all about it thanks to the gossipy relatives who'd raised him after his parents died.

Your mother always was the black sheep of the family.

Now, that no-good father of yours...

Swept her right off her feet...

No-good dragons...

Liam's gut twisted at the memories.

Electra went on. "However, in this rare case, the bloodlines appear to have combined in a way that makes her royal lineage more potent than any of the original threads. She may be a mere human, but her blood runs thick with royal power."

Every shifter in the room leaned closer as Electra paused.

"Just think of the potential." The old woman's eyes gleamed. "Not only in her, but for our future. If we can arrange for this woman to mate with a suitable individual, she may produce even stronger offspring."

Liam's eyelids twitched. This could not be happening.

Sergio hissed to Liam, "How can anyone suggest such a thing? Mating is the most sacred bond in the world."

Spoken like a true wolf, and for once, Liam agreed.

"This Fire Maiden will help us stabilize the current situation, and her offspring will allow us to sustain that power into the future," Electra said.

Everyone nodded, but Liam was aghast.

Electra smacked her hands together to silence the murmurs of approval. "Now, then. I have a plan."

Everyone leaned closer, but Liam eyed the exit. Whatever that plan was, he couldn't stomach it. Even if the Fire Maiden had been just anyone, he would despise whatever Electra had up her sleeve. No one had the right to manipulate — even force — a woman into anything for their own gain.

"We shall identify a suitable mate and lure this woman in," Electra started.

Lure? Liam wanted to scream.

"Then we settle her among us. Watch her closely. Choose a few petty areas in which we allow her to dabble and maintain the illusion of power."

Liam's gut roiled.

"Meanwhile, we shall make use of her power to secure the city. And when she falls pregnant. . . "

Liam's eyes bulged. How far did Electra's crazy plan extend?

". . . we'll make sure to take that child. . . "

She said that in a way a person might take a flowerpot or a fruit bowl.

". . . and raise it properly."

Liam couldn't believe his ears.

"A brilliant plan, is it not?"

Electra scanned the council, and for some reason, her eyes landed on him. Then she flashed a bright smile — the one that broadcast *Danger!* with a thousand volts — and pointed to him.

"And you, Mr. Bennett, play a prominent role."

The blood drained from his face. "Me?"

"Yes, you. The unfortunate circumstances of your breeding may have a bright side after all."

A wave of anger rushed through his veins, and if it hadn't been for Sergio's elbow in his ribs, who knew what Liam might have done?

"Mr. Bennett. What say you to my plan?"

Much as he was attracted to Gemma, this was wrong. So, so wrong. Yes, he'd wanted Gemma, but not like this. Not as a pawn in someone else's game.

"It's disgusting. Unethical. Immoral," he snapped. To hell with the consequences of crossing Electra.

"On the contrary, Mr. Bennett. It is practical." Then she smirked. "Are you turning into your poor, deluded mother? A closet romantic who puts love ahead of duty?"

"Shouldn't love come before duty?"

Other than Sergio, whose eyes flashed, everyone in the room looked blank. Well, a few of the dragons scuffed the flagstones uncomfortably, and for a moment, one of the unicorns looked as if she might start spouting poetry about destiny and desire. But no one spoke. No one even peeped a word of protest. They just waited for Electra to steamroll along.

Electra crooked a finger. "Come down here, young man."

Liam wanted to dig in his heels, but he wasn't a kid anymore. He was a member of an elite military group. The veteran of countless battles. A grown man. He could stand up to Electra, right?

So he stepped down the stairs. Creaky stairs in a room gone deathly quiet, making the instinct to run away more urgent. But he had never run from danger before, and he sure wouldn't run now. He kept his chin high and walked to the group of elders at the head of the room.

Behind him, the stairs creaked again, and Sergio, bless him, appeared at Liam's side.

"Did I summon you? I think not." Electra sniffed at the wolf shifter.

Sergio kept his expression neutral. "No. You didn't."

Liam made a mental note to buy his buddy a drink — the good stuff — later.

Electra turned up her nose and continued as if Sergio weren't there, starting with Liam's name. Did she know how much he hated that? Probably.

"Mr. Bennett, your mother put love before duty, and look where it got her."

His lips twitched, but he managed to keep them sealed.

"Now you have a chance to atone for her mistakes and to serve your pride."

Liam stared straight ahead, refusing to meet Electra's eyes.

"Come now," the older woman purred in a totally different tone. "A young man such as yourself must know how to. . . shall we say. . . get friendly with young women. I can all but guarantee Miss Archer will be receptive. After all, you're. . . you," she said, letting her eyes travel his body slowly.

Liam felt sick.

". . . and she is rather plain."

Liam snapped his head up. Gemma wasn't plain. She was gorgeous. Smart. Independent. Amazing in every way.

"Then there's the fact that she's young and impressionable. And a Yank. They love the accent," Electra concluded.

A few men nodded wisely, while others snickered.

"It will be child's play. All you have to do is find her. Get friendly. Seduce her."

Liam clenched his fists. He wanted to get to know Gemma. To fall in love with all the facets of her personally, no matter how quirky. And yes, he would love to make love to her too. But seducing Gemma? Tricking her? Never.

"As soon as you deliver the mating bite—" Electra went on.

"As soon as I what?"

29

The lioness's eyes went cold. "There seems to be an echo in here. You were hired to take orders, not to ask questions. Is that clear?"

Liam kept his lips sealed.

"And if you cannot follow such simple — dare I say, pleasurable — orders..."

More snickers broke out across the room.

"...we will turn to the next best candidate. Archibald, what say you?"

A young lion shifter stepped forward, touching his golden hair. "Nothing could be simpler, madam. I live to serve my pride."

Liam rolled his eyes. Archibald lived to serve his ego — and to bed as many women as he could.

Electra held up a hand. "Of course, Mr. Bennett's breeding makes him the better choice. Not only would he bind this Fire Maiden to our fair city forever—"

Against her will? he wanted to scream.

"His dragon blood, when crossed with this Maiden's, may even produce a Fire Maiden of the next generation. One we can raise properly, with a full understanding of her duties."

An eager murmur went through the crowd, and Liam stared. They were talking about Gemma like some kind of broodmare, and him as the stud. Worse, if Electra's twisted plan actually worked, any children he and Gemma had would be manipulated by the pride. Electra would raise them, groom them — in a word, brainwash them — to believe her warped vision of the world.

Liam looked at the other shifters in the room. Electra's plan might serve the city, but it smacked of lion supremacy. Surely, they wouldn't approve.

But the unicorns simply shrugged or nodded along, as did the giant deer. The Welsh dragons exchanged glances that suggested they'd find a way to turn the situation to their advantage. The lions, meanwhile, practically rubbed their paws — er, hands — together in glee.

Deep down, Liam knew they all supported a just cause — that of peace and prosperity for shifters and humans alike.

But, hell. Did they dare control a woman's future? Worse, did they really expect him to go along with their outrageous plan?

"Remember, if we don't get her first, the Lombardis will," Augustus added.

Liam's blood ran cold, and a murmur went through the crowd.

"We must act quickly," Electra agreed. "First, to protect this Fire Maiden, and second, to get her mated to one of our own." She turned to Liam. "It's for her own good, you know. If we don't step in, the Lombardis will. What mercy do you think they will show her? What freedom?" Electra shook her head. "They will use this woman to gain power, whether they attempt to establish themselves here or elsewhere. They must be stopped."

"We'll stop them, madam." Archibald thumped his own chest.

He may as well have grabbed his crotch, the way lust glittered in his eyes.

"That's the type of loyalty I expect," Electra gushed, giving Liam a dubious look. "However, Mr. Bennett, by virtue of his dragon blood, has first rights to this Maiden."

First rights? Liam wanted to cover his face with his hands.

"You have seventy-two hours, Mr. Bennett," Electra declared. "If you do not secure the Fire Maiden by then, the others may stake their claims."

And I thought the Guardians of Rome dwelled in medieval times, Sergio muttered into his mind.

Archie, meanwhile, practically rubbed his hands. So did Daniel, Thomas, and a few others — all young males from families of moderate rank. Mating with a Fire Maiden would be their ticket to the big time, giving them power, money, and prestige.

"Well, then," Electra concluded. "Is everyone clear?"

No, Liam wanted to scream. *I want someone to wake me up from this nightmare.*

But everyone nodded. Archie checked his watch and nodded like the race was on.

31

"Fine." Electra studied Sergio briefly. "Mr. Monserratti, you are to patrol the city for any trace of the Lombardi clan. Let's see if wolves are as good trackers as they say." *Though I doubt it,* her tone said. "And you, Mr. Bennett..."

Liam looked up miserably.

"Get moving, young man. Claim this Maiden before it is too late." Then Electra flashed him a dirty little wink that made it all too easy to imagine what kind of sexual games she may have played in her youth. As if Liam's stomach needed to churn one more time.

"And who knows?" she summed up. "You may even enjoy yourself."

Chapter Four

"How was the rally?"

Gemma stared blankly out the window and onto the street.

"Gemma? The rally?"

Gemma gave herself a little shake and turned to her boss, Steven. Boy, she really had to get her head out of the clouds. Or out of the gutter, where it had been for the past twenty-plus hours, ever since she'd met Lancelot — er, Liam. She really had to stop thinking of him as her knight in shining armor, and she really, really had to stop fantasizing about what he might be like in bed.

"It was great," she mumbled, guessing that would be an accurate way to describe a night with Liam, too.

And, *zoom!* Her mind rushed right back to those steamy visions. Dammit, the rally was far more important than a brief — and all-too-chaste — encounter with a hot guy. Where were her values? And, yikes. What was with her hormones these days?

"Did many people attend?" Steven asked as he sorted through the *Decorative Prints* section of the map shop he owned in Notting Hill. The tweed-clad man was a friend of her father's who had offered her a job when she'd arrived in England with no plan other than getting away from Petro.

She cast a covert look out the window. Those memories and the creepy man in the Underground ought to have made her worry. But somehow, she felt more secure than ever. Watched over, almost.

"Yes, the organizers were really pleased," she replied.

It had been a good rally, though progress in terms of effecting social change was slow. But someday, she would look back

33

in pride at being part of an important movement. A little like a student who protested in the 1960s could, she supposed.

Still, she felt guilty about spending most of the rally — and the previous night — thinking about Liam. She'd even picked up her phone and stared at his number a few times, compelled to get in touch. It was a need, an itch. As if some outside force was trying to tell her something.

But that was crazy, and there were enough loony people in her family as it was. She had to be the reasonable one. So, she hadn't called, but she hadn't deleted Liam's number either.

The bell chimed over the front door, and a customer stepped in. The type that looked like a born scam artist, perfectly happy to post pictures of Steven's maps on eBay.

Sure enough, the guy took out his phone and aimed it at a 1789 chart of Batavia.

"No pictures, please," she said, pointing to the sign.

Click. The bastard took one anyway. "No harm, right, honey?"

She stuck her hands on her hips. She was not his honey, and a rule was a rule. "No pictures."

The man put away his phone and spent the next few minutes pretending to browse. But then he snuck his phone out of his pocket and—

Gemma jumped between him and the map. "What part of 'No pictures, please' did you fail to comprehend?"

He grinned as if he really thought she'd fall for his nonexistent charms. "Sorry. I forgot."

She pointed to the pair of antique swords hung on the wall. "I know how to use those, you know." Then she scowled — really scowled, giving him the evil eye.

His eyes went wide, and his cheeks paled slightly. Then he hurried to the door, muttering under his breath.

Steven popped his head up. "Well done, Gemma. Can I hire you full time?"

She frowned, because it had happened again — one of those episodes in which she'd grown so angry, her eyes burned. *Really* burned, sending people scurrying away. Then she sighed. Why couldn't she summon that trick with stalker types?

"Sorry. Part time is perfect for me."

"More time for social justice?" Steven looked around and sighed. "I suppose that is more important than old maps."

She smiled. Her degree was in sociology, but that minor in geography was finally proving useful.

"A little of both is perfect for me."

Over the next hour, she did the usual — sorting through new stock, helping customers, and checking for online sales. The job wouldn't make her rich, but it paid the bills, and she loved working with maps. Each of them was a treasure. One of her favorites was the historic map of Wales on the wall. Just one look, and she could dream herself right back to her favorite view in the Brecon Beacons — the one with all the mountains, a lake, and that castle she'd always loved.

Then the bell chimed again, and her father entered with his walking stick and slobbery bulldog.

"Hi, Dad. Hi, Winston." She stooped to pet the dog on the head.

Her father closed the shop door, yanked the curtain across the glass, and peeked back out onto the street.

Gemma sighed. Her father's brow was furrowed in worry, his features drawn.

"How are you, Dad?"

"The question is, how are you?" He took her by both shoulders. "I had a dream last night."

"Another one, huh?" She nudged the curtain open and went back to sorting charts of the Pacific.

Her dad was brilliant, and on most days, relatively normal. But other times, he'd fall under the spell of the fantasies that played out in his head. The ones that had made her mother leave him when Gemma was four. Ever since then, Gemma had shuttled between two continents, walking a tightrope between cultures — and between her parents.

"Nothing bad happened yesterday? This morning?" her father asked.

"Nope. Not a thing," she fibbed. There was no use encouraging her father's delusions, right?

He leaned in and whispered, "No dragons?"

Nope, just a creepy guy on the subway. But Lancelot took care of him, she nearly said.

"Not even one. But there were several vampires hanging around the rally," she threw in to test how nutty her father was at that moment.

He made a face. "Don't be silly. Most vampires are in Paris these days."

Gemma sighed.

He called to Steven. "Would this be a good time for an old man to take his daughter to lunch?"

"I had lunch, Dad."

"A cup of tea, then. Steven?"

Her boss laughed. "As long as you bring her back. I don't know what I'd do without her."

Gemma shot him a grateful look. Steven had helped her father after her parents' divorce — and dozens of other crises, most involving figments of his imagination. Dragons, fairies, werewolves — they had all featured in her father's visions over the years.

She pulled on a windbreaker and followed her father to the door, bumping into him when he stopped abruptly. "Dad..."

"Oh dear," he muttered, eyeing a delivery man.

Gemma sighed. *Oh dear* was never a good sign when it came to her father.

"Dad," she barked, making a move for the door.

"Just checking. They were after your mother too, you know."

Gemma refrained from rolling her eyes. That was another of her father's delusions — and the principal factor contributing to the divorce. Alastair Archer was kind and smart, but his imagination had a way of tipping to the dark side.

She hooked her elbow through his as they walked down Portobello Road, hoping to anchor him in reality.

"Tell me about your latest case. Another pro bono?"

Her father had always been passionate about the cases he took on as a retired lawyer, but he didn't take the bait.

"Our court date is months away. Anyway, how is your mother?"

Gemma pursed her lips. He meant if her mother was safe, but she wasn't going to humor him on that one. "She's fine. They found a new sponsor for the reclaimed swamp project."

Her father patted her hand, but his eyes were still on the sky, as if a dragon might appear at any moment and spout fire.

"Look. Isn't this nice?" She extended her arm to show off her latest treasure, a bronze-tinted bracelet. "Doesn't it look real?"

The five embedded rubies glinted in the daylight, and the intricate filigree winding around them shone gold.

"Very nice." Her father barely turned his head.

Gemma heaved another sigh. When she'd found the bracelet, she could have sworn it had called to her from all the way down the street. She hadn't been shopping, but out of nowhere, the urge to track down that special something had come over her. She'd hunted it down, stall by stall, and when she finally found the piece, it had taken her breath away. The gold, bronze, and rubies couldn't be real. Not for the five pounds she'd paid, and definitely not with the disinterested way the stall keeper had all but tossed it to her. But, still. They looked so real.

"It's just like grandma's," she added, showing him the matching one she'd worn for years.

Her father didn't even glance over. "Lovely."

It was lovely, dammit, even if no one else noticed. Gemma shook out her sleeve, covering it again in case a thief with a discriminating eye noticed.

No one did, of course, and despite her father's fears, no dragons swooped out of the sky during the five-minute walk either. Together, she and her father passed the first three houses on his street — pastel yellow, pastel blue, and pastel pink, respectively, each with white trim. Then he unlocked the door to his house — pastel green — and they stepped in. Bright colors were one of the things she loved about Notting Hill, and she loved her father's house most of all. Every inch of the place was covered in books, maps, and ancient manuscripts.

"I'll put the tea on," he said as Winston flopped onto his dog bed, panting from the short walk.

Gemma wandered around her father's office, revisiting all the familiar things. The photo he kept on his mantelpiece, showing her beaming mother holding a bundle — baby Gemma. Dozens of black-and-white photos hung on the walls — even one of Gemma's great-grandmother in traditional Chinese garb from back before she'd moved to the West. Then came her father's framed degree from Oxford, with thank you notes stuck into the edges from the pro bono cases he had devoted much of his career — and all of his retirement — to.

She looked up at a higher shelf, where he kept the trophies and ribbons she'd won in fencing tournaments. Nothing big, really. Just a fun hobby she'd pursued through college.

A good skill. You never know, her father had always said.

She could have snorted. It was the twenty-first century. No one used swords any more.

"That looks great," she said when her father came in with a tray of tea, cream, and biscuits.

He set down the tray, poured the tea, and settled in his worn leather chair. "Now, about that dream I had."

Gemma suppressed a groan. "People dream all the time, Dad. It doesn't have to mean anything. I once had a dream about getting stuck on an elevator."

He shot upright. "You were stuck on an elevator?"

"No! That's the point. Our brains make up weird things."

He shook his head sadly. "That's what you've been taught to believe. In reality. . . "

And off he rambled, describing all the supernatural beings that populated the world.

"Dragons. . . werewolves. . . werebears. . . "

Gemma's eyes drifted to the photo of her mother. No wonder the marriage hadn't lasted. Then she took in the leatherbound volumes on his shelves. Somehow her father's mind took all those old legends — "research" as he liked to call it — and turned them into reality.

"I dreamed there was a new dragon in the city. An evil one. . . "

"Riding a double-decker bus, I suppose?" she joked.

38

Her father frowned. "No, he was flying. But I suppose a shapeshifter could ride a bus when he changed to human form."

Gemma dropped her face into her hands. What an imagination.

"Then the dream changed, and I saw him riding the Underground," her father went on. "You were there too."

Gemma looked up, startled. Then she dismissed any connection. Just because she'd encountered a creepy man didn't mean she'd spotted a dragon.

"He was following you..."

She set down her tea with a bang. "Would you stop that? You'll make me paranoid too."

"I just want you to be safe. Are you sure you didn't see anything?"

"I'm sure. Nothing."

She looked into her teacup. It wasn't that she enjoyed lying to her father. It was simply a necessity. The man worried about so much, and half of it wasn't even real.

A truly lovely man, but off his rocker, her mother still sighed about the decades-older man who'd once wooed her.

"Are you being careful, though?" her father persisted.

She mulled that one over. With the stalker, yes. With Liam, well... She had resisted the urge to share any details, like her phone number, address, or where he could find her naked that night. But damn, it had been close. If it hadn't been for that urgent phone call he'd received, who knew? He might even have come to the rally, and they would have had a chance to get to know each other.

A pang of regret hit her — a feeling so intense, she winced. It was as if she'd allowed an incredible opportunity to slip through her fingers. An adventure. A future. A life-altering encounter broken off with a polite goodbye. Why?

Then she caught herself. In real life, there was no love at first sight. People didn't bump into future partners on the subway or on plane rides or in crowds. They got to know each other gradually before racing into decisions they might regret for the rest of their lives.

Like letting him go? part of her cried.

She stood quickly. "I ought to get back to work. I promise to be careful, all right?"

She bent to kiss her father's cheek then gave Winston a little pat.

"You could stay here, you know," her father offered.

She took a deep breath. Much as she loved her old bedroom, no. She was almost thirty, for goodness' sake.

"Thanks, but I like the place I'm renting. I'll see you soon, though."

Her father walked her to the door, peering out between the curtains before letting her go. "All right. You take care."

She hugged her poor, delusional father then stepped outside. "You take care, too."

He watched her go just the way he had when she'd been five, ten, or fourteen. Then, finally, she turned a corner, and—

"Sorry," she murmured to the person she crashed into.

"My fault," the man replied.

Then they both stood and stared.

"Liam?" Her cheeks flushed.

"Gemma." He broke into a huge, innocent grin, as if bumping into her was a dream come true.

She stared a moment longer. Wow. It really was Liam. And, whoa. Her cheeks weren't the only part of her body heating up at the sight of him.

"What are you doing here?" she asked when her overjoyed nerves settled back into place.

Liam's smile slowly morphed to a slightly pained look, and he stuck his hands into his pockets.

Gemma tilted her head. "What?"

He considered for a moment, and she swore his eyes brightened to a glow, then faded slightly, only to brighten again.

"How are you?" he asked out of the blue.

Changing the subject. Why? And, damn. Did he have to have such a great smile?

"I'm fine. And you?"

"I'm well, thank you. How was the rally?"

"The rally was fine. How was your... your... " She motioned vaguely.

"Nice. Fine." Then his face fell. "Actually, no. I was called away to a meeting."

"Didn't go well, huh?" she asked, remembering something about a demanding boss.

The shine went out of his cheeks, and his eyes dulled. "Not so well," he admitted, then brightened. "Not as nice as meeting you."

For a moment, they stood there, grinning at each other like fools. Then a bus rattled by, making Gemma jolt and check her watch.

"Shoot. I have to get back to work."

"I'll walk you," Liam said with an eager, puppy-dog look.

And off they went, with Gemma's mind spinning. Was Liam a creepy stalker, or was he as sweet as he seemed?

"What are you doing in Notting Hill?" she asked, testing him.

He ran a hand through his hair, distracting her in a wildly wicked way.

"Just...er...shopping."

She halted, sticking her hands on her hips. "Shopping?"

He drooped, then took a deep breath. "No. I came to...to..."

The previous day, he'd been the picture of confidence and certainty. Now, something was eating at him. What?

She stirred the air with her hand, prompting him along.

He gulped. "To find you."

Coming from another man, those words might have rattled her. But somehow, she couldn't bring herself to be suspicious of Liam. His eyes were too clear, his expression too honest.

"Why?"

"Because of that man. In the Underground. He hasn't turned up again, has he?"

"No, but you've turned up," she pointed out.

He winced and ran a hand through that beautiful mane of golden hair. "I suppose I have. But I swear, I'm not stalking you."

"Then what are you doing?"

His shoulders straightened, and he went back to that invincible warrior look. "Protecting you."

"Protecting me. From what, exactly?" When he hesitated, she went on. "The truth, Liam. No bullshit."

They'd stopped in the middle of the sidewalk, and after a pause, he pulled her aside to a gate to a private garden, overhung by leaves and vines. There, he stalled, shifting from foot to foot.

"What if you don't like the truth? What if you don't believe it?"

Her stomach sank. That didn't sound promising.

Still, she tapped her foot and crossed her arms. "Try me."

He studied her for a minute before speaking. "That man in the Underground — I can't be sure, but I think he may belong to the Lombardi clan. Trouble, in other words."

Gemma's eyebrows shot up. "Sounds very mafia-like."

"Worse than mafia, if he really is a Lombardi."

"And if he is?"

"Then your life is in danger."

She paled at that echo of her father's worries but made sure to keep her voice a steady monotone. "My life is in danger."

Liam nodded quickly.

"And I need you to protect me," she went on slowly.

Liam's chin jerked up and down. "You do."

"Because that man was a criminal?"

Now, Liam looked really uncomfortable. "I suppose you could call him that."

Gemma snorted, losing patience. "What would you call him? Exactly, I mean? What's the danger? And how can you be so sure?"

Liam wavered for a moment. "The truth?"

She jerked her head in the most commanding nod she could muster. "Yes, Liam. The truth, the whole truth, and nothing but the truth."

Liam shot a covert glance down the street then leaned closer. "Because he's a dragon. A dragon shifter, I mean."

She stared. This was not happening.

But Liam sputtered on. "I think he could be after you because of your royal blood."

Gemma's jaw swung open. God, not this again. She'd heard the same crazy warnings from her father again and again.

Then it hit her. "Have you been talking to my father?"

Liam looked at her like she was the crazy one. "No. Wait. Your father knows? Hardly any humans do."

Gemma blinked. "Humans? As opposed to...?"

"Shifters," Liam said, all matter-of-fact.

"Dragon shifters?"

"And other types."

She narrowed her eyes. "Other supernaturals?"

Liam nodded so earnestly, it broke her heart. Then he frowned. "What?"

He was so eager, so innocent. Speaking the truth, at least, as he saw it.

Gemma slumped back against the gate, closing her eyes. She should have known Liam was too good to be true. Handsome, honorable, determined to help...and as batty as her father.

She opened her eyes again, determined not to get mad. The poor man needed help, not a yelling-at.

"Sure. Dragons. Danger. Royal blood."

Liam's hopeful expression faded. "You don't believe me, do you?"

Gemma pursed her lips, trying to let him down gently. Mental illness came in all shapes and sizes. What a pity, though, that this case had struck someone who was so together in every other way.

She shook her head a teensy, tiny bit. "Sorry. No." Then she checked her watch again. She really had to get back to work.

Liam looked at his feet. "Of course, you don't believe me."

A long, awkward moment ticked by, and she wondered if she'd done the wrong thing. Who knew what rejection might do to his fragile state of mind?

Then Liam brightened. "Can I still protect you, though?"

She stared. Was he serious?

He was, and she knew the answer should be no. A big, insistent no. A woman had to watch for danger at all times.

But, dammit, people with mental illnesses shouldn't be ostracized. They needed help. And besides, she couldn't believe he was dangerous. Not to her. He was so sweet. So kind. So...so...deluded.

She slumped. God, she didn't have the heart. And, hey. There could be an advantage to having a big, handsome — er, powerful — man around, even if he was a little crazy. So she took a deep breath and started walking again. Fast.

"Fine. You can protect me."

Liam jumped into step beside her, looking pleased as punch.

She stuck out a finger. "But no stalking. No pestering. No weird stuff, you got it? When I tell you no, I mean it."

He stuck his hands up, smiling again. "Wouldn't dream of it. I'll just keep away the dragons."

She looked at him, then at the sky, and finally sighed. "Sure. Just the dragons."

Chapter Five

Liam knew Gemma didn't believe him. She thought he was crazy, in fact. He could see it written all over her face. But she hadn't called the police or pushed him away. She had just sighed and walked back to work after one final warning.

"I mean it. No weird stuff. No stalking."

Gemma could put on a hell of a fierce expression, and the way she held her hands, karate-chop style, showed she meant business too. Which was good. Very good. Any shithead would think twice about bothering her.

On the other hand, even a black belt wouldn't help Gemma against a dragon, so once she was safely inside the shop, Liam found a spot across the street to stand guard. There, he leaned against a wall and crossed his arms, feeling rather pleased with himself. Not only had he located Gemma, he'd managed to win her trust, and he hadn't even had to lie. For the first time ever, he had come straight out and told a human about the shifter world. It was refreshing, really, even if she didn't buy a word.

He hid a smile. It was kind of Gemma not to actually call him mad.

Inside, his lion crooned happily, imagining a dozen different happy endings for himself and his mate.

She loves me. Deep inside, she knows we are mates.

But then his smile faded. That was exactly what the Council wanted. What they'd ordered, even, and that made him sick. Even if he succeeded in winning Gemma over, she would be furious when she found out about the Council's orders. She might think he was only after her as part of a deal.

She's not a deal! She's my mate, his lion growled.

He stood on guard all afternoon, thinking it through while studying every passerby for any hint of danger. All in all, it was like some of the guard posts he'd been assigned in the Legion, without the sandbags and mortars. Plus, there was a huge bonus because Gemma would peek out the shop window from time to time, making his soul sing.

He waved to her each time, wishing he could call out, *Hello, my mate. Don't fret. I will keep you safe.*

It amazed him how quickly he'd accepted the whole mates thing. But as Sergio had said, when you knew, you just knew, as surely as you knew the shape of your hands, the beat of your heart, or the sound of your own voice.

I know, his lion rumbled.

The next time Gemma peeked out, she wore that annoyed, *Are you still there?* look. But then a shy smile emerged, and he swore her eyes glowed.

So, yes. She must have shifter ancestry. And yes, she must feel what he felt, too.

She knows we belong together, his lion sighed happily.

Eventually, she gave herself a little shake and remembered to look annoyed, but he knew that was just for show.

And that was how the afternoon went by — with glorious little glimpses of Gemma, and lots of glares at suspicious types in the street. He didn't bother concealing himself, making damn sure any shifter who happened along would leave Gemma alone. Delivery trucks came and went, tourists snapped photos, and eventually, shopkeepers started locking up. Not long after six, the bell over the map shop door jingled, and Gemma exited, calling goodbye to her boss. Then she stopped, put her hands on her hips, and looked straight at Liam.

Her expression wavered between *I can't believe you're still here* and *It's so nice to see you*, and Liam was glad too. Then she spun on her heel and headed down the road. The twisted bun she wore her long, blackish-brown hair in that day bounced as she strode along.

He hurried over and fell into step beside her. "Did you have a good day?"

She threw him an exasperated look. "Yes. No dragons."

He gave his chest a little pat. "See? It pays to have a bodyguard."

Too late, she hid the smile and whatever flirty comeback she'd had on the tip of her tongue. "How exactly are you going to protect me against dragons? Are you a knight or something?"

He laughed. "No. Just a lion."

Her step hitched, but she covered it up. "I see. A lion."

Boy, she really did think he was crazy. But that was all right. Even liberating, in a way, not having to be constantly on guard against letting the truth slip.

"A lion shifter, actually. We can change back and forth."

"I see. Your whole family?"

He decided not to go into details, like the fact that his father had been a dragon shifter. "Most of us, anyway."

"Aha. And how exactly would a lion protect me from a dragon? Dragons can breathe fire, right?"

That was exactly the question he'd been mulling over all afternoon. "The trick will be to keep them on neutral territory where they can't shift into dragon form. They wouldn't want to be seen."

"Oh no. They definitely wouldn't want to be seen," she said in that indulgent tone.

He motioned around. "Open streets, the Underground — that should be all right. We'll have to be careful of wide-open spaces, though."

She shot him a piteous look, then glanced away again.

"Military training helps too," he added. "You know, in case it comes to hand-to-hand combat."

It was a joke, but Gemma looked dead serious. "You were in the British Army?"

"No, the Foreign Legion."

Her jaw swung open — the usual reaction he got. "Really?"

He nodded. "I was rebelling. You know — not wanting to conform to what the family wants for you."

Funny how some things don't change, he almost added.

"Where did you serve?"

47

"Oh, you know..." He motioned around, summing up thousands of miles and ten years with a wave of his hand. "Mali. Burkina Faso. The Middle East." He fingered the scar on his abdomen, then brightened. "We also had some joint training operations in Martinique."

Her expression oozed sorrow, and he could just about read her mind. Gemma probably thought he was suffering from a bizarre case of PTSD in which he transformed human enemies into dragons, lions, and wolves.

He changed the subject. "What about you?"

She shook her head. "I decided against joining the Foreign Legion."

For a moment, he stared, then burst out laughing. "You got me there."

She smiled one of those starburst smiles that warmed him from the inside. "No military. I did fence, though." She swiped a wrist expertly, and he pictured a sword flashing.

"That might come in handy."

"What? Against dragons — or strange men who follow me around?"

He chuckled. "Touché, fair lady. Touché. Did you fence professionally?"

She burst out laughing. "I wish. There's not much call for swordplay these days. After college, I focused on work — first for a political campaign, then for an environmental NGO, plus a few side jobs to pay the bills. Then I came here."

Her face fell, and he wondered exactly what had precipitated that move.

For the next few minutes, they walked in amiable silence, making their way to the Underground, where she led him to the Central line.

"Are you from London?" she ventured once they boarded the subway.

"On the outskirts. Richmond." He pointed over his shoulder.

She laughed. "You're sure it's right there? The Tube does take a lot of turns."

He nodded and leaned in to whisper. "Felines have a great sense of direction."

She bit her lip, and that *Poor, pathetic you* expression clouded her eyes.

"Brothers? Sisters?"

He shook his head. "An only child. But after my parents died, I lived with my cousins, so they feel like siblings. How about you?"

Gemma shook her head. "I'm an only child." Then she paused. "I'm sorry about your parents. How old were you when... when..."

"When they died? Seven. But it's all right. I barely remember them."

His lion grumbled inside. *I remember.*

Well, he did and he didn't. Little snatches, mostly, like the sound of his mother's laugh, or the booming voice his father would call out in when he came home from a midnight flight. He remembered the exhilaration of his father swinging him in circles, saying, *Just wait, my lad. Someday, you'll be able to fly like me.*

Liam pursed his lips. Maybe it was a good thing his father hadn't lived to discover his son could only change into lion form.

He sighed. There were those little snapshot memories, and then there were dreams. Things that hadn't happened — they couldn't have happened — but they felt so real. In some dreams, he flew alongside his father, wingtip to wingtip, and watched the world sweep beneath. In other dreams, he could breathe fire, making his mother go, *Tsk, tsk. Be careful, my boy.*

He dragged himself away from those thoughts — crazy thoughts, because he couldn't shift into dragon form, and dangerous thoughts, because they stirred emotions he'd locked away for a long time. Also, Gemma was studying him with those wide, sad eyes, probably tracing his unstable mind back to losing his parents so young.

"Sorry," she murmured, touching his arm.

They were on a rattling subway car surrounded by dozens of strangers, but the contact made him feel as if the two of them were alone, and that nothing in the past mattered. Only the future, which was sure to be sunny and bright, because they would be together. Forever.

Forever, his lion hummed.

Forever, the sparkle in Gemma's eyes seemed to agree.

If an announcement hadn't blared out — *Next stop, Tottenham Court Road* — well, hell. They might just have ridden all the way to the end of the line and back before budging from their cozy cocoon.

But budge they did, from the platform of one line to another, followed by another few stops on the Northern line. Eventually, they exited to street level and wound along a couple of curving roads. Liam looked around, wondering where Gemma lived. At the top level of that townhouse near Primrose Hill? Or was she renting one of those cellar apartments, down three stairs from street level?

None of those things, as it turned out. One minute, she was leading him along a perfectly normal street. The next, she turned at a bridge and detoured down a flight of steps to... the towpath along a neglected canal?

"Well, I'm home," Gemma announced. "Safe and sound."

He looked around. Nothing but fences and gated gardens. Then he followed her gaze and did a double take. "You live there?"

"Yep," she said proudly.

"In that?"

She nodded, grinning. "Isn't it great?"

He rubbed his chin. "It's a boat."

"A narrowboat, to be precise. And it has a name." She pointed at the faded gold lettering across the stern.

"Valhalla?"

"Valhalla. Viking heaven. The owner is away in Mallorca, so I'm house-sitting. Boat-sitting, I guess."

It looked tiny, run-down, and totally impractical. But Gemma looked delighted.

"I suppose it does have... character," he tried.

"Where do you live?" Then her face froze, and she waved her hands. "Never mind. I suppose you have a lair somewhere. None of my business."

He chuckled. What would she say if he told her about his penthouse views over Hyde Park?

"Well, it's late," she added.

It was only seven, but it was pretty clear he was being dismissed. Much as he would have liked to stay, the smart thing to do was to give her space.

"I'll see you tomorrow, then."

Once again, Gemma wore an expression that was partly delighted, partly suspicious. "Tomorrow?"

He nodded. "To keep you safe."

She pursed her lips. "Don't you have a job you have to get to?"

Telling her his job was protecting her wouldn't go over well, and he wasn't going to hint at everything else the Council had demanded.

"I work flexible hours," he said, leaving it at that.

Gemma didn't look so sure, but she didn't ask either. She just looked at him and finally waved. "Well, good night."

"Good night." He stuck his hands into his pockets to stave off the urge to hug her.

But Gemma didn't move, and neither did he. A gnat wafted by, and a dog barked in the distance. A car drove over the nearby bridge. But all that faded into the background as they gazed into each other's eyes.

Gemma, he wanted to whisper.

Liam, her eyes said.

He leaned closer, and she did too. Her mouth moved a little, as did his, and her lips looked so near. Near enough to kiss.

So, kiss her, his lion whispered.

Kiss her, a low, rumbling voice echoed.

Her eyes fluttered a little, and she tilted her head, as if obeying the same command. Because that was the voice of destiny, telling them what to do.

Kiss her, his thumping heart said.

He inched closer, as did Gemma. She'd undone her hair clip somewhere along the way, and her silky locks tumbled over one shoulder, begging him to run his fingers through them. Her lavender scent wafted through the air, mesmerizing him. Make that, intoxicating — more than any liquor or drug. His inner lion jumped with glee, and his soul sang just from having her near.

Then a cyclist came barreling down the towpath, making them both jolt.

"Look out," the cyclist called over his shoulder as if *they* were the hazard.

Liam was tempted to shift into lion form, sprint after the fool, and teach him who was supposed to watch out for whom. Instead, he turned to Gemma.

"Good night," she said, glum as he was, because that magical moment had passed.

"Good night," he whispered, stepping back.

He stayed long enough to watch her unlock the door, slide back the hatch, and step inside. Then, with a last little wave, she ducked out of sight and slid the hatch shut. A light went on inside, and Liam fought the urge to wave again. Instead, he walked along the towpath and back up the stairs to the street.

There, he paused, looked back, and whispered, "Good night, my mate."

Chapter Six

Liam didn't go far, though, because with night came danger in its myriad forms. The Lombardis were out there somewhere, and so were countless other foes. Ordinary criminals, too, making Liam consider things he'd never thought about before. How safe was a single woman in London, really? Did Gemma walk that deserted towpath alone every morning and every night? And, hell. How solid was the door of that barge?

Cyclists came and went. Shadows lengthened. Lights came on in a few boats. Liam tiptoed down to the towpath, ducking when a bat flew overhead. Then he set off to assess the surroundings carefully. It was a nice neighborhood, but the canal created a strip of open airspace a dragon could swoop through, and there weren't many escape routes. The narrow banks of greenery along the canal abutted a solid line of walls. On the other hand, there were plenty of bushes for a lion to conceal himself in.

A house cat flitted by, and Liam looked around. Tempting. Very tempting. Usually, he ran in Hyde Park, but he would love to explore a new part of town. The darker it grew, the quieter the area became. Surely no one would notice if he was careful.

His lion snorted, reminding him of all the covert missions he'd run. *Of course, no one will notice.*

So he stepped into the bushes, stripped out of his clothes, and bundled them inside his jacket. Then he tilted his head back, looking at the sky. The moon was rising, and a few stars shone through the city's glow. Funny how he'd never wanted to fly before. But tonight. . .

He shook his head. Flying was for dragons, and he was a lion, right?

He shook even harder, letting his mane grow out. The stubble on his chin burned in a good way, as did his back as tiny hairs extended and thickened, warming him against the chilly night. He dropped to all fours, hands turning to paws before they hit the ground. He flexed his claws in the dirt, savoring that connection with the earth. Then he worked his jaw from side to side, letting whiskers extend from his cheeks. Within a minute, his tail was lashing the air in anticipation, and the urge to roar was stronger than ever. His mate was near, and he would protect her forever. Surely that was a message worthy of bellowing through the night?

He had to be content with prowling instead. Up along the embankment, then back to the bridge, strutting every time he passed Gemma's boat. How good would it feel to stand before her in lion form and show off how powerful he was? He would roar his love into the night, and—

He sneezed, shaking the urge. He was there to protect Gemma, not to preen, right?

For a while, he curled up nearby, silently keeping watch. Then he set off on another loop, venturing farther than before. Bright lights clustered ahead, and he slowed. Gemma's immediate neighborhood was peaceful, but from somewhere around the bend came voices...music...cars...

Camden Town Locks, he realized. A place he'd dragged Sergio to one night just for fun. A little drinking, a little dancing, a little carousing. Everything a young lion might desire.

But suddenly, none of that interested him any more. Only Gemma and the warm yellow light illuminating *Valhalla's* curtained portholes. Heck, he could even picture spending quiet evenings in rather than wild nights out.

He turned around and prowled back, mulling it all over. Could a man really fall in love so quickly? So eagerly? His parents had mated young — much younger than most lions. Did that carry over to him?

When you know, you know. Sergio's words echoed through his head.

Liam considered. Maybe he'd inherited a few dragon traits from his father after all.

Then he halted in his tracks and growled under his breath. Someone — or something — was out there.

Then an answering growl came, and the bushes near the bridge swayed.

Archibald, Liam muttered, recognizing the young lion's scent. Daniel and Thomas were there as well, along with a big, older lion.

Rutland, Liam sniffed in disdain.

For years, the Guardians had tolerated the mercenary who came and went, occasionally hiring him for dirty jobs they didn't want to sully their own reputations with. Dozens of scars demonstrated his status as the veteran of a hundred back-street campaigns. From the look of things, Archie and the others had hired Rutland as backup.

Liam snorted. Years earlier, the hair along his back would have stood at that challenge. But a decade in the Legion had taught him plenty, so he puffed out his mane and stepped into the open, more annoyed than alarmed.

What are you doing here? he snarled, using the mental link most shifters shared.

How satisfying it was to see Archie skitter away. With his buddies there, however, the arrogant lion quickly recovered his swagger.

I am visiting my Fire Maiden. Making sure she's safe.

She's safe. I guarantee it. Liam circled the others.

It was laughable, how Archie, Daniel, and Thomas bumped and tangled in response.

Amateurs, Liam's lion sniffed. All but Rutland, who stood his ground a few steps away.

Archie and Thomas collided a second time and rumbled at each other. Which should have made Liam laugh, but instead, his anger grew. A Fire Maiden deserved better than second-rate guards.

The thought must have slipped out, because Archie chuckled in an all-too-familiar mocking tone. *So what are you doing here, half blood?*

Liam clacked his teeth an inch from Archie's face, making the lion leap back. A reaction that would have been far more satisfying if the reality of his situation weren't so grim. How was he ever going to win over Gemma on his own terms?

Daniel and Thomas looked at each other uncertainly, then inched forward, flanking their friend.

Run along, boys, Liam growled. *Before you really tick me off.*

Archie sneered. *You really think she'll be interested in you, half blood?*

That was just like the old days, when Archie had been a merciless tease. Never within earshot of adults who would shush him out of consideration for Liam's powerful relatives. But otherwise, Archie and the others had been relentless. And back then, Liam had felt powerless to react.

Well, no more. Unlike Archie, Liam had left the luxuries of London and hardened up. The Legion didn't put any man above another — not unless he earned it through brutally hard work. In hindsight, the shifter politics that had seemed so insurmountable in his youth were laughable now. London was full of old-timers who battled with words and young guns who hid behind the shield of their noble family names. All of them were so tangled in tradition, they had lost track of the real world.

Liam leaned forward, feeling taller and more powerful than ever. He was a warrior. Archie and the others were nothing. Rutland was a lowly mercenary without any real cause.

Liam growled, letting the sound echo through his chest. *The Fire Maiden will choose the man she wants, whomever that may be. But a man he will be, not a boy like any of you.*

Daniel backed up, and Thomas gulped at the threat in Liam's voice. Archie bared his teeth in a gesture that held more fear than defiance. Meanwhile, Rutland's eyes shone, eager for a challenge.

Why would she choose you, half blood? Archie taunted. *Are you such a master of seduction?*

The others laughed, but Liam fumed — literally. His lungs felt strangely hot. His tongue burned, and his throat filled with an ashy taste. But those sensations were nothing compared to the fury in his heart. He would never, ever stoop to the means the Guardians had suggested. If Gemma chose him, it would be out of love, not from any trick.

He prowled forward, lashing his tail.

Run along, boys. Leave real work to real men.

Or you'll what? Archie challenged.

Liam dug his claws into the ground, wishing he could do that to Archie's flesh. If he had left the Legion after the first five years, he might have done just that. But time and experience had taught him to recognize when fighting caused more trouble than it was worth. If he beat up Archie now, the Council of Elders would have his hide, and where would that leave Gemma?

Liam was no such fool. But Archie was a conniving bastard who might be willing to gamble on such a plan.

I have had enough of you, Liam growled in a voice so deep and gravelly, it surprised him. *I will not waste any more time. Go.*

Archie, Thomas, and Daniel cowered, but they didn't move. Rutland watched, ready to follow their cue. Liam roared into their minds, ready to end the juvenile encounter.

Go, I said! Go.

Daniel and Thomas scurried behind Rutland. Archie shook but stuck out his chin.

Make me.

Liam knew he shouldn't take the bait. But, hell. He was a soldier, not a diplomat. And he had had enough of Archie's bullshit.

So he crouched, ready to jump. Archie crouched too, making every mistake in the book, such as neglecting to edge away from the canal to gain maneuvering space or angling himself to take advantage of the glare of streetlights. The kind of errors a lion could get away with if all he ever did was play-fight in his noble family's domain.

Rutland, meanwhile, sidestepped into a more advantageous position on the sloping high ground, proving he was no fool.

Make me, Archie taunted a second time.

Liam twitched his tail in one final warning. A moment later, he sailed through the air, calculating how much claw to let out to send Archie packing without actually killing him. Archie skittered sideways, barely dodging the blow. Liam made a last-second adjustment, batting Archie across the muzzle without actually drawing blood. No sense in making the situation worse. Then he sprang back, giving Archie one last chance.

Time to pack up your little gang and go home, boy.

Archie's eyes shone with fury, and he swiped at the air. *Get him, dammit!*

The words were aimed at Rutland, who flicked an ear in a bored expression that said, *I'm only obeying because you paid me, asshole.* Then a rumble sounded in his chest, and he bared his teeth at Liam. *Ready?*

Oh, Liam was ready, all right.

They circled one way then the other, sizing each other up. Then, just when Liam was sure the mercenary would chuckle and retreat, calling off whatever deal he'd struck with Archie, Rutland whipped around and lunged, claws bared.

Liam ducked, sidestepped, and sprang at Rutland. He drew first blood, but Rutland landed a glancing blow a moment later, tearing into Liam's shoulder.

The next few minutes blurred in the most brutal, yet strangely silent cat fight Liam had ever been part of. Even when claws tore through flesh, neither he nor Rutland let more than a grunt slip. And, hell — Rutland was good. Very good. A master of every trick in the book, with superior body weight, to boot. But Liam was fighting for a greater cause, and he countered every lethal move. He even found himself relishing the action. His first few months as a civilian had been full of alerts but no real action, and his lion had been itching to fight.

Rutland grinned as if he enjoyed the action too, though he didn't let up his relentless attacks.

Get him, Archie cheered, slashing from one side.

Daniel and Thomas inched closer, too, and Liam sneered, seeing through their cowardice. Obviously, they were content to hang back and try to score whatever sneaky side blow they could. Then they would claim to have beat Liam on their own. He could hear them sniggering to each other now.

Well, he wouldn't give them the pleasure.

So he battled harder, digging his claws deeper with every blow. Thomas yelped and rolled away. Daniel stuck his tail between his legs and backed up. Rutland's grin vanished, replaced by a look of grim concentration. And Archie—

Liam slashed at Rutland, then slammed the bigger lion aside. That left Archie unguarded, and Liam rushed forward.

Archie's eyes grew wide. And, hell. If Liam hadn't been possessed by something greater than himself, he might have been surprised too. But that force — that raw strength like nothing he'd ever experienced before — felt right. It was his to command — some power emerging from a locked chamber deep in his soul.

Something sparked in the air, and flickers of orange and red reflected in Archie's terror-filled eyes.

You will never have her. Never. Do I make myself clear? Liam bellowed.

He had only aimed the words at Archie's mind, but wow. It was easy to imagine them echoing through the night the way a dragon's challenge might.

Yes, a deep, scratchy voice inside him whispered. *Yes. Let me out.*

Liam pushed the unfamiliar sensation aside and roared one more time. *Go!*

Archie stumbled backward. With a yelp and a gratifying splash, he plunged into the murky water of the canal.

Much as Liam would have loved to watch Archie sputter and curse, he was too possessed by that inner force to let up. He spun to face Rutland, no longer bothering to mask the deadly glow in his eyes. He was willing to fight to the death. Was Rutland?

The mercenary glared for a moment, going perfectly still other than the calculating sweep of his tail. Then he glanced behind Liam and sniffed.

Liam snarled. Did the bastard think he could claim Gemma?

Then, with one final jut of his chin, Rutland inched back as if to declare, *Enough.*

Enough, Liam agreed, though he didn't budge. Despite the fatigue of fighting, his feet felt light, as if he might tiptoe upward and soar into the air. Like a dragon. Like his father. Like—

He puffed sharply, pushing those thoughts away. They were as crazy as Gemma believed him to be, and he wasn't going there.

Rutland turned to the others with a disdainful gaze. With one disparaging snort, he strutted quietly up the stairs. Archie, meanwhile, splashed around like a half-drowned rat. Finally, he dragged himself out of the filthy water with Daniel's help. Then he stood, shaking with rage.

Liam snorted. The effect would have been a lot more impressive if Archie's mane hadn't been plastered all over his face.

I was generous with these before, Liam growled, displaying his claws. *But I'm not feeling so generous now. Get moving, you little ass.*

Archie staggered, dripping, to the stairs that led away from the canal and up to the street, squeaking, *You have no right.*

Liam huffed and followed, snapping at Archie's heels. *Oh, I have the right. And the might.*

How satisfying it would have been to chase Archie through the streets.

Oh, let's, his lion begged.

But he'd risked too much already, making such a racket. He'd made his point, right?

He stood panting at the top of the stairs, yearning to make the point to every other lion in London as well.

Finally, he turned and descended the stairs. Every step closer to his mate calmed his mind, and every breath—

He paused. Every breath burned. Less with each passing minute, but still. What was wrong with him?

Nothing wrong, that deep, scratchy voice chuckled. *Only what's right. What's within you.*

Liam considered for a moment, then stopped attempting to puzzle that out. He'd had enough drama for one night. It was time to find a soft patch of earth where he could curl up and keep watch over his mate for the rest of the night.

Chapter Seven

Gemma yawned, padded down the narrow hallway of her floating home, and peered out one of the portholes. It was one of those beautifully quiet mornings, with mist blanketing the canal and a light drizzle thickening the air. As usual, her little neighborhood felt a hundred miles away from the bustle of the city.

She'd slept fairly well, though there'd been some kind of ruckus outside at one point. A cat fight? A couple of drunks? Whatever it had been, she had done what her neighbors did — hunker down and avoid trouble. Now that daylight was breaking, she was prepared to deal with whatever might be out there. The houseboat was low, and the windows came to about ankle height of anyone on the towpath beside the canal. But there was no one outside, just the bushes, a flitting sparrow, and—

Wait a minute. Liam?

She raced up the four gangway stairs, slid back the overhead hatch, and threw the door open.

"Whoa. Are you still here?"

He was, indeed, sitting on a bench, tightly wrapped in his jacket. When she called out, Liam blinked away his sleepy look and waved. "Of course I am." He stood, stretched, and came closer. "You know. Danger."

She made a show of looking around the deserted towpath. "The only danger I see is you."

He folded his hands over his heart and made a face. "You wound me, fair damsel."

She had to laugh. God, was he cute.

Then he grew serious, pointed upward, and whispered. "Not me. Dragons."

She sighed. "Right. Dragons."

He nodded earnestly. "Lions too."

"Lions like you?"

He scowled — really scowled, as if she'd hit a sour note. "Like me but not like me." Then he shook his head. "Anyway, they're gone now."

She studied him. His hair and clothes were disheveled, but his smile was merry. Was he always so upbeat?

Mostly yes, she decided. He did have gloweringly dangerous moments too, but never aimed at her. Just others, like the man in the subway.

"You spent the whole night out here," she said slowly. "Protecting me."

He nodded happily then cocked his head. "What?"

"I'm trying to decide whether that's creepy or cute."

He laughed. "Call it devoted."

The morning air was chilly, but she warmed all over. Devotion was a fitting word. Liam's eyes shone with it, and it was impossible to believe he meant her any harm. Still, a smart woman had to keep her guard up.

"Well, thanks. I'm going in now." She stepped down one rung.

Liam waggled his fingers. "Ta-ta."

She closed the hatch and peeked out a different window. Would Liam sneak over when he thought she wasn't looking?

But, no. He just stretched, backtracked to that bench, and sat there. Looking left, right, and even up, as if a fighter jet might zoom into view and dive-bomb her boat. Or a dragon, she supposed.

She hesitated, weighing up what to do. Allowing Liam to walk her home was one thing. But spending the entire night beside *Valhalla* was another. Really, she ought to send him packing. A woman had to be firm, as she'd learned from her mom. Especially with the quiet ones who made your heart weep.

Still, Liam was so sweet — and so hopelessly crazy. Every time she set out to tell him enough was enough, her resolve crumbled.

"Dammit," she muttered.

She headed to the galley and put the kettle on the stove. A peek out the window told her the drizzle was letting up, and the sun was slowly burning through the mist. Liam had tilted his chin up and let his eyelids droop, like a cat sunning itself. Or a lion, she supposed.

She stuck two pieces of bread into the toaster then paused at her dish rack. One plate or two?

A moment later, she found herself calling out from the entry. "Tea or coffee?"

Man oh man. She was supposed to keep her nutty stranger at arm's length, not offer breakfast. But Liam flashed that winning smile, and she melted all over again.

"Tea would be lovely, thank you."

"Earl Grey?"

"Yes, please."

"Toast?" The moment she offered, she nearly slapped a hand over her mouth. What the heck was she doing?

He beamed. "I wouldn't mind."

She headed back down, shaking her head at herself. Who was the crazy one now?

She stomped to the galley, humming — humming! — while she made breakfast for two. Then she looked over it all. The toast, the jam. The cream, sugar, and saucers. How was she going to get all that up on deck?

She thumped a fist on the counter. No, she was not going to invite Liam in. No way. Even if he begged.

The thing was, he didn't beg. He simply sat outside, not expecting anything from her at all except the honor of guarding her. And finally, she gave in.

"Would you like to come in?"

His eyes lit up, and for some reason, her heart soared. "Aren't you a gem." Then he grinned. "Gem — Gemma. I reckon your parents knew what they had when you came along."

She stood, torn between laughing and crying. He was so charming. So mixed up. Which was tragic, really. A nice, young, good-looking guy like that. He'd probably had a great future before it all got to be too much and his mind went. She looked around. The canal was fronted by some posh Georgian mansions, and she pictured his poor mother, wondering where her son, the emotionally scarred war veteran, had wandered off to.

Except, he didn't appear emotionally scarred. He was big, tough, and totally in charge of his world. And, oops, she'd been staring too long, because he tilted his head.

"Everything all right?" His smile faded. "Oh. It's all right. I can stay out here."

She waved her arms. "No, come in. Please."

Then she caught herself. Yeesh. Now she was the one begging him.

"I don't mind. It's fine out here."

She buried her face in her hands. Was it legal to be so disarmingly cute?

"Um, Gemma?"

God, what a sucker she was. "I mean it," she insisted. "Come in."

Which was how she found herself serving breakfast for two, not one, in the compact living room of the boat. Telling herself that it was perfectly safe with Liam squeezed in behind the table like that. He cupped his hands around the mug, warming them, and she felt guilty for not inviting him in sooner.

"Milk? Sugar?"

"Both, please."

He looked around her tiny home as she brought everything over, making her slightly self-conscious.

"Sorry. It's not as tidy as it should be."

He chuckled. "You should see my place."

She laughed, and he motioned to the papers she'd left on the table. "May I?" When she nodded, he leafed through them. "Wow."

"Wow?"

He sipped his tea, then pointed to the fliers and brochures. "Safer Parks Panel. Reptile Rescue Center. The Towpath Task Force..."

"You don't think those are worthwhile causes?"

"I do. They are. Absolutely. It's just..." He considered for a minute. "I suppose I wonder what makes a Yank so committed to local causes."

Sometimes, she wondered too. She'd sworn to keep a low profile for a while, but she hadn't been able to help herself from pitching in.

"I see rubbish in the canal, and I want to do something about it — something more than picking up a piece today and another piece tomorrow. I want to stop it for good. I see people treated differently because of the color of their skin, and I have to speak up. I want to see things really change."

Liam shot her a smile. "I suppose I shouldn't get you started on animal rights."

"Don't," she agreed. Then she thought back. "I get it from my parents. I went to my first rally in one of those baby backpacks, and I've been going ever since."

"And are you satisfied with progress on these causes?"

She snorted. "Far from. Sometimes it's like Sisyphus — the guy who's destined to roll a boulder up a mountain for all eternity, only to have it roll back down. But when I really think about it, yes. There has been progress — slow but steady, thanks to people who keep chipping away."

She hurriedly set out the toast and jam, giving her guest an easy out. Most people politely tuned out when she got going on the causes she cared about. But Liam chewed thoughtfully on his toast, and she could see him considering what she'd said.

"Fitting," he murmured.

She cocked her head. "What?"

He jolted a little then hurriedly patted his belly. "Um, filling. Thank you. Delicious."

She laughed. "Would you like more?"

"I wouldn't mind." He gulped his tea, then looked into the cup. "It's funny, that."

She put two more slices in the toaster and waited for him to finish.

He studied the depths of his tea. "I went into the military thinking I could fight for a good cause — literally fight." He flashed a weak smile. "And for the most part, we did. But the more I think about it, the more I think your way is better. And there are fewer casualties. That's a plus." His tone made clear that was a joke, but his eyes didn't play along. "Definitely a plus," he murmured before taking another long sip.

"I guess there are pluses to both ways," she said, trying not to imagine the toughest situations he must have witnessed — the kind that had tipped him over the edge.

Liam waved around, changing the subject quickly. "How do you like living on a boat?"

That brought back her smile. "I love it. It's cozy."

He laughed. "Cozy, huh?"

"Yep. I have everything I want in arm's reach." She demonstrated, extending her arms to each side. "The boat is barely six feet across and only forty feet long, but I have everything I need. Well, at least for the next month or so."

His eyebrows furrowed. "What then?"

"Then the owner comes home, and I have to find a new place. If I'm still in London, that is."

Liam's face fell, and she felt a pang of regret. She only had the vaguest of plans, but none of them involved staying in London more than a few months, which wasn't very long. Just enough time to get to know a charming young stranger and possibly convince him to get psychiatric help. Not enough time, really, but plenty to fall in love.

Their eyes locked, and she could feel him mourn too. But then the next batch of toast popped up, and she hurried to transfer it to his plate. Liam slathered it with butter and jam and devoured it in two bites. Boy, did he have an appetite.

"Anyway, I've got everything I need. A miniature woodburning stove, a fridge, a view..." She popped open the window just as a dragonfly flitted past. "It even has a shower."

"You're joking. This place has a shower?"

She nodded proudly. "Look. Over here."

And oops, there she was, giving him a tour, allowing him ever deeper into her private world.

"Bathroom... Closet..."

She led him down the length of the boat, trying not to get flustered. But the narrow passageway forced them to get close — nice and close — and her cheeks started to heat.

"Bedroom," she said then turned quickly. That brought her practically into his arms, and the worst part was, she wouldn't have minded staying there. But she skittered away. "Sorry."

Liam's eyes shone. Or was that a trick of the light?

"That bunk is a little tight, isn't it?"

She looked him over. Yeah, for a guy his size. As it was, he had to stoop slightly to avoid hitting his head in the hall. But the place suited her perfectly.

"That bed is cozy," she corrected.

He laughed and stuck up his hands. "Got it. Cozy. Can you even stretch out in there?"

She was tempted — so, so tempted — to show him just how much space there was to stretch out — not just for one person, but for two. Instead, she motioned him back down the hall. "It's really comfortable. The engine compartment is down there."

He turned with a grin. "Engine compartment, huh?"

Then she stopped in her tracks — so suddenly, Liam bumped into her again.

"Everything okay?"

She nodded. "I just remembered. It's the eighteenth, right? I have to move the boat."

Liam nodded sagely. "Smart move. Dragons can't trace your scent over the water."

She closed her eyes. Just when she got to thinking Liam wasn't so crazy, he'd remind her how off his rocker he was.

"No — my two weeks here are up. Shoot." She stepped into the kitchen and started stowing things. "I'd better get going. No telling how long it will take to find a new spot."

Liam handed her the dishes. "Can I help?"

69

The answer, she knew, had to be no. She'd already let down her guard too far. But when she considered the dock lines and the tight corners she would have to navigate around...

"Don't you have someplace you have to go?" she asked.

"I have time."

And thus, she found herself with a deckhand for the next hour and a half. One who proved himself to be more than mere eye candy as he hopped efficiently around deck.

"Ready?" she called once she'd coaxed the engine to life.

Liam held up the stern line. "Aye-aye, Captain."

That was the best part — he didn't try to take over as so many men might have. No suggestions, no amused looks, no *If I were you, I'd do it this way* comments. He simply followed her directions — and, wow. He even fished some plastic out of the canal while he was at it. Finally, he untied the lines, hopped aboard, and stood beside her as they got under way.

"Nice," he murmured as she piloted *Valhalla* into the center of the canal.

"It is. A whole new perspective on London, huh?"

It was magical, in fact. The mist was slowly rising, and shafts of light angled down as the sun steadily broke through the clouds. The boat puttered along at two knots — a slow walking pace, in other words — and the scenery slipped silently by.

"So, tell me about dragons," she ventured. "Lions. All those...shifters, right?"

Liam glanced her way, but she kept her eyes straight ahead. "You don't believe in them."

"Let's say I wanted to educate myself."

He chuckled. "All right, then. A group of shifters watches over the city. They're called the Guardians. Most of them are lions, but there are also bears, dragons, and other types."

"What other types?"

He flapped a hand casually. "Oh, you know. Wolves. Giant deer. Unicorns."

"Unicorns?"

"Just a few. Traditionally, lions rule London. They have for centuries. See that?"

He pointed to a mooring ring embedded in the stone wall — a ring held in the mouth of a bronze lion's face. Gemma looked at Liam. That was his proof?

"Think about it," he went on. "There are lions all over London. Trafalgar Square. Buckingham Palace. All along the embankment."

"That's because lions are a symbol of England."

"Because we guard the city." He sighed. "At least, we try to. Oh — I have another one. The South Bank lion."

He continued in that vein, and Gemma's pursed lips grew ever tighter. Was Liam in cahoots with her father? Unlikely. Her father's warnings were all vague and centered on dragons. Liam's went into so much detail, it was tempting to believe him at times. And, hey. Who wouldn't want to believe in a world of good guys, bad guys, and unicorns?

But she wasn't a little girl any more, and she had enough real-world problems. Why use her imagination to create more? Liam, on the other hand... Well, she decided not to push him on it. Maybe he needed to transfer wartime experiences into a fantasy world. Maybe someday, that would help his poor, damaged mind heal. But until then...

"Maybe it will turn out to be a nice day after all," she said, changing the subject.

"It already is." Liam made a sweeping motion. "I get my own little cruise."

She laughed — it was impossible not to around Liam — and abruptly swung the wheel to starboard. "Oh — there's a spot."

Soon — too soon, really — they got *Valhalla* tied up again. She checked her watch. If she hurried, she could even make it to work on time, and to the Safer Parks meeting afterward. She ordered Liam out while she showered and changed, then rushed around, locking up the boat.

"Where are you going?" Liam asked when she stepped onto the towpath.

"Work." She paused and tried to get herself together. No matter how nice it was to have Liam around, she had to get real — and so did he. "Look. I have a life. A job. A meeting to attend. And you..." She paused, then spoke more gently. "You need to get help. There are lots of counseling services out there and lots of people like you dealing with PTSD."

He waved a hand, unconcerned. "I need to see you safely to work."

She stuck up a hand in a stop sign. "No. Absolutely not. You will do no such thing."

And yet, he followed her. Happily, it seemed.

"Liam," she started.

He sighed. "All right, all right. If I promise to get help, will you let me walk you to work?"

Just the thought of another half hour with him made her heart skip, and — against her better judgment — she gave in again.

"All right already. But really — you have to promise to get help. I mean it, Liam."

His eyes swirled and danced as he put his hand over his heart. "For you, anything. I promise."

Chapter Eight

"Now what?" Gemma muttered, glancing up at the commotion outside.

She had been reading in her bunk on *Valhalla* — make that, trying to read — as she would on any other night. Three days had passed since that morning on the Tube, and she hadn't seen that Petro look-alike again. Either she'd been imagining things, or having Liam around was paying off. Liam was probably outside at that very moment, as he had been every night.

How he managed, she had no clue. But he seemed perfectly content hanging around all night and keeping watch over her for most of the day. Whenever Liam left, his friend Sergio would take over guard duty. Gemma didn't know whether to laugh or cry at how seriously they took their fantasy world. Had they undergone some kind of mental experiments in the military that had warped their minds? It was a pity, because Sergio, like Liam, had everything going for him, from smoldering good looks to startlingly quick reflexes and an amazing sense of fashion. The man could have modeled for Armani, Hermes, Rolex, or any other high-end product.

But, boy. They were so earnestly committed to their misguided cause, Gemma found it hard to draw a line — especially with Liam. She knew she shouldn't allow herself to grow too close to him, but he was so adorably sweet, and the chemistry between them... Well, it was off the charts. Every time she saw him, her nerves would jangle and she would bump into things. Every time he left, no matter how briefly, something in her ached. And every night, he featured in her dreams.

On that particular evening, however, she was starting to

get fed up. First, there'd been a bump on the roof of the boat. Then, she was sure she'd heard Liam and Sergio whispering outside. After that, they appeared to have gone off in two different directions, and things were peaceful for a while. But then a dog began to snarl, and a minute later, someone hammered on *Valhalla's* hatch.

"Gemma!" Liam called in a low, urgent voice.

She slammed down her book. Living on a barge along London's canals meant putting up with passing drunks or late-night pranksters. But having someone jump on the roof or smash a bottle was hardly a life-threatening crime. So what was Liam so agitated about?

"Gemma," he hissed.

She swung her jaw from side to side. Responding would only encourage his fantasies. But if Liam kept up that racket, one of her neighbors would surely complain. She'd already gotten strange looks for having two strapping young men checking in on her all the time. The last thing she needed was for someone to file an official complaint — or, worse, to spread rumors that she was involved with two men.

"Gemma!" Liam called hoarsely.

She huffed and stood. Fine. She'd see what he wanted and then sit him down for a long talk. He had to get help, and soon.

"Liam, you can't keep doing this," she muttered as she unlocked the door, wrapping a flannel shirt around herself.

With the boat lying low in the water and Liam standing so tall, he loomed over the entranceway, more agitated than she'd ever seen him.

"You have to come with me. Right now."

She shook her head firmly. "No way. I am going to bed, and you are going to calm down."

He peered over his shoulder, barely listening. "Hurry. Quick."

She backed down the stairs with a sigh. "Why don't you come in?"

Liam got worked up sometimes, but she had a knack for calming him down — the way he had with her when she got stressed or uptight.

Liam motioned urgently. "It's not safe. You have to get out of here."

"Liam, I live here. It's late. I—"

A huge shadow swooped behind him, and Gemma froze. Liam ducked and held a finger over his lips.

"Quiet. It hasn't located you yet."

What hadn't located her yet? She tried peering around Liam, but he blocked most of the gangway.

"Liam..."

Dammit, now she was whispering too.

He turned and uttered a sharp word to someone behind him.

"Who...?" she started, then froze as a low, furry shape trotted away. Was that a wolf?

"That's Sergio. He'll try to buy us time."

She peered around Liam. That was definitely a wolf. But in London? Then she studied Liam's eyes. She'd been sure he wasn't into drugs, but—

"Hurry. It's homing in on you," Liam urged. "The dragon."

She took a deep breath. "I told you already—"

That was all she got out before something huge swooped through the sky behind Liam, and her jaw dropped. No way. It couldn't be...

Liam reached down. "Come on, we have to get you out of here."

He pulled her on deck, hurried her ashore, and started hustling her toward a bridge.

"Keep moving." He tugged her hand, because Gemma, without realizing it, had slowed to a stop to stare.

"Holy shit." That really was a dragon, with two huge wings — bigger than any bird — a long, snakelike neck, and an equally long tail. The beast soared in circles, peering down. Searching, obviously. For what?

The wolf that had started trotting away glanced back as if to say, *Searching for you. Get moving.*

"Now do you believe me?" Liam asked.

Her mind spun, hoping for an alternative explanation. That could be a trick of the light or some kind of projection. But moonlight glanced off the dragon's wings, showing them to be leathery and marked with veins. The belly was smooth with natural armor, and the tail flicked gracefully when the dragon turned. All of it far too real to be a hoax.

She nodded dumbly. Holy crap.

"Come on," Liam said.

But all she could do was mumble in awe. "Oh my God. A dragon."

Stating the obvious was stupid, but she couldn't help it. All these years, her father had been right. Boy, did she owe him an apology.

You must watch out for dragons. They are ruthless, greedy things. If they discover your heritage, they will hunt you.

Liam's face was grim. "We need to get out of sight."

One more tug was all it took to get her running. Liam led her to the bushes at a crouch. Then he stopped, looked up, and pushed her ahead.

"Now! Go!"

They rushed under the bridge then stopped and looked back.

Her hands shook. "Someone will call the police, right?"

Liam shook his head. "Regular humans can't see them, not with the spell in place."

She stared. Regular humans? What did that make her? And, whoa. A spell — as in magic?

"Come on. . ." Liam's eyes flicked between the dragon and the wolf disappearing around a corner. Then he shook his head, displeased, and started stripping out of his clothes.

She jumped back. "What are you doing?"

"Shifting. If Sergio and I can distract the dragon, you can get away. Wait here."

Her eyes went wide. "You're leaving?"

He whipped off his shirt and started tugging at his shoelaces. "Not for long, I hope. But if I'm not back in five minutes, go. Stick to the shadows. Make for the Underground, then get as far from here as you can."

It was all too much to process, especially now that Liam was unzipping his pants and—

She jerked her eyes toward the sky. This could not be happening.

But it was. The dragon was still wheeling like a hawk in search of a field mouse, and the wolf had started to howl. Liam was buck naked, and as much as she tried not to peek... Well, it was hard not to, what with the way his shoulders tapered to his waist. The rippled stack of muscles along his abdomen drew her gaze lower, and—

He thrust his clothes at her. "Five minutes. If I'm not back, go."

"Go where?"

He gulped, stopping to think. "Your father's. I'll find you there."

She blinked. Wait. He knew where her father lived? She supposed so, given how he'd shadowed her around Notting Hill.

"But what are you going to do? Whoa..." She stared.

Liam hunched his shoulders, balled his hands into fists, and grunted. "I'm shifting. Don't panic."

Don't panic? How could she not stutter and gag when hair broke out all over his back?

"Liam..."

He shook his head — violently — coaxing out more hair. The stubble of his jaw thickened, extending into hairs that grew longer and denser.

A mane. Her crazy/not-crazy friend was growing a mane. Soon, his entire body was consumed by fur.

"Liam!"

She jumped back as he fell to all fours.

His limbs became more compact, and his joints took on an unnatural curve. Unnatural for a human, at least. But perfectly normal for a... a...

She stared. A lion?

The golden-green eyes that met hers were one hundred percent Liam, and the thick mane fit too. But the rest of him...

Well, wow. She took in the powerful lines of his feline body and his long, tufted tail.

Wait here, those eyes begged. *I'll come back. I swear.*

When he spun and raced off after Sergio, Gemma nearly ran after him. Then she halted in her tracks. Surely, she ought to run away from a man who could change into a wild beast?

Something swooped overhead, making moonlight flicker. The dragon was gliding about a hundred feet up and to her left, its eyes glowing yellow as they searched the ground.

Gemma inched deeper into the cover of the bridge. A howl broke out from the distance — Sergio? — and the dragon flew toward it. But when she stumbled, a bottle lying on the path rattled into the canal, and the dragon whipped its head around. A split second later, it backwinded its wings, peering her way.

Gemma ran to the middle of the bridge, where it was darkest. Pitch black, in fact, moist, and absolutely, positively creepy. The dragon wheeled quickly, coming directly toward the bridge.

She cowered in the shadows. Oh God. She should have listened to Liam and to her father. Panic threatened to seize her, but she fought it away. She had to think, and fast.

The bridge was too low for the dragon to fly under — or so she hoped. The dragon's eyes pierced the dark sky, jerking side to side often enough to suggest she hadn't been spotted. Which wasn't all that comforting, given the way the beast was speeding toward her hiding place. She pressed herself against the mossy inner wall and held her breath.

The dragon rushed directly to the mouth of the bridge, then — *whoosh!* — banked upward at the last possible instant. Air rushed, and leaves tumbled in its wake. Gemma glanced up, trembling, looking left and right. Where was it?

For a moment, the night was eerily still, and she strained for any sound. Then the limp flag at the stern of a distant barge flapped wildly, and a scrap of paper flew across the towpath. A heartbeat later, those yellow eyes appeared at the far end of the bridge, and Gemma nearly screamed. The dragon hovered, kicking up dust and leaves. Gemma covered her mouth, willing herself not to cough.

It hadn't spotted her — yet. But how long until it did?

As the dragon panted, little sparks spun out of its mouth and nostrils. Then a roar sounded in the distance, and the dragon snapped its head around.

Gemma blinked the dust out of her eyes. Was that a lion?

A howl broke out next, and the dragon raced off. When it disappeared around a bend in the canal, Gemma crumpled to the ground. Holy shit.

Eventually, she stood, trembling. Once, the dragon rose high enough for her to spot it over the rooftops before diving again. Another howl broke out — a shorter, more urgent one — but that was all.

Gemma dug her fingernails into the mossy wall. Should she run? Wait for Liam? And, God. Were Liam and Sergio all right? She'd lost all sense of time, unable to judge whether a minute had passed or ten.

A car drove over the bridge, and she considered running after it. She even took three hurried steps into the open, but she couldn't bring herself to leave. Not without Liam.

So, she waited — and waited — until she couldn't stand another minute. Then she waited a little more, her hopes fading, stomach churning. What if Liam was hurt?

Then something moved in the distance, and she gasped. Something fast and low to the ground with glowing yellow eyes. A warm yellow, not the fiery color of the dragon's eyes.

"Liam," she whispered.

Somehow, he was instantly recognizable, even in that different body. His blondish-brown mane flowed in the wind, and his wide shoulders heaved with every powerful step. Even so, it took everything she had not to back up in fear. Not with a full-grown lion rushing straight at her.

At the last second, the lion pulled up abruptly and made a low, chuffing sound.

Are you okay? He didn't actually speak — he only raised a paw — but the question was clear.

Gemma gulped then nodded quickly. "Are you okay?"

He chuffed again, then turned to check the sky, whiskers twitching. When his tail banged against her shins, he spun back, looking horrified that she might flip out. But, hell. She'd held herself together — mostly — so far. She wasn't about to freak out now.

"It's okay. Really." She rubbed her shins. "But I'd love it if you could change back." Then she froze. "You can change back, right?"

A tiny glimmer of amusement showed in Liam's eyes. Then he lowered his head, tucked his tail, and—

Gemma looked on breathlessly as he shifted back to human form. His mane receded, as did his tail. Although he started out on four feet, by the time he reared up on his back feet, his paws had transformed to hands. The last bit of fur disappeared, and—

Gemma looked away, blushing, as Liam grabbed his clothes.

"What about Sergio?" she asked, keeping her eyes on the towpath.

Liam shook out his pants and yanked them on. "He's buying us time, but we have to be quick. He can only keep it up for so long."

Gemma gulped. "I'm so sorry. I didn't believe you. I'm sorry I dragged you into this."

And just like that, all her emotions bubbled up at once, and she was a mess. A teary, babbling mess. Liam tried shushing her, but she couldn't stop. So much for not freaking out.

"I'm so sorry..."

Gently, Liam pulled her closer, then wrapped his arms around her. *Really* wrapped them, nice and snug, making it feel as if evil couldn't possibly squeeze past. "You'll be okay. I promise."

"But what about Sergio? What about you?"

Liam held her until she stopped shaking. Until her heart rate settled, in fact. But then it took off again, because her face was tucked up against his neck, and he smelled so good. Like oak and raw leather. She breathed deeply, claiming that little bit of him. Her body was pressed against his, and her curves complemented his perfectly. Her arms fit, too, looped comfortably around his waist. And Liam — boy, was he a good hugger. Not just using his arms but tucking in all around her. His chin snuggled her in, and his shoulders dipped. Even his feet were close.

She turned her face slightly, intending to pull away, because she wasn't used to falling apart in front of anyone. But she couldn't quite bring herself to, and in the end, the motion only brought her closer to his lips. Close enough to kiss. Close enough to *have to* kiss, though she wasn't entirely sure why. All she knew was that kissing was suddenly an urgent, burning necessity.

When Liam looked down, their eyes met, and for a few heartbeats, they wavered. But that kiss was something unstoppable, inevitable. Something directed — even demanded — by fate.

Gemma closed her eyes and leaned in, surrendering to that force field. Liam did too, and my, my... What a kiss. One of those rare kisses that could go down in history, if anyone kept track of such things. Their lips parted and moved in silent little mumbles. Their noses bumped softly, as did their hips, because every part of their bodies wanted in on that kiss.

Gemma found herself threading her fingers through his thick hair and making little whimpering noises. She swept her tongue over his lips, then paused as if he'd begged to do the same. And when he did... Wow. His hungry, lingering touch made her feel wanted. Needed. Revered. A new batch of tears welled up in her eyes, driven by a rush of emotion. Emotions she couldn't even name, because she'd never felt anything remotely similar.

She broke off for a breath of air — a gasp was more like it — then dove right back in. The kiss stretched on and on, and she never wanted it to end. But gradually, the wave that had swept her up began to recede.

There, it might as well have said. *Now you know how amazing a kiss can be. If you behave, you can have more later. But right now...*

Gemma clutched Liam's shirt and spent the next few seconds panting into the comfortable nook between his shoulder, chin, and neck. Then she pried herself away and gazed into his eyes. They were glowing an intense gold, and his expression was just as awestruck as hers.

"I knew it," he whispered.

She tilted her head. "Knew what?"

He bit his lip, looking absolutely gobsmacked. "Not sure I should say this."

The corners of her mouth curled up. "Right now, I'm pretty sure I'd let you say anything."

He smiled then grew serious again. "I knew that would be good."

She blushed. Had he been thinking about her the way she'd been thinking about him? And were his thoughts limited to kisses, or were they full-blown fantasies like hers?

Then she shivered and looked around. That dragon was still out there. They had to get moving.

"Where can we go? What do we do?"

"Someplace safe," Liam murmured in a way that said he was still mulling over options. Options she couldn't begin to guess at, because how exactly did one evade a dragon?

Then Liam took her hands and turned her to face him. "Do you trust me?"

Her heart hammered as the rational part of her mind threw on the brakes. Liam was a near stranger. A lion shifter. A mystery in so many ways.

But she did trust him, dammit. She had from the very start. She gulped and nodded briskly, turning herself over to fate.

"Of course I trust you."

The smile he flashed was a thing of beauty, full of hope, relief, and even a little fear. Was he just as awed at what they were getting into as she?

"Let's go, then."

"Go where?" she asked as he tugged her into the open and made for the street.

He shot her a grim look. "The safest place I can think of. Into the lion's den."

Chapter Nine

Liam hurried down the street, scanning the sky. Gemma stuck close by his side, her eyes wild and wide.

"Are you sure Sergio will be all right?" she whispered.

He gulped. No, he wasn't sure but, wow. How many rescue ops had he conducted in which the victim worried about the soldiers? His unit had carried out plenty of extraction operations, and the answer was...none.

"Sergio can handle himself," he said for lack of a better reply.

"Against a dragon?"

He let that one go. His job was to hustle Gemma to safety. Sergio's was to distract whichever of the Lombardis that was back there. If either of them stopped to worry about the other, the mission could break down. That was how it worked, and it was one of the biggest lessons the Legion had taught him: teamwork counted, especially when everything was on the line.

"There," he murmured at the sight of the nearest Tube stop.

Gemma broke into a run, and he loved that about her too. She charged ahead. Not only that, but when they got to the turnstiles, she vaulted right over.

"Are you coming?" she called while he stood staring.

A minute later, they sprinted into a departing subway car. Then they stood, gulping for air as the station blurred past.

"Okay. Where to?" she panted.

The destination was easy. The question was how best to get there.

"Richmond," he said, trying to think it through.

ANNA LOWE

"Wait," she protested when he indicated the exit a few stops later. "This is too early. Richmond is at the end of the line."

"It is, but we're driving the rest of the way, and my car is here."

His heart rate should have settled down by then, but it hadn't. Though he'd carried out dozens of operations that paralleled this, he'd always had an earpiece and a team to back him up. Above all, there had been someone giving orders. Now, it was all on him. Of course, like every other man in his unit, he could operate on his own. But this was the point when a team ought to regroup and strategize their next moves.

He looked at his phone. Nothing from Sergio, and that was all the team he had. His friend Tristan was in Paris, and the other members of their unit were spread throughout Europe. It was all up to him.

With every step, an intimidating, *What if I fuck up?* feeling haunted him, but he shook it off, concentrating on his next moves.

"Four minutes," he murmured, checking his watch.

Gemma tilted her head. "Four minutes?" Then she waved her hands, seeing his haste. "Never mind. Just go. I'll follow."

And she did, all the way up to his penthouse, where he scrambled for his car keys and a wad of cash. No time for anything else.

"Wow. Nice apartment." Gemma stared at the view of Hyde Park. The Serpentine was a long, curved line, glittering with moonlight. The lawns were pools of darkness, while Marble Arch was brilliantly lit.

"Not as cozy as a boat," he pointed out.

That coaxed a grin out of her, though he didn't have time to enjoy it. Instead, he hurried her back down to the building's subterranean garage.

"Over there." He rushed for his car.

Gemma halted in her tracks. "That one?"

He motioned her in, revved it up, and peeled up the ramp.

She ran a hand along the dashboard. "Wow. An Aston Martin. 1964? '65?"

84

"1962 Zagato. It was my father's."

One of the only reminders of his father he kept around, actually. One of the few the lion side of the family tolerated, now that he thought about it.

She turned to stare at him then finally murmured, "Mr. Bennett, you are an enigma."

He burned to take her hand, kiss it, and say, *Ms. Archer, everything about you fascinates me. It has from the very start.*

Instead, he hit the blinker and roared down the road.

"How fast does this puppy go?" she asked.

He threw the Zagato into the next gear. "Let's find out."

With the windows down, the wind whipped his hair, and the lights of Knightsbridge blurred past. Harrods... The Oratory... South Kensington with the Victoria and Albert Museum... All in all, it would have been fun if he hadn't had to crane his neck to check for dragons. He itched to turn around and take Gemma for a joyride past London's newest skyscrapers and oldest landmarks. Instead, he pursed his lips and drove west.

"What's in Richmond?" Gemma asked when they crossed the Thames.

The streets were empty, and the sleek car raced along, alone and unchallenged.

"My family." A silent moment ticked by. "My aunt and cousins, I mean. Where I grew up."

She nodded, all matter-of-fact, but he could see her throat bob. "Your lion family."

He tapped on the steering wheel. It would have been easier to explain if she still thought he was crazy. Then he could have just rattled it all out. *They're the only family I knew from the time I was seven. I owe them everything.* Then he frowned and rubbed the leather stitching of the steering wheel. His aunt and uncle had shown him every kindness, but they'd never uttered a positive word about his father, the dragon shifter who'd wooed his mother away from her tightly knit lion clan.

"They're all right," he said at last. "Maybe a little stiff. A little old-fashioned. A little..." He searched for the word, then sighed. "Posh. Imagine a distant relative of the queen."

Gemma's eyebrows jumped up.

The phone rang, thank goodness. And better yet, it was Sergio.

"*Ça va?*" Liam asked, trying to play it cool.

Gemma whipped around, and he nearly said, *Old habits die hard,* like speaking to his buddies in weak, slangy French.

"*Ça va,*" Sergio replied in that understated, *I nearly just died, but that's okay* manner they'd developed in the Legion. "And you?"

Two minutes was all it took to brief each another. Sergio had shaken off the dragon in a series of tunnels, having gotten a fairly good look at the bastard. Unfortunately, he couldn't tell which direction the dragon had flown off in.

"What about the Guardians?" Sergio asked.

That was the tricky part. The Guardians would want a full report, especially if the Lombardis had grown bold enough to stage an aerial ambush in central London. But Liam was in no rush to divulge too much either, not when it came to Gemma.

"Wait until morning, all right?"

A long pause told him what Sergio thought of that idea, but a moment later, the wolf shifter signed off. "*À demain.*" *Talk to you tomorrow.*

By the time Liam clicked the phone off, he and Gemma had passed Kew Gardens, on the outskirts of Richmond. Not long after, they came to the winding lanes of Petersham. Finally, he coasted up to a massive golden gate at the end of a long, tree-lined road.

Gemma sat very still, eyeing the lion statues adorning the entry.

He took a deep breath, second-guessing his plan. It was almost two a.m., and everyone would be asleep. Did he really want to rouse the entire household?

He eased the car into first gear and cruised a little farther down the lane to the service gate, then cut the engine and reached for his phone.

"New plan?" Gemma asked.

He nodded as the phone began to ring. "New plan." Or so he hoped.

∞∞∞∞

Twenty minutes later, he finally exhaled. "Thanks, Brianna."

His younger cousin bounced on her heels, far too peppy for that late hour. But that was Bri.

"You owe me, big guy. May I suggest a drive in that sweet car of yours?" Then she sighed theatrically. "Anything else?"

Liam looked around the guest cottage Brianna had helped them slip into. "All set. Thanks again."

"Thanks," Gemma called as Liam walked his cousin to the door.

Brianna waved then whispered in his ear. "She's cute. Is this your hot date — on the run?"

Liam snorted. If only Brianna knew. And wouldn't she like to, as a sixteen-year-old who was far too curious for her own good.

He pushed his cousin out the door. "Good night, Bri."

She shot him a mischievous look. "No, you have a good night."

He shut the door firmly, then turned to Gemma, hoping she hadn't heard.

"This is beautiful." She waved around the thatched cottage.

There were fireplaces at both ends, each big enough to roast a pig. Windows set in the foot-thick walls let in a little bit of moonlight, augmenting the flickering candles Bri had lit.

"My aunt had it redone. When I was a kid, it was all cobwebs and mice." Then he winced. "No need to worry about mice these days."

Gemma cocked her head. "You mean, with all the cats around?"

He grinned. She meant lions, and he knew it. Either she was coming to grips with the idea of shifters or she was as exhausted as he was.

"Bedroom's this way." He led her up the stairs.

They halted at the top, staring at the queen-size bed. The only bed.

Liam looked at Gemma, but when she glanced his way, his eyes hit the floor. Now what?

She cleared her throat and motioned. "I call this side. You get that side. Okay?"

He smiled. Thank goodness for assertive Yanks.

He could have offered to take the couch, but he was too tired for the polite argument that was sure to ensue. Instead, he made a quick bathroom run, then stripped down to his boxers and slid into bed. There, he lay perfectly still with his eyes squeezed tightly shut.

Gemma had gone into the bathroom after him, but a few minutes later, he heard the door softly open and close. The air in the room swirled with every motion she made, and he sniffed her flowery scent. His mind matched every sound to a gesture as she took off her sweater, shuffled around, and unclipped her bra. Then she rearranged her shirt, removed her hair clip, and shook out those long, silky strands.

He inhaled deeply, dreaming of finger-combing it for her. Then she sank down on the mattress, making him roll ever so slightly as she took off her shoes and pants.

Nice, his lion hummed. *Nice and close.*

Not only that, but he was fairly sure she was down to just a shirt and knickers — er, panties, as she would call them. He fought to keep his thoughts clean when she blew out the candle. The sweet scent of beeswax drifted around the room, and the sheets rustled.

"Good night," Gemma whispered.

"Good night."

Liam lay stock-still, listening to the familiar sound of the river gurgling past. And for a moment, everything was silent.

Then Gemma turned to face him — he could tell without looking — and slid her hand over his shoulder. "Liam. . . "

He did his best to sound half asleep. "Hmm?"

It came out pretty well, too. And thank goodness, because if Gemma knew how little it would take to push his inhibitions away. . .

"Thank you. For everything."

He tried not to open his eyes, but he couldn't help it. Worse, he found himself gazing into those deep, amazing eyes with their little hint of Asia that only showed at times. "My pleasure."

Definitely my pleasure, his lion said.

Her eyes remained on his, steady and sure. Glowing, if he wasn't mistaken, like a shifter's would. Not red with anger, but with the warm hue of arousal.

He clenched his fists. He should not — could not — touch her.

But dammit, he found himself tucking a wisp of hair behind her ear and cupping her cheek. She leaned into his palm like a cat, slid closer, and nudged his legs with hers.

No, no, no, he ordered his lion side.

He might even have succeeded in leashing the beast's instincts through sheer willpower, too. Gemma, on the other hand, didn't let up.

"We shouldn't—" he tried.

"Shh."

She pressed a finger to his lips, then drew it along the seam. Her eyes twinkled, and her lips twitched. Then she leaned in and kissed him. A sweet, slow, honeycomb kiss — the type you took your time with, savoring every pounding heartbeat. A kiss that had to be real because his imagination couldn't produce anything that rich. It was soft, yet yearning. Grateful, yet bold. Practiced, but as innocent and breathless as a first kiss.

Gemma slid closer, and he nearly reeled her in. They were so close to tipping completely over into desire. He could picture it already — the flurry of clothes tossed over each side of the bed, the rush of raw need, the surrender to sheer instinct.

"Gemma," he whispered, trying to find his emergency brake.

She murmured into another kiss, making him teeter over the edge. "Need this... Want this..."

He tried telling himself it was wrong. That they were too exhausted to think straight, and that Gemma was too vulnerable after all she'd been through.

Then why does it feel so right? his lion growled.

It did feel right. Desperately so, as if he'd found an oasis in the middle of a desert and simply had to drink. Circumstance, instinct, destiny — they were all ganging up on him. And, hell. Gemma definitely knew what she wanted. She slid a hand down his rear, then swept her tongue over his.

From that point on, his mind shut down, and the deal was sealed. Everything unfolded just as he imagined, only better. The silent whoosh of clothes tossed to either side of the bed. The quiet little whimpers Gemma made. The soft goodness of her body, begging him to explore. Suddenly, nothing was off-limits, and he could touch — taste — smell her anywhere he desired.

"Yes..." Gemma breathed. Her hands were just as busy as his, and when she gripped his cock, he hissed.

So good, his lion rumbled, eyeing her neck.

All he had to do was plant a love bite there, and Gemma would be safe. She would be his mate, and he would protect her forever. She would be safe from the Lombardis, from Archie and his swaggering friends, and from the influence of the Guardians.

But, damn. Would he be able to live with himself? He had to talk to her first, but he sure as hell wasn't going to try that now.

So he forced his aching canines not to extend and shut away the thought of a mating bite. As it was, everything was a heated blur. Their bodies, grinding against each other. The insistent tug of Gemma's hands.

"Liam..."

He was about to roll and take the top, but she beat him to it, straddling him. Which, together with everything else — the dragon attack, the exhaustion of the late hour, and his latest rush of adrenaline — made his mind go blank to everything but that moment in time. Gemma gasped, slowly taking him in.

When she started to rock and moan, the back of his mind issued urgent warnings, but the sensual haze kept those faint. Wasn't it too soon to get intimate with Gemma? No, it couldn't be, because she was his mate. And as for using a condom — well, that warning faded just as quickly. He and she were destined for each other, so what did that matter? At that moment, his world was pure sensory experience, not consequences or reactions.

Gemma's breasts swayed as she leaned back, and her mouth moved in silent cries. How was he supposed to think of anything at a moment like that?

His soul sang, and a whole happy future played out in his mind.

"Yes..." Gemma moaned, moving faster.

The heat inside him became an inferno, and his whole body ached for release. Gripping her hips tightly, he thrust upward again and again. Gemma pushed down at the same time, and a wave of ecstasy built inside.

If it had been any earlier — or his mind any clearer — he would have drawn out the pleasure. But he was a puppet to destiny — and to Gemma's out-of-control desire. On the next hard thrust, he hissed, and Gemma cried out. One more thrust, and he exploded inside her. Gemma shuddered and yelped at the very same moment. A wave burst, roaring through his ears and sweeping his mind around and around. Nothing had ever felt better, nor had he ever felt less in control of his own fate. But somehow, that wasn't as terrifying as it might have been.

Gemma shuddered again, then went limp over him, murmuring. His chest heaved with deep breaths as he held her tightly.

Mate, his lion mumbled again and again.

"So good," she whispered, melting against him.

They were a mess, as was the bed, and he still couldn't think straight. But, hell. She was right.

So good, his lion echoed.

Rolling slightly, he shifted to his side and used a corner of the sheet to clean up. Then he spooned Gemma against his chest and lay still, listening to her heart beat. His eyelids drooped as exhaustion caught up with him again, and soon, he couldn't tell if it had been real or just a dream.

Real, his lion murmured. *The real deal.*

Chapter Ten

Four hours of sleep shouldn't have felt that good, but Liam woke feeling so, so satisfied. Gemma was still looped in his arms, and he snuggled her a little closer.

To think, you nearly ruined everything, his lion grumbled.

Well, he'd been trying to do the right thing. But raw need for his mate had gotten the better of him, and he'd been a goner from that point on.

Thank goodness Gemma knew what she wanted, his lion huffed.

His lips curled up. She certainly did.

He rubbed his chin gently over Gemma's shoulder, marking her with his scent. Then he kissed her cheek, and after that, her shoulder, holding her close while a glorious dawn broke.

Then he eased away again, remembering where he was. Not in his own bed in his own place where he could lock the world away. He was at his aunt's and, bugger. His presence — and Gemma's — wouldn't go unnoticed for long.

"Gemma," he whispered.

She snuggled deeper into the sheets. "Too early."

He sighed. "You don't know my aunt."

Gemma didn't react, which was just as well. He slipped out of bed, then stood quietly, taking it all in. Her bare back. The twisted sheets. The sweet scent of sex that perfumed the air. His lion wanted to strut around and roar, showing off his amazing mate to the world. And although creeping worry invaded his human side — What would the repercussions be? — it was too early to think straight.

So, first things first. He forced himself to shower — thoroughly. Then he brewed two coffees and sat on Gemma's side of the bed, swirling one of the mugs.

Gemma's nose twitched, and she blinked. She smiled, and for a moment, his world was twice as bright as it had been in the early dawn light. Then a blush spread over her cheeks, and she sat up slowly, looking adorably mussed.

"Morning."

"Good morning." He handed her the mug.

She rearranged the sheet to cover her bare body and took the mug, then looked at him.

"As good as last night was..." she started, making him grin. "What makes me think I'm going to need this?"

He sighed and sipped from his mug. "Because you will. We'd better find my aunt before she finds us."

Gemma lifted one eyebrow as if to say, *That kind of aunt?*

He sighed. If only she knew. "She's okay, really. Just a little...domineering, I suppose you might say. She's always trying to save me from myself."

Gemma considered that for a moment. "Seems to me you can take care of yourself."

Her eyes heated, and he swore he could read her mind. *You took pretty good care of me, too.*

Steamy images from the previous night filled his head, and his lion gave a lusty growl. *I can take care of you any time you need. And you can take care of me.*

Then he cleared his throat and laughed it off. "One would hope, yes. But in her mind, I'm still eighteen." Then he frowned. "That, and she's worried I'll turn into my father."

Gemma blew on her coffee. "Was he that bad?"

His first instinct was to joke it off and change the topic, as he usually did. But he was comfortable enough around Gemma to stop and think.

"Honestly, I don't remember much. According to my aunt, he stole my mother away and corrupted her."

"According to your aunt, huh?"

A good point, he supposed. There were two sides to every story. The problem was, no one had ever filled him in on the other side. He gazed at the misty morning scene outside. A bee meandered over the flower bed, and dewdrops sparkled with soft pink light. A perfect little world, just the way his aunt liked it.

Gemma shot him a wry grin. "Maybe I'm the one corrupting you. But you've been a knight in shining armor, coming to my rescue again and again."

He laughed, pulling her into a hug. "Definitely not a knight. And believe me, my thoughts have been — let's say... impure — for a while now."

She snorted. "Not as impure as mine."

"We'll have to compare notes someday."

She chuckled. "Someday."

But then her eyes fell to his lips. Her hand slid over his knee. And dammit, he couldn't help but guide her around to face him. A moment later, they were kissing. Gently, then harder. A hum sounded in his ears, like the sound of the ocean washing over a rocky shore, and the longer he kissed her, the closer his ship drifted to that lee shore.

Yes, his lion rumbled. *More...*

But someone started hammering on the door, and ever so slowly, they eased apart. His body moved first, but his hands fought to hang on, and his lips resisted most of all. He and Gemma ended the kiss with long, stretched-out lips, drawing out the magic as long as they could. When they finally separated, their eyes locked.

"Nice," Gemma whispered, flashing a smile.

"More than nice," he replied, sliding back for more.

But the hammering grew louder, and Bri hollered through the door. "Rise and shine."

Liam groaned and made for the door. When he opened it, he threw an arm across the threshold before his cousin could charge in.

"That good a night, huh?" She waggled her eyebrows.

"No comment."

She sniffed then grinned. "Definitely a good night. When's the wedding?"

95

He crossed his arms, trying to look menacing, but it was hard with someone who was practically his kid sister. "Watch it, Bri."

She sighed. "It's not my fault I don't get any fun, not with the way Mother watches over me." She frowned, motioning behind her. "Anyway, consider yourself warned. Mother saw the car."

He groaned. Of course she had.

"She nearly marched over here, too, but I told her you were with a lady friend."

He winced. "What exactly did you tell her?"

Brianna flashed a smug smile. "Not as much as I could have. Anyway, I talked her out of coming over to inspect the happy couple for herself. She's ready to receive you now."

Liam slumped against the doorframe. So much for a quiet morning of considering his next steps.

"Do me a favor, please."

Brianna rolled her eyes. "Another one?"

It took him five minutes to convince Brianna to run back to the main house, and another ten for Gemma to shower thoroughly enough to — mostly — cover the lingering scent of sex. By that time, Brianna had come over with some fresh clothes for Gemma, and Liam braced himself for a half-hour ordeal of his cousin mulling over fashion choices. But Gemma came down the stairs a few minutes later, wearing jeans, a white T-shirt, and her flannel shirt thrown over that. Her hair was clipped in a half-up, half-down arrangement that echoed the lines of her cheeks.

She twirled once, inviting him to look. "I went for practical, not stylish. Will your aunt mind?"

Liam shook his head, then his whole body. Now was not the time to think of how he'd had Gemma's beautiful, naked body to himself the previous night.

"Mother always finds something to mind," Bri said cheerfully. "Just ignore her."

Liam snorted. Easier said than done.

"She's very bossy. Very businesslike," Brianna continued. "Daddy was the down-to-earth one."

Liam shot her a sad smile. Bri was right. His uncle had been warm, patient, and kind. Indulging, if a little disengaged, like most male lions who settled down late and let their mates run the household. And boy, did Liam's aunt run that household. She had ruled it with an iron fist even before his uncle passed away.

"Shall we?" Brianna motioned outside.

Gemma didn't look so sure, but she stepped to the door gamely. "Let's go."

Liam marveled yet again. If anyone could face his aunt, Gemma could. But, whew. He had yet to master that art form himself.

"Beautiful garden." Gemma skimmed her hand over the flowers crowding both sides of the twisting path.

Liam looked around. The oaks were hundreds of years old, standing strong and steady. Bright daffodils sprung up around their roots, forming a swaying blanket of green and yellow. Thick hedges that meandered this way and that, all lined with flowers. As a kid, he'd never really considered the aesthetics, but now... It really was beautiful, and a great place to grow up. His very first shift into lion form had happened in that garden, and many since.

But among the feelings of nostalgia lurked frustrations that had plagued him for so many years.

Be a good boy, Liam. Not like that no-good father of yours...

Lions are the best. Dragons, you can never trust.

Your poor mother. She could have done so much better...

"It's so quiet here," Gemma whispered as they crossed a stretch of open lawn.

Liam followed her gaze. The property ran between the Thames and the former hunting grounds of Richmond Park, so, yes, it was quiet, if you didn't count the flights heading in and out of Heathrow.

"Too quiet. Not much nightlife in Richmond," Brianna grumbled, much as Liam had, once upon a time.

Gemma slowed. "Wow. Is that a tennis court?"

Bri sighed. "I have to take lessons and everything."

Liam tugged Gemma onward. Yes, the property included a tennis court. If he took her on the grand tour, she would also discover the stable, a boathouse, and the *Orangerie.* Lions liked making an impression, and that extended to their homes.

When they turned a corner, coming into view of the main house, Gemma trailed behind. "Wow."

Liam frowned. "It is rather... large."

"Large? That is huge."

Liam looked over the manor house with its sweeping east and west wings, all facing a row of fountains and, farther downslope, the Thames.

"Not big enough to get away from my mother," Brianna muttered.

Liam took Gemma's hand, hoping she wouldn't think less of him for that obvious display of wealth.

"Nice terrace," Gemma offered as he led her over the flagstones.

"Great place to sun yourself — if and when the sun comes out," Brianna said.

Gemma's step faltered, and Liam winced. If she was picturing a pride of lions resting in the afternoon sun, then yes, that really happened sometimes.

Peaceful lions, he wanted to explain. *Ones that wouldn't hurt a fly.*

But that wasn't entirely the truth, as he'd come to learn. His family — and by extension, the lion Guardians of London — were a lot like the Foreign Legion. Their ideals might be lofty, but sometimes, the ends justified the means. Woe be the shifter — or human — who stood in the way of the Guardians' goals.

He pulled Gemma a little closer, promising himself that would never be her. But his stomach turned, remembering the task Electra had set out for him. He shouldn't have succumbed to sheer need the previous night. Not before explaining everything to Gemma.

But it was too late — in more ways than one, because Brianna was already leading them into the house.

"Liam, darling." His aunt rose as they entered the sunny breakfast room. "So good to see you again." She hugged him with stiff arms, then thrust him away. "Now, who is this beauty?"

Her voice was perfectly even, but something in it put Liam on red alert.

"This is my friend, Gemma. Gemma, meet my aunt, Lucinda."

"A pleasure to meet you, ma'am." Gemma took her hand with a tiny curtsy.

Bri looked impressed, as did his aunt. Even better, confused. Gemma had an American accent but British manners, at least when she chose to switch them on.

"The pleasure is all mine, dear."

She didn't demand Gemma's last name, and Liam prayed she hadn't yet heard about the Fire Maiden sought by the Guardians. On the whole, his aunt refrained from mixing in politics, leaving that to the indomitable Electra and others. But Electra was his aunt's aunt, so he couldn't be sure. And as for Lucinda's expression — well, it was always hard to differentiate. Was that crafty calculation or innocent curiosity that made her eyes glint?

"Come along. I've asked Jensen to lay out a few things for breakfast."

Gemma's eye caught Liam's and said, *A few things?*

He sighed. The table held everything from salmon to scones and fresh strawberries with cream — enough to feed a dozen hungry lions. Then again, his aunt always liked to impress.

Still, he sensed something brewing under her cool exterior. Something not entirely normal, like the way she silently tapped her nails on the tablecloth. Or was it just him? He hadn't spent much time at home since leaving the Legion, and people changed. He certainly had.

"Now, my late husband..." His aunt set off on the long-winded tale of how his uncle Hendrick had amassed the art collection decorating the walls.

Gemma spread clotted cream and jam on her scone and listened politely. Brianna rolled her eyes. Liam frowned. His uncle had been the one prone to droning on with long stories, but not his aunt. Never. Why was she dragging things out now?

"And then we renovated the cottage. Isn't it lovely? I started by choosing the color palette..."

Jensen, the butler, appeared at a door, quiet as a mouse, then backed away without fluttering an eyelid. Liam's aunt didn't miss a beat, but she did tilt her head ever so slightly.

"Mother, you're boring our guest," Brianna complained.

"Don't be ridiculous. Am I boring you, dear?"

Gemma put down the spoon she'd been doodling on her empty plate with. "Not at all."

"You see?"

Brianna made a face. "You're boring me."

"Nonsense, child. Now, hush."

She'd been exactly the same when Liam was seven, seventeen, and everything in between. Any comments he made, any theories he proposed — especially about his parents — were greeted that way.

Maybe my daddy tried to be good. Maybe dragons aren't so bad.

All were greeted with those same, abrupt words. *Nonsense, child. Now, hush.*

"We knew the cream tones needed contrast, and that's why the curtains are sage..." Lucinda went on about the guesthouse.

Liam knew damn well his aunt didn't care about curtains, color palettes, or any such thing. And yet, she rambled on. At the same time, her gaze kept darting around, and, like a lioness crouched in the savanna, she kept perfectly still.

When the butler nodded from the door and Lucinda half nodded back, Liam's alarm grew. Something was definitely off.

Bri... he called into his cousin's mind. *What's going on?*

But Bri just frowned in confusion. *What do you mean?*

Obviously, Brianna wasn't in on whatever his aunt was plotting. He pulled out his phone and peeked down. On his first glance, he tapped in the code. On the second brief glimpse, he scrolled to his messages. On the third—

Even before he saw the message from Sergio — the one marked with a red exclamation mark — it hit him.

His aunt had been in touch with the Guardians. Whether she had contacted them or they had called her didn't matter. The point was, the Guardians were on their way over. That was why Lucinda was stalling.

Bri, he all but shouted in his cousin's mind. *I need a favor.*

She looked up, startled.

Pull up my car. Please. Quietly, and no questions asked. The key is in the ignition.

Brianna's eyes slid between him and her mother. Then she shot him a mischievous wink. Slowly, she stood and pressed a napkin to her lips, mumbled something about the ladies' room, and slipped away.

"Now, the roofing was really difficult," his aunt continued, barely noticing.

Liam gnashed his teeth, and the next few minutes felt like an eternity. Finally, the hum of the Aston Martin's straight-six engine reached his ears. He jumped up, toast in hand, and pulled Gemma to her feet.

"Thank you for breakfast, but we really must get going."

Gemma blinked. "We do?"

He nodded firmly and made for the door. But Lucinda was there in a flash, blocking the way.

"My dear boy. What's the hurry? Gemma and I are only starting to get acquainted."

Her voice was cheery, but her eyes were hard. *Don't you dare ruin this. Everything is going according to plan.*

What exactly that plan was, he didn't know. Would the Guardians sweep in, grab Gemma, and take her away? Would they drug her up and force her to do their bidding?

"We have urgent business to attend to," he insisted.

"Nonsense, child. You can't leave." It was a command, not an admonition.

Liam had always been grateful for his aunt's help, and while he'd always known there was a hidden agenda at work, he had usually trusted her judgment. But now, he'd had enough.

"What's going on?" he demanded, feeling his face flush. "What have you done?"

Lucinda's eyes flashed. "What I had to do. It's for your own good." Her gaze went to Gemma with a satisfied glow. "And hers."

Gemma frowned. "What are you talking about?"

"My dear girl, there's so much you don't know."

Liam could have throttled his aunt. Instead, he made a beeline for the door.

"Liam!" his aunt shouted.

"Goodbye," he barked, breaking into a jog.

Gemma followed without a peep, and he wished he had time to explain. But he didn't, not with his aunt rushing off for the old-fashioned landline she still used.

Outside, the car was already facing the manor gates, its engine purring. When Bri slid out of the front seat and held the door open, he hugged her.

"I could kiss you sometimes."

"Yuck. You're practically my brother. Now, go. And remember, you owe me."

"You'll be okay?"

Brianna shrugged a little too nonchalantly. "Maybe I'll be the next Elspeth around here."

"God, I hope not." He tousled her hair. "Thanks, Bri."

The second he and Gemma were buckled in, Liam peeled away, scattering gravel. Brianna — bless her — had opened the gates, and within minutes, they were zooming out of town.

"What exactly is going on?" Gemma asked. "And who is Elspeth?"

He ran a hand through his hair. "My mother."

Gemma fell silent, and he pursed his lips. There was so much he had to explain, but did he really want to get into the details of his mother, the wild child of the family, at a time like this? It was far more important to contact Sergio and warn him. Above all, he had to figure out where Gemma would be safe.

His mind was spinning, and it must have shown, because Gemma touched his arm. "Sorry. Maybe you can explain some other time."

God, he loved her. "I swear I will."

Gemma swiveled in her seat, looking back. "Just one thing. Will Brianna be okay?"

He snorted. "That girl can sweet-talk her way out of anything."

Gemma didn't look convinced, but she kept her lips sealed. A moment later, she opened the glove box and pulled out a map. Then she unfolded it and spread it out on her lap. "Where to?"

His heart warmed. Boy, did he love her pluck. When he threw her a grin, his gaze caught on the left side of the map, and a whole new plan unfolded in his mind. One he hadn't even considered, but all of a sudden, there it was, beckoning him.

Wales. His father's homeland. A place he hadn't visited in years.

Wales? his lion protested. *It's filled with dragons allied with the Guardians. And the Guardians are after Gemma. We can't bring her there.*

But the more he thought about it, the more he was convinced. For every Welsh dragon who cooperated with the Guardians, there were a dozen others quietly holding out in the hills, the way his father's clan had.

He glanced in the rearview mirror, and an image of his father popped into his head. Not the vague blur most of his memories had become, but perfectly clear. The upward sweep of his eyebrows, the sharp curve of his cheeks, and the angle of his jaw — all the features that hadn't passed through to his son. And yet Liam saw them in the mirror, superimposed on his own.

That face was young. Honest. Hopeful. That face was calling him home.

"Motorway coming up." Gemma's eyes darted between the map and the roadside signs. "Do we head back to London or follow the M4?"

103

Liam scratched his jaw. According to his relatives, Wales was a wild, unruly place. Undesirable, just like his father. He glanced in the mirror again.

"Liam? Which way?" Gemma asked.

He could practically hear his relatives clamoring for him to turn Gemma in to the Guardians. The Guardians were old and wise, and they worked for the common good.

But a lone voice drew him the other way. His father's voice — one he recognized from his dreams.

Liam looked at Gemma, then in the mirror. Whatever decision he made would affect her life forever.

A truck moved into the lane beside him, and a Land Rover was accelerating from the other side. If he didn't act fast, one of his options would be cut off. Wales or London?

"Liam..." Gemma motioned urgently at the rapidly approaching fork in the road.

At the last possible second, Liam threw on the blinker and pulled a sharp left.

Gemma yelped. The Land Rover swerved. The truck blared its horn. Liam cursed both vehicles, then exhaled. A minute later, he and Gemma were speeding along the motorway.

Slowly, Gemma unwrapped her fingers from the handle she'd grabbed. Then she compared the map with the signs overhead. "M4 heading west. Are we going to Bristol?"

Liam shook his head. "To Cardiff. Then we'll hang a hard right."

Her eyes went wide. "The Brecon Beacons?"

Liam's jaw swung open as he remembered what she'd said. *I love it there.* It was as if all the loose threads of his life and hers had tangled together and were pulling them to one place. As crazy and impulsive as his last-minute decision had been, it felt right.

Maybe it's not crazy, his lion murmured. *Maybe it's destiny.*

Chapter Eleven

Gemma spread the map on her lap, tracing their position as Liam drove. For a while, she'd remained mute, trying to settle her nerves. Then, an hour outside London, she'd finally let out the barrage of questions that had built up in her mind. For what seemed like hours, Liam had patiently answered. Now, she was silently digesting everything Liam had explained.

Dragons... Lion shifters... Guardians... And above all, Fire Maidens. Like her.

She gulped and put a finger on Cardiff, the next landmark on the drive. Somehow, that map felt like her lifeline to the normal human world — the boundaries of which had been burst over the past twelve hours.

"So, my father really is descended from dragons. My mother too," she said slowly.

Liam nodded without taking his eyes off the road.

"What exactly would the Guardians want me to do, if I really am their Fire Maiden?"

She waited as Liam weighed his response before speaking. His forehead was deeply lined, his eyes dark. Gone was the fun, easygoing charmer who bubbled with energy. Now he was a mute soldier in a battle she struggled to comprehend.

"At a superficial level, simply having a Fire Maiden in the city reinforces the power of the ancient spell."

"The one cast by the dragon queen, Liviana," Gemma murmured, trying to piece together what she'd learned.

"Witches cast the spell. But, yes — Liviana ordered it. The spell protects the city from evil, but it has been waning. The only thing that can strengthen it is the presence of a Fire Maiden."

105

Gemma frowned. "Just her presence? I mean, will it suck away my energy or something?"

He shook his head firmly. "No. On the contrary — it can give you power, too. Power you can use for good. My friend Tristan in Paris..." He trailed off, and a mix of emotions passed over his face. "His mate, Natalie, is a Fire Maiden, and she's thriving. They both are."

When he gulped and looked away, Gemma wondered why. Then he hurried on.

"From what I know, some Fire Maidens have been content to simply... well, hang around. They live in the city, and that's it. But the greatest Fire Maidens — the ones who go down in history — are the ones who harness that power and put it to good use."

"Like what?"

"Honestly, I don't know the details. The past few generations of lions have downplayed the significance of Fire Maidens. All I learned about was how high and mighty lions are. Not too much about dragons." His voice grew bitter, and then he sighed. "But from what I gather, a strong Fire Maiden can accomplish a lot, like forging new alliances. Supporting public projects. Working toward peace and prosperity." Then he attempted a little chuckle. "Right up your alley."

She snorted. "I'm just one person contributing to movements that could take decades to bring lasting change. Most of those causes started before my time, and most of them will continue long after I'm gone." She looked out the window. Once upon a time, she'd actually believed one person could change the world. Now, she wasn't so sure.

"Natalie is doing a great job in Paris," Liam said. "She set up a counseling network for homeless people, placing them in jobs and homes. She's helping single mothers, as well, and she's even working with the gargoyles to speed up reconstruction efforts at Notre Dame."

Gemma felt the blood drain from her face. Gargoyles?

She tried distracting herself by studying her bracelets, but that didn't help. According to Liam, the Guardians had set one out to lure in a Fire Maiden — her — and she despised the idea of being used. On the other hand, she loved having a matched pair, and somehow, she felt stronger with them. More complete, and more powerful in some mysterious way. Why?

A few minutes later, she gave up trying to figure that out. She had enough to come to grips with as it was. Instead, she studied the landscape. They were high on the Severn Bridge, crossing the mighty river while a storm swept down the valley, coming right for them.

"So, I could be a Fire Maiden," she continued once they approached the far shore. "And the Guardians need me to stick around London. That's it?"

Liam made a face and mumbled, "More or less."

She had the distinct impression there was a lot more, but for now, that would do.

"All right, then. If the Guardians are the good guys, why are we running?"

Liam looked stuck, and she wondered if his instincts agreed with hers. That they were smart to run even though she couldn't explain why. It simply felt right — and more urgent — than anything she had ever felt before.

He tapped the steering wheel, thinking. "The Guardians serve London. I genuinely believe that. But individuals don't matter to them. They want to control their Fire Maiden in every possible way." His voice dropped and wavered. "They would protect you, but they would clip your wings and keep you in a gilded cage."

His words came from the heart, and she wondered whether the bitterness came from personal experience.

"What's to keep them from coming after us in Wales?"

Liam snorted. "First, I doubt they'd think of it. Hell, I'm surprised I thought of it. They wrote off my father a long time ago, and I guess I did too." His expression grew morose, and he paused before going on. "Second, Wales is the realm of dragons. As high and mighty as the lions of London consider themselves, they rarely venture from the heart of their empire. So, no. The Guardians won't come after us here. At most, they'll send an emissary and try to woo us back."

Gemma made a face. There was no way she'd be wooed by those bastards. But they were only one part of her problem.

Outside the windows, the sky was a swirling maelstrom of gray clouds that grew ever darker. Sneaking up, almost, like the stalker of her nightmares. Within minutes, visibility dropped and raindrops splattered the windscreen.

I want you, Maiden. And soon, I will have you. Petro's words echoed through her mind.

She suppressed a little shiver. "My father always warned me about dragons. He never said a word about lions."

Liam shrugged. "Maybe he doesn't know about us. Anyway, dragons lie at the heart of the problem."

"The Lombardis," she said.

He nodded. "Sergio got an ID on the dragon who attacked last night. Lorenzo Lombardi — brother of Petro, last seen in Boston."

She gulped. So she hadn't been crazy about the man in the Tube.

Reaching for his phone, she mumbled, "I ought to call my dad. May I use your phone?"

But Liam shook his head so vehemently, she stopped. "Not yet. The less he's involved, the safer he is. We have to understand exactly who we're dealing with first. The Lombardis are bad news, no matter which one of them is involved or where they strike. The Guardians are right not to want the Lombardis to find you first. If they do..." Liam's hands clenched so tightly over the wheel, his knuckles turned white. "It would be bad for the city, and it would be bad for you."

Though Liam hadn't gotten into the details when he'd first explained about the Lombardis, Gemma could read between the lines. She would be stolen away like a princess in feudal times, completely at the mercy of powerful men who took whatever — and whomever — they wanted. Living in a gilded cage sounded like a walk in the park compared to the hell her life would be under the Lombardis.

She clenched and unclenched her hands, studying the lines on her palms. She'd always been an average, girl-next-door type. Now, powerful forces vied for control of her life. She closed her eyes, determined not to bang the dashboard. How the hell had that happened?

Outside, rain hammered the roof, and water splashed the wheel wells, creating a constant, washing sound. The sound of a life spinning out of control. But then Liam wrapped his fingers around hers, halting the chill that crept into her bones.

"We'll think of something."

She squeezed his hand and forced herself to smile. She had her very own Lancelot, and the Aston Martin was his trusty steed, carrying them both to safety. But, still. She could no sooner overcome powerful shifter forces than she could halt the storm outside.

"Welsh weather, huh?" Liam joked. "Welcoming us home."

They rushed past a sign, and she straightened the map over her knees, trying to ground herself in reality.

"Cardiff, coming up," she said, trying to be matter-of-fact. Then she dipped her head and looked out the driver's side window. Somewhere to the north, hidden by swirling clouds, were the mountains.

Liam nodded and whispered, more to himself than to her. "The Brecon Beacons." Then his lips moved a little more, and though no sound came out, she swore she heard one word whisper through his mind. *Home.*

∞∞∞∞

By all rights, the drive should have taken them four hours, what with the distance, the weather, and the winding mountain roads they followed over the last few miles. Gemma had driven the same route with her father, and his cautious driving often stretched the trip out to five hours. Liam, on the other hand, made it in closer to three. She didn't need to ask if they were close, only to watch the furrows in Liam's brow deepen.

Finally, he eased the car around a tight turn and cruised to a stop, staring ahead. Gemma caught a glimpse of a roof on a hilltop, but Liam shifted into first gear and moved forward before she got a good look.

"That's it. Home. My father's place."

She'd never heard his voice go that tight or the contours his face pinch so deeply.

"When were you last here?" She craned her neck as he navigated the last turns. The hill was so steep, it hid the house, somewhere over the ridge.

"Ten years ago, just to stash my things. Before that..." His chest rose and fell with each uneven breath. "Not since my parents died, though I barely remember."

His eyes drifted over the landscape, and she wondered how much of that last statement was a fib.

The storm was disappearing over the horizon, leaving gray skies and one of the most dramatic — if soggy — landscapes she had ever seen. Carved between craggy peaks were long, sweeping valleys sliced by rocky outcrops. All in all, a windswept, uninhabited expanse without the villages, stone walls, or sheep they'd passed in the lower slopes.

Wales, the land of dragons. Who would have believed it?

She looked around. It was all so familiar, she wondered how close she'd come to this very part of the Brecon Beacons on walks with her father.

Then Liam turned the last corner, and her breath caught.

"That's your house?"

Liam nodded wearily.

It was a goddamn castle, but somehow, that didn't surprise her. What made her jaw drop was that she recognized it. The structure was imprinted in her fondest memories and a recurring sight in her favorite dreams.

"I know this place," she whispered as Liam turned onto a twisting driveway.

He waved a hand around. "Yes, you mentioned. The Brecon Beacons."

"No, I mean I know this exact place." She pointed at the castle. "I've been here. At least, close." She swiveled around, trying to locate the viewpoint she'd seen it from. "I know this castle. I know that tower."

She gulped, deciding not to mention how often she'd dreamed herself into a life at that castle, with a man and some dogs and her very own happily-ever-after.

Liam looked dubious. "Precisely this place?"

She nodded. "There's a row of trees around the back, right? And a ruined chapel."

Liam stopped the car. Those things weren't visible from this angle, so he had to know she was right. For a long, quiet minute, they looked at each other, then at the castle.

"Wow," she murmured. "Some coincidence."

Liam shook his head slowly. "Destiny."

Destiny, an inner voice told her at exactly the same moment.

She sat, stunned. The concept of fate had always given her the shivers, but somehow, being at that very castle with Liam felt perfectly right. Maybe destiny was more of a guardian angel, not the cruel mistress she'd always assumed it to be.

A huge raven flew over the car, cawing loudly, and Liam jutted his chin. "Bugger. Some things never change."

She tilted her head.

Liam made a face. "That's Gareth."

"Gareth?" She watched as the raven circled one more time then settled on a windowsill.

Liam sighed. "You'll see."

They drove on, and a drawbridge came into view. Liam made a hard right and pulled up to a barn, where they both got out to open the double doors. Gemma stood aside as Liam parked, then ducked as a bat flew over her head. The place was musty but neat as a pin.

"This way," Liam muttered in a *Let's get this over with* tone.

Gemma gawked as he led her onward. "Wow. You have a moat and everything."

"A moat. A portcullis. Suits of armor. Brace yourself." He sighed. "Many, many suits of armor."

He lifted the huge iron knocker on the door-within-a-door of the entry, then hesitated. Finally, he slammed it against the door as if to make a statement. Was it *I'm back but not to stay* or *Destiny, here I come?*

Either way, it was loud. Plenty loud. Gemma put a hand on Liam's shoulder, and the next three bangs were a little less forceful. More... resigned, almost. Then he waited a minute, lifted the knocker again, and—

The door opened, and a tall, thin man in a dark suit scowled at him.

"I was on my way. Sir."

Liam broke into a wide grin. "Hello, Gareth. And here I was, thinking you might have gone deaf."

"Not yet. Unfortunately," the man said dryly.

His hair — jet-black peppered with a little gray — was freshly windswept, and the sweeping motion he made to usher them in echoed the motion of the raven's wings.

"This is Gemma," Liam said as they stepped in.

"Miss." Gareth gave her a stiff bow.

Gemma did her best to bow back. "Nice to meet you."

As they walked, she peeked out of the corner of her eye. Was Gareth the caretaker? A butler? And, whoa — if he was a raven shifter, what other species existed? Did tiny mouse shifters reside in the castle pantries?

"Gareth has been here since before I was born," Liam said as they walked through a lofty hall lined by arches, each occupied by a suit of armor set in a stand.

"Since before your father was born," Gareth corrected. "Sir."

Gemma pinched her lips. Poor Liam. He might have proven himself to her, but not to Gareth.

Not yet, she decided, squeezing Liam's hand.

The entrance hall led to a dining room that could have hosted an entire medieval court. Gemma pictured knights, ladies, and jesters consuming steaks and drinking from horns. She quickened her pace to keep up with Liam and Gareth, who headed into a smaller room on the left. A library, from the looks of it, with floor-to-ceiling shelves packed with leatherbound books. There, she nearly ran into Liam, who stopped to stare at the huge oak desk in one corner of the room. Had his father worked at that desk? His grandfather?

She touched his back without saying a word.

"May I ask how long the young master and his guest intend to stay?"

Gareth's face was perfectly neutral, but Gemma could guess what Liam's answer would be — namely, as brief a stay as possible.

"Not sure yet," Liam murmured, still looking at the desk. Then his eyes drifted to the window. Gemma's did too, checking the sky for enemy dragons.

A chill went through her. How safe was this place? And for how long?

Chapter Twelve

Hours later, Gemma sat on a couch with her feet pulled up beside her, staring into the crackling fireplace of the parlor. Man, was she exhausted. Liam was too; she could tell. He'd spent the afternoon coming and going, tending to business with Gareth. Every time he stepped out, he looked weary and forlorn, and every time he returned, his face lit up upon seeing her. She lit up too. Liam hadn't been part of her life for long, but somehow, it felt as if he belonged.

Forever, a scratchy voice whispered in her mind.

She watched the fire snap and swirl. It was as if there'd been a hole in her life she hadn't even been aware of, and now it was filled. But, damn. She'd had a hell of a couple of days between the dragon attack and their rush to leave London. The fact that she'd slept with Liam — without second thoughts of any kind — made her wonder how off-kilter she really was.

Please, please, let this not all turn out to be one huge mistake, she prayed.

He's no mistake, that scratchy voice replied.

That voice was something deep inside her she'd heard at different times in her life, though never as often and as clearly as now. Was it the voice of her ancestors? Her inner dragon? Destiny?

She'd had tea with Liam and, more recently, dinner — a hearty stew with thick slices of dark bread that could have come from a medieval kitchen. Outside, rain came and went, and the wind howled, though the tapestries insulating the walls kept any draft from sneaking in.

Finally, she stood, studying the tapestries. Liam was a lion shifter, so what accounted for all those dragons in the scenes? In one, a dragon flew over a castle, breathing fire. Did that relate to the shifters who'd owned the castle before Liam's family? In another scene, two dragons flew over a flowery landscape, and they didn't even look too menacing. On the contrary, that scene radiated hope, happiness, and love, contradicting everything her father had ever said about cruel dragons. Of course, there were unicorns, too, and bunnies, and even monkeys. Who knew what those elements represented to the person who had woven the tapestries centuries ago?

A door creaked open, and Gemma whirled, then smiled.

"Hey," she called softly.

"Hey," Liam whispered.

And there they remained for a long minute, doing nothing more than exchanging dopey grins.

Finally, Gemma gave herself a shake and spoke. "I know it's not that late, but I'm ready for bed."

"Me too. I'll show you to your room."

Her room implied a separate *his* room, and she would have much preferred to curl up next to him. Maybe even do more than curl up with him. On the other hand, they were in his family's home, and Liam might need time to process all his stirred-up memories.

But, drat. He'd lit a fire inside her from day one, and her desire had grown steadily since then.

"So, the bedrooms are up here..."

Liam led her up a spiral staircase, then down a wide hallway on the third floor. Portraits lined the walls, and every archway housed a suit of armor. Lots of armor, as Liam had said, all shining to high heaven as if ready to kit out the Knights of the Round Table.

"I can't decide whether this would be a great place to grow up or a spooky one," she murmured.

Liam laughed. "Mostly great, as far as I remember. I used to sit on my dad's shoulders and ride him around like a knight." His smile stretched from ear to ear then slowly subsided. "At least, I think I did."

Gemma had always thought it was a curse to have divorced parents and an eccentric father. But to have lost one's parents so young, and to have heard so little about them from relatives... That was much worse.

She slowed, studying the next suits of armor. Some had pikes, while others held lances, and still others...

A sword glinted, catching her eye, and she touched it. "Can I try this one?"

Liam was so deep in thought, he didn't turn. He just called over his shoulder, "Of course."

The sword zinged as she pulled it from the scabbard, and the blade flashed. *Really* flashed, brighter than any of the bulbs in the hallway. A surge of energy went through her as her bracelets reflected the light back.

She sliced the air experimentally. Wow. That blade was perfectly balanced. She cut to the left, then shuffle-stepped forward and thrust toward a different suit of armor.

Liam jumped back, his eyes wide. "You know your sword-play."

"Not playing," she murmured in an echo of her father's words.

Using tiny wrist movements, she circled the tip of the sword. It felt like an extension of her arm.

"Careful," Liam said in a strangely guarded voice. "That blade is spelled against shifters."

"Oh yes?" She turned the blade this way and that. "I'd love to put it to use against a dragon."

Liam winced and put up his hands. "Yes, well..."

She slumped a little. He was right. Even with a sword that felt as magical as Excalibur, how could she possibly fend off a dragon? She slid it back into place and trudged down the hall.

Liam showed her into a spacious corner room with a huge four-poster bed, a cushioned window seat, and gorgeous stained-glass panels. When he started a fire in the huge hearth, the shadows made the figures on the tapestries dance.

Gemma made a face. Great. More dragons. Between her exhaustion, the gloomy weather, and the reminder of her own helplessness, she found herself dreading a night alone.

Liam must have noticed, because he glanced around the echoing room glumly. "Not exactly cozy, huh?"

She forced a smile. "It's great. I mean, how often do I get to stay in a castle?"

Still, he didn't look satisfied. He looked around, then stuck up a finger and announced, "I'll be right back."

"But—"

"Just a tick," he called, trotting out the door.

Gemma rubbed her arms. Castles were great for sightseeing, but not so much for spending the night, especially in a vast, spooky chamber. Outside, the wind howled, making shutters bang and groan.

Within minutes, Liam hurried back in, half hidden behind a mountain of pillows and blankets that threatened to spill out of his arms. Gemma scurried out of the way as he made for the bed.

"All right, then. Commence Operation Make Castle Cozy," he announced.

She laughed. "Operation what?"

He started tossing pillows into place. "Ha. You think it can't be done? That's what they told Churchill during the Blitz. Just watch."

With one hand, he yanked off the gold-tasseled bedcover and flung it aside. Then he pulled a thick, woolen blanket from the pile he'd brought and threw it open with a snap.

"First, you get your happy colors," he said, spreading it over the bed.

She laughed. The blanket was white with sky-blue stripes that flowed like waves as it fluttered into place. The pillows were bright yellow and green, like the flowers and grass at the shore of a lake they'd passed.

"Now, if Gareth weren't so slow..." Liam muttered.

"Say again, sir?" Gareth appeared at the doorway with two steaming mugs.

"Finally," Liam declared. "What took you so long?"

If his aunt had uttered those words, they would have sounded hopelessly snobbish. But Liam made them more of a tease.

118

Gareth paced in, unperturbed. "I dare say, the cocoa powder hasn't been called for in years. Not since you were a wee lad."

Gemma hid a grin. Gareth had a way of following orders while putting Liam in his place.

Liam grinned, and Gemma swore Gareth had a twinkle in his eye. They liked testing the boundaries of the boss/servant relationship, didn't they?

"Well, we need it now." Liam motioned to the four-poster bed. "Leave the cocoa there, please, and help me push this thing."

Gareth's face pinched. "*That* is not a *thing*. It is a seventeenth-century heirloom from the house of—"

"Yes, yes. A very old bed. Come on, put your back into it."

"Really, it's fine where it is," Gemma protested.

But Liam was a man on a mission. "It is not fine. It's not cozy."

Gareth frowned. "Cozy?"

"Cozy," Liam declared. "Ready?"

Gemma put her shoulder to one corner, while Gareth and Liam pushed at the others, and slowly, the monolith scraped along.

"It will scratch the floor," Gareth protested.

"Which is made of stone," Liam pointed out.

"Like the soul of an Englishman," Gareth muttered.

Liam laughed. "I'm half Welsh. Come on already. We're nearly there."

Once they'd maneuvered the heavy bed into a corner, Liam trotted back, dragged over the rug, and surveyed his handiwork.

"Better. We need a table, though. A place to put a book and a drink. Come along, Gareth. Chop chop. Make yourself useful."

"Useful. Indeed," Gareth grumbled, heading for the door.

"Really, it's fine," Gemma tried.

But Liam didn't pay attention. Instead, he called after Gareth. "And not one of those oak monstrosities that weigh ten stone. Something cozy."

"Certainly, sir. Something we have an abundance of on the premises."

Liam ignored him, turning back to the bed. "So, if we pile these up. . ." He tossed a few more pillows around. "And close these. . ." He drew the curtains on three sides of the four-poster bed, then hopped in and patted the space beside him. "What do you think?"

Gemma crawled in, sitting with her back to the wall and her shoulder against Liam's. Their feet stuck out before them, and they sat there, watching the fire as if it were a television.

"Cozy? Not cozy?" Liam asked.

Gemma smiled and held both thumbs up. "It's great. Thank you."

The curtains closed off most of the huge, echoing room, reducing the view to the best parts: the bright, comfy blankets, the crackling fire, and the window seat with its stained glass, barely lit by moonlight.

"Maybe not as nice as your bunk on *Valhalla*, but it's a start. Oh — except for one thing." Liam scurried out and returned with the drinks.

Gareth had used big, earthenware mugs for the hot chocolate, and when Liam transferred one to her hands, his fingers played over hers. For a few breathtaking moments, they remained close, hands touching, eyes locked. Her breath hitched, and she swore Liam's did too.

Stay, she wanted to say. *Stay and make me feel as good as you did last night.*

But a heavy thump sounded at the door, and they broke apart.

"A table for the young lady," Gareth announced.

The table was a light, pretty thing, painted with colorful flowers and vines. Something narrow enough to fit through the door without trouble, though Gareth bumped and banged as he went, announcing his presence. Gemma blushed. Had she and Liam been that close?

Her blush deepened, because yes — Liam had kneeled between her legs to hand her the drink. Quite innocently, she was sure, but what had it looked like from behind?

It would look good, the dirty part of her mind decided. *It would feel good too.*

And, *zoom!* Her mind took off with wild fantasies of Liam crouched in exactly that position, minus the hot drink — and his clothes.

Of course, Liam didn't blush. Was the man even capable of feeling self-conscious? She doubted it. He simply extracted himself and waved Gareth over, helping him position the pretty table at the bedside.

"Perfect," Liam announced.

"If you're quite finished making the room cozy, sir..."

Gareth held the bedroom door in a hint. Obviously, he was an old-fashioned, *no boys and girls in the same room* type.

Liam waved cheerily. "Thank you, Gareth. That will be all. Good night."

Gareth paused, looking at Gemma in a way that begged her to show more decorum than Liam did. He waited and waited, then muttered something in Welsh — a string a syllables far too long and loaded to mean *Good night.* But Liam turned back to Gemma, and a moment later, Gareth closed the door, leaving them alone.

A few minutes earlier, they'd been all but cuddled up on the bed, but suddenly, Gemma didn't know what to do. It was one of those awkward moments when she was caught between being a nice girl and the burning desire to tear off her clothes and declare, *Let's get down to business, baby.*

Even Liam seemed stuck. His eyes glowed honey-gold with desire, but his hands clenched and unclenched at his sides. He wanted her — she was sure of it. So, what made him hold back?

"What else can I get you?" he whispered after an excruciating pause.

You, she burned to say. *Just you, curled up next to me.*

Instead, she said, "I'm fine, thanks," and regretted it immediately. Which left her little choice but to sip her drink.

Liam sat beside her, drinking just as quietly. Gemma did her best to stretch out the moment, sipping slowly. But at some point, her mug was empty, and his too.

"I guess I'm all set," she mumbled lamely, setting her mug on the table.

The clock on the mantelpiece ticked, hinting at the late hour. But when she was sure Liam would utter a polite, *Well, I guess I'd better go,* she blurted out something — anything — to extend his stay.

"How do lions sleep?"

His laugh echoed through the room. "That's what I like about you. You're very... unexpected."

I like a lot about you, she wanted to say.

"Sorry. Rude question?"

"Not in the least. Most nights, I sleep in a bed, just like this." He motioned over his human body. "But in lion form, I find myself a nice spot — a cozy spot, you might say. Then I lie down and sleep."

"Like a cat?"

He shook his head. "Cats curl up. Lions are above that. Kings of the jungle and all that. You know." He raised his chin and looked down his nose in a regal way.

"Actually, I don't know. I'm new to all this."

"Well, then. Lion Sleep Patterns, Lesson One. Pay attention, please." He clapped like a schoolteacher. "First, you sit back." He went down on all fours on the rug and sat on his haunches. "Like this. Sort of like... like..." He moved around but couldn't settle into a comfortable position. "It doesn't work in this body. But basically, you get into the position of a sphinx."

She burst out laughing. "A sphinx?"

He grinned, then grew serious. "I could show you if you want."

Her lips trembled, and her whisper barely made it past her lips. "I'd like that."

He stood and glanced around, then said, "Don't be alarmed." It was a joke, but the little hitch in his voice said he was nervous too. "I have to strip first."

Gemma decided not to say, *Fine with me.*

She did lean back slightly, because a girl shouldn't come across like a total voyeur. That put Liam partway behind the curtain, mostly out of view. Good enough?

Liam slipped off his shoes and shirt as the fire popped and crackled over burning logs. Something popped and crackled in Gemma's gut too. All that muscle, rippling and sliding like tectonic plates.

Liam turned and slid down his pants, giving Gemma a view of his nice, tight buns. Then he sank to his hands and knees, and—

Gemma's jaw dropped as his body began to transform. His shoulder blades bulged, and hair sprouted along his back.

She wanted to turn away, but she was too fascinated. It was all so smooth, so seamless. One minute, he was Liam. The next, everything blurred as his fur covered the details. Then he was a lion, giving his mane a firm shake. Slowly, he turned, faced her, and—

Their eyes locked, and her breath caught. Those beautiful, honey-gold eyes were all Liam. The way he held his head was similar, too. His body was completely different, yet she could see echoes of the man in his bearing. Proud, but not arrogant. Powerful, but not pushy. And those eyes...

With a twitch of his whiskers, Liam lowered himself to the floor — butt down, front legs stretched forward, his head held high. Just like a sphinx, ready to watch several centuries unfold.

"Wow," she managed to finally find her tongue. "That's amazing."

Liam puffed out his chest.

"Can you roar for me?"

He rolled his eyes, making her laugh. "Okay, maybe no roaring." She thought for a minute. "You said sphinx pose was the first part of going to sleep. What comes next?"

Slowly, he lowered himself to his side. For a minute, he lay there, ribs rising and falling with every deep breath. Then he popped his head up, and in one graceful movement, rolled to his feet.

The sight of all that feline muscle, hair, and teeth surging closer nearly made Gemma scuttle away. But her fear was tinged with wonder — and trust. That was Liam, and he would never, ever betray her. Deep in her heart, she knew that.

So, she didn't budge. In fact, she slid to the edge of the mattress and reached out. Liam inched closer, sliding his head under her hand. Her fingers twitched in an awkward attempt to scratch his ears.

Liam chuffed and closed his eyes.

God, that's good, she could practically hear him sigh.

When he settled back on his haunches, her heart swelled with hope.

"Are you really going to stay here?"

Those deep, golden eyes searched hers, saying something like, *If you want me to.*

She gulped. "Seriously? Would it be comfortable?"

He gave her a look that said, *I served a decade in the Foreign Legion, lady. Who cares about comfort as long as you're safe?*

She nodded slowly. "Wow. My own lion guard."

He bobbed his head and marched back and forth in front of her door, baring his teeth. Really big, really scary teeth, though he would only use them on the bad guys.

"Aha. Are you going to keep that up all night?"

He shook his head, then went back to sphinx position on the rug at her feet.

Her heart thumped a little harder. God, he was sweet. And not at all crazy. Just incredibly loyal. Lovable.

Mine, that voice growled in her mind.

She cleared her throat, stood, and tiptoed around him carefully. "I just need a minute..."

In the end, it took her five to get ready for bed. Liam's ears twitched, tuned in to her every move. When she finally slid under the sheets and blew out the candle at the bedside, the room went silent but for the quiet crackle of the fire.

Slowly, she slid one hand from under the sheets. And as sure as if she'd called out for him, Liam nestled his head against her palm.

She closed her eyes, marveling at the silky thickness of his mane. His *mane*, for goodness' sake!

Part of her burned for Liam to shift back to human form and join her in bed. To touch, kiss, and make love to her all over again. But they were both worn out, and she needed to step back before she got in over her head.

She snorted to herself. There she was, tucked into bed with a lion at her side. Hell, she already was in deep.

She curled her fingers, caressing his thick mane. "Nice."

His tail tapped gently against the rug. *Very nice.*

Touching him settled her jumpy nerves, and soon, exhaustion tugged at her eyelids, beckoning her to sleep.

"Liam?" she murmured into the soft glow of the firelit room.

The lion's left ear flicked back, listening.

"Thank you. For everything."

He chuffed quietly — twice. Once to say *You're welcome*, or so she imagined, and once to say, *Good night.*

Given everything that had transpired, she had good reason to fear sleep because of all the nightmares that were sure to follow. But with Liam, the cheery fire, and the castle walls...

"Good night," she mumbled, drifting easily, peacefully to sleep.

Chapter Thirteen

The fireplace crackled, and Liam sighed, glancing around. It had been a long time — too long, really — since he'd slept an entire night in lion form. It had been too long since he'd been home. Too long since he'd thought enough about his parents to feel connected to them...

Too long since we really cared about something, his lion whispered.

He leaned into Gemma's hand. Her fingers had stopped moving when she fell asleep, but the contact felt nice. So nice that he sat thinking for a while in spite of his exhaustion.

Lots of guys came home from the military feeling numb, but in his case, the numbness had set in much earlier. Way back to some point in his childhood, even. Now, for the first time in years, he felt alive and burning to succeed in one incredibly important thing.

He huffed in a quiet lion chuckle. Gemma had so many causes, and for the first time in ages, he did too.

He had to protect her. To eliminate the bad guys. To make her his mate — not because the Guardians had ordered him to, but because he loved her.

The question was, how to proceed? His relatives had betrayed him. The Guardians of London had probably declared him a rogue for spiriting Gemma away. Worst of all, he had no idea where the Lombardis were or what they were planning.

He stared into the glowing embers. Funny, he'd never realized how easy life in the Legion had been. He'd been told what to do, when to move, and when to rest. He'd been handed causes to fight for and weapons to accomplish that with. But real life was far more complicated, and not just because a man had to figure out complex issues on his own. As it turned out, the line between good and evil was blurrier than he'd been led to believe.

The wind howled outside, and a shutter rattled.

We need that Fire Maiden, Electra had said. *When the shifter world is at peace, the human world tends to follow.*

He growled under his breath. Electra was right. London needed its Fire Maiden, and Gemma was it.

You have a chance to atone for your mother's mistakes. To serve your pride.

He wasn't so sure about his mother's mistakes, but serving his pride was one reason he'd taken the job in London — to finally earn his place among his lion kin. But fitting in wasn't all that attractive. Not now that he knew how the Guardians operated.

Find her. Protect her. Claim this Maiden before it is too late.

He wanted to — desperately. But, hell. What next? Should he come out and tell Gemma about the Guardians' twisted plans? Or should he explain mating first? Then there was the matter of his mixed heritage. Gemma didn't know he was half dragon, and she seemed convinced all dragons were enemies. How would he ever explain?

Tiny flames danced and swirled. His eyelids grew heavier, and he nodded off, hoping nightmares wouldn't find him.

But the dreams that visited him were good ones, if a little warped. Some featured Gemma, while others backtracked to his childhood, and still others overlapped. In one dream, his mother patted him on the back and grinned at what a nice girl he'd found to settle down with. His father smiled too, and spoke to Liam man-to-man, not father to child.

You found your mate? Good. Now love her. Protect her. Make her happy, no matter what it takes.

Which was nice, but strange. Everyone had always said his father was a selfish rogue. In Liam's dreams, the man was utterly devoted to his mate.

I love her. I would die for her, Liam heard his father swear.

He did die for her, a little voice whispered.

Which only went to show how mixed up he was. According to his aunt Lucinda, his father had been killed in a senseless fight, leaving Liam's mother to die of sorrow.

He woke with a start and tapped his tail, thinking. Eventually, he snorted and put his head down again. It was late, and he was tired. Too tired to think straight. If he didn't get some rest, he wouldn't be able to protect Gemma.

So he concentrated on happy thoughts, like the weight of Gemma's hand on his mane and the quiet, steady sound of her breath. And before he knew it. . .

He woke suddenly, feeling cranky because he'd only just gotten to sleep.

But sunlight was flooding through the windows, and birds were chirping outside. Somehow, the entire night had slipped by. He yawned and looked around. Wow. Apparently, he'd fallen into one of those rare, deep sleeps that felt like an instant but were actually hours long.

His mane ruffled under Gemma's hand, which meant she was awake. Awake and watching him, as he discovered when he turned. Her smile was as bright as the sunshine pouring through the windows, and her dark eyes shone.

"Good morning," she whispered.

He twisted his head under her hand. *Good morning to you, beautiful.*

She chuckled. "I see you want to pick up where we left off."

He bobbed his head. In truth, he had business to attend to, but he hadn't been able to enjoy a quiet morning for a long, long time. And he hadn't ever had the pleasure of spending one with his destined mate. So he indulged himself in a few minutes of tuning in to Gemma. He couldn't read her mind, but if he really tried, he might be able to pick up on more subtle clues. Had she slept well? Did she like his ancestral home?

He closed his eyes and flared his nostrils, testing her scent. She was calm. Happy, with thoughts that seemed to be drifting around.

He let his drift too, and while they meandered for a time, he kept circling around to the raw, rushed sex they'd had in

Richmond. Damn, had that been good. And wow — they'd been perfectly in tune, barely needing to utter a word to communicate. He pictured the look on Gemma's face when she'd crawled over his body and—

He threw on the brakes, trying not to venture too far down that slippery path. But, whoa. A sniff revealed the air to be thick with the scent of arousal, and not just his. Had Gemma been thinking along those lines as well?

A peek showed that her eyes were vacant, her hands gripping the sheets.

"Hey," she whispered when she caught him watching.

He held his breath. Would she blush and pretend she didn't feel what he felt? Or would she embrace the instinctive need to bond?

Her eyes held his for a long, quiet minute. Then she considered for a moment and finally spoke. "What if I invited you up?"

Liam's heart revved, and he flicked an ear. Did she mean what he thought she did?

She chuckled. "As you, I mean. Sleeping next to a lion is pretty amazing, but in bed, I have a strict rule. No animals. Just humans." Then she turned crimson and rushed to explain. "Oh my. That sounded wrong. I mean, one at a time. I mean, not just anyone. I mean. . . " She flapped her hands, trying to find the right words. "You. I mean you."

Oh, he knew what she meant, all right. So, he shifted — the fastest, smoothest shift of his life. Gemma's eyes went wide, but she held the sheet up, and he slid right in — into her arms and into a kiss.

"You're like a drug, you know," she mumbled when they came up for air. "I never used to be like this."

He really had to explain about mates soon. Because he'd never felt anything like this either. It was as if he had three gears: protect Gemma. Admire Gemma. Burn with desire for Gemma.

They had started out side by side, but soon, he rolled, gently coming out on top. Gemma's eyes glowed like coals — a sure sign of her shifter heritage — and her fingers spread out on his chest. When they kissed again, her legs snuck up along his sides, and her chest heaved.

"I want you so much..."

He traced her lips with one trembling finger, mouthing a silent message. *I want you — to be safe. To be happy. To be mine.*

Her eyes shone, and he could sense her inner animal reply. *I want you to be mine.*

She knew they were mates, even if she didn't know exactly what that meant.

"Liam..."

Her needy whisper set him off again, and he went back to kissing her. Inhaling her, practically. He was naked, while she was wearing a shirt and knickers, but not for long. Within seconds, he'd helped her wiggle out of both.

"So beautiful," he whispered, rolling her nipple between his lips.

She gasped and arched off the mattress.

He could have caressed her soft flesh all morning, but hell. He needed some more of her sweet lips too. Meanwhile, his legs were a step ahead, nudging hers apart while he lowered a hand to her core. The minute he traced her folds, she moaned.

"Yes..."

Her voice was muffled, because his mouth covered hers. His heart hammered, and his body ached with need. The more he slid his hand around, the more Gemma pushed back, and the slicker she became. When she wrapped a hand around his cock, his breath caught. And when she started sliding up and down, his eyes rolled back.

Mate... his lion murmured again and again. *My beautiful, perfect mate.*

Her hair fanned over the pillow, and her mouth formed silent cries as he circled a finger inside her. Wider and wider, feeling her body cry for his.

Then he pulled away with a gasp and tumbled out of bed. "Condom..."

The first time they'd slept together, neither of them had been thinking clearly. This time, he had no excuse. But someday, when she was his mate...

Gemma grumbled a little, though nowhere near as loud as his lion protested. Still, he fumbled in a pocket of the pants he'd stripped out of the night before. He'd felt like a cad when he'd bought a pack of condoms at a petrol station the previous day, but now, he was fairly proud of himself. A smart lion was a prepared lion.

A smart lion claims his mate, his inner beast grumbled.

Gemma stuck out her hand. "Allow me."

He handed over a condom and hurried back into bed. Boy, was it nice to be with a woman who knew what she wanted. And nice to turn a practicality into searing pleasure as her fist dragged along his shaft. The moment the condom was on, Gemma lay back, opening her arms to him. His limbs fit perfectly around hers, and his hips dipped. For one long, aching minute, he slid along her body, dragging out the pleasure. Then he anchored his arms beside her head, took a deep breath, and thrust in.

Gemma cried out, a sound of pure pleasure that begged for more. He withdrew and waited as long as he could before hammering back in.

"Yes..." She tipped her head back and hugged him with her legs.

His blood was on fire, his muscles tight with need.

"Gemma..."

More, her eyes begged. *More.*

He plunged deeper, barely holding off the explosion building within. Every time he pumped his hips, Gemma bucked back. She slid her hands from his hips to his ass, pulling him closer. Soon, he lost track of which thumping heartbeat was his and which was hers. He lost track of himself, too, because his canines started to extend, preparing for a mating bite.

There, his lion whispered, watching the pulse beat in her neck. *Right along there.*

He kissed her neck, sniffing his way to the perfect spot, guided by an instinct he'd never felt before. All it would take was to sink his teeth deep and Gemma would be his forever. It all played out in his mind, from the smooth slide of his teeth to the heavenly sigh she would heave and the tsunami of pleasure that would consume them both. He sensed exactly how to seal his lips around his bite, keeping her safe while his shifter essence mingled with hers. He could practically feel the satisfaction that would come afterward, knowing she was truly his. Forever.

"Liam..." she moaned, arching under him.

He was so, so close to biting her. But instinct served up another image, catching him off guard. He pictured himself holding Gemma in the mating bite, then exhaling, sending a puff of fire through her veins.

Marking her as ours, a deep voice murmured in his mind.

But, wait. That was a hallmark of dragon mating, not of lions. What was up with that?

He gave himself a little shake and beat back the crazy urge. Now was not the time to mate, but he could give her the high of her life. So, he put everything into pleasuring her — hard and fast enough to make that oak bed creak. Then every muscle in his body pulsed at the same time, and he came.

"Yes!" Gemma cried, shuddering beneath him.

He tossed his head back in a silent roar that echoed through the castle walls. The frequency was too low for human ears, but clear in his mind. Outside, birds fluttered off the windowsills, and the last, burned-through log collapsed in the fireplace.

"So good..." Gemma groaned, still clenched around him.

Images rushed through his mind, most of Gemma in ecstasy. A few were proud lion images in which he roared from a hilltop, staking his claim. Others showed the castle from above, with a feeling of cool air rushing under wings. That contrasted with the heat of the fire he exhaled in a long, fierce breath, daring any enemy to take him on.

Which was confusing as hell. He was a lion, not a dragon. Why was he even imagining such things? A holdover from his dragon heritage, he supposed.

He held on to his climax as long as he could, then sank down over his mate and panted into the sheets. Holy hell. Was it even possible to feel that good?

Gemma went limp too, though she cried out a moment later, shuddering with an aftershock that zinged through his bones, making him go hard once more. Then they both drooped and held each other, counting every pounding heartbeat.

"Mmm," Gemma mumbled sometime later. She was still wrapped around him, her hands patting his back. "Cozy."

He laughed and pulled back for a look at her. Her hair was a mess, her cheeks pink, her expression more peaceful than he'd ever seen.

"This might be cozy. But *that* was. . ." He searched for the word. *Amazing* was such a cliché. So was *earth-shattering*, and neither came close to describing what he'd felt.

"Good," Gemma filled in. "Really, really good."

Her tone captured the feeling more than the words, and he nodded. "Beyond good." Then he kissed her, held her, and gradually drifted back to sleep.

∞∞∞∞

Liam knew he had business to attend to, but once he and Gemma had woken — and made love — a second time, then eaten breakfast, he took her for a walk instead.

"Oh!" She stopped in her tracks and checked her watch before they'd made it too far. "There's a meeting of the Safer Parks Panel today."

He looked at her. Wow. The woman's life had been turned upside down in the past twenty-four hours, but she was still committed to her causes.

"You're going to miss it," he pointed out as gently as possible.

She frowned. "I guess so. Damn." Then she looked around, took a deep breath, and strode on. "First World problem, I guess. This is beautiful, by the way."

He grinned. With the previous day's storm off to soak some other part of Britain, the sun was shining brighter than ever, and every bird on the moors sang at the top of its lungs. Liam nearly sang too, but he settled for swinging Gemma's hand as they walked.

"Correction. This isn't beautiful. It's gorgeous." Her voice was soft and lyrical, fitting in with their surroundings.

He gazed around, taking in the rust-colored slopes, the purple patches of heather, and the lush moss growing along ledges.

"It is gorgeous."

A brook babbled, and a hare bounded from one bush to another. A bird of prey circled above, the forks of his tail casting a distinctive shadow over the landscape. Every sight, every sound, and every earthy scent set off memories. Nice ones, like his mother laughing or his father carrying him on his shoulders.

Liam paused, looking over the miles of untouched landscape. Maybe his father hadn't had to steal his mother away from London to this place. Maybe she'd loved it as much as Gemma did.

His eyes fell to Gemma's feet. He'd found a pair of rubber boots that fit her, as well as an old wax jacket. Had they been his mother's?

"I'd love to live in a place like this," Gemma murmured.

He looked at her, bursting to bare his heart and soul. *So, stay,* he nearly said. *Be my mate, and we can be together forever.*

But all he got out was a quiet, "Maybe you could."

She smiled wistfully, not quite catching on. "You offering me a job?"

Then she did catch on, because her eyes went wide, and her throat bobbed.

Yes, he meant it. But for some reason, he shrugged, trying to play it cool instead of dropping to one knee and uttering the words on the tip of his tongue. *I love you. I need you. Please be my mate.*

Fool that he was, all he said was, "We could call this the interview."

It came out a little breathlessly, and for a long, quiet minute, they looked at each other, unmoving, unblinking,

135

hearts pounding. The cheerful little brook gurgled, and the wind whispered through knots of wild grass.

Gemma's eyes shone, and her whisper was a little uneven. "I'm not sure. How long would the contract extend?"

He swallowed away the lump in his throat. "Quite a long time. Maybe even forever."

A butterfly flitted past on delicate, powdery wings.

Gemma bit her lip. "I see. And what exactly would the job entail?"

"I guess that's open to negotiation," he murmured, though his lion cried, *Anything you want. You name it. Just stay with me.*

She took his hands and rubbed her thumbs over his, gazing into his eyes. "I like the sound of that. A lot. But I wouldn't consider anything less than a full partnership, you know."

He smiled. "I wouldn't want it any other way."

She nodded slowly. "Of course, I'd need some time to think it over. The job offer, I mean."

He slid his arms around her shoulders, slowly reeling her in. "As long as you need."

Her lips moved, but she ended up kissing him instead. The first was a soft peck. The second was a long, lingering kiss, and on the third, her chest pressed against his. The sweet scent of arousal joined the peaty scent in the air, and Liam couldn't resist sliding his hands down her rear.

Then a raven cawed overhead, and they broke apart.

"Gareth?" Gemma shielded her eyes against the sun for a closer look.

"Gareth." He sighed. "I swear he still thinks I'm a child."

She laughed. "Maybe he's just looking out for you."

Liam snorted, though that was the truth. Gareth had always looked out for him, though the raven shifter was careful to hide his feelings behind a mask of indifference. In fact, Gareth had dedicated himself to looking out for generations of Liam's family.

Much as Liam appreciated that, a stubborn urge took over as the raven circled overhead.

"No. Wait." Liam reached for Gemma. "If we want to kiss, we'll kiss, dammit. No matter what anyone thinks."

She grinned and wove her fingers through his hair. "You're right."

He kissed her harder and more defiantly than before. Let Gareth caw all he wanted. Let the fates be damned. Gemma was his mate, and no one could tell him otherwise.

So they stood high on that bluff, kissing in plain view. Not that there were many witnesses — not once Gareth swooped away with a huff, leaving them alone in the surrounding wilderness.

That kiss might have started as an act of defiance, but it rapidly gave way to a raw, smoldering need. His kisses grew deeper, and his hands started wandering upward from her ribs.

"You know, I was thinking," Gemma mumbled.

"Yes?" he whispered, still peppering her ear with kisses.

"We ought to head back to my room. You know, to check the fireplace. We wouldn't want to set the castle on fire."

He chuckled. She'd already set fire to his soul, and nothing would extinguish that blaze.

Still, he hesitated. He really, really had to tell her about the Guardians' plan. He had to assure her that he'd fallen for her first, and that his love had nothing to do with job requirements. But Gemma's eyes were glowing with need, and her hands wandered down the rear of his jeans. He could tell her afterward, right?

"Liam," she whispered, coaxing him home.

Chapter Fourteen

No matter how many deep breaths Gemma took, she couldn't pull herself together. Did all lion shifters possess magic power that drew in women? Or was her heart correct in insisting that Liam was the one? Maybe it was the extraordinary circumstances, preventing her from thinking straight. Whatever the cause, it wasn't even lunchtime, and she was already starving to wrap herself around Liam again.

Just the *again* part blew her away. She couldn't believe she'd slept beside a lion all night, not to mention having slept with a lion — er, a lion shifter. Yet there she was, strolling back to the castle — *his* castle — for another round of fun.

Hand in hand, they walked through the grand hall and climbed the stairs to the upper floor. Liam kissed her hand, and his eyes glowed in the dim light. Neither of them spoke, and Gemma hardly breathed, already flushing with anticipation. Silent suits of armor saluted her and Liam, and a sword glinted as she passed — the one she'd wielded the previous evening. Her bracelets shone back, and part of her mind hung on to that fact, but the rest fast-forwarded to the bedroom.

"Why do you do this to me?" she finally demanded. "How?"

Liam looked stricken. "What did I do?"

She chuckled and ran a hand across his back. Okay, closer to his ass than his back, but who was counting? "Around you, my brain turns off, and the rest of me — well, everything else turns on." She slid a hand into the rear pocket of his pants.

His eyes flashed with some wisecrack that was sure to make her laugh. But a moment later, he went serious and took both her hands.

139

"Shifters have fated mates. Like...soul mates. The one person in the entire universe that destiny sends your way. The one you're meant to be with. Forever." He gulped. "I'm pretty sure you're mine. No, I know you're mine."

Her mouth cracked open, because what exactly did one say to something like that?

Say yes, a little voice prompted. *Say, "Liam, you're the one."*

"Mates, huh?" she whispered.

He nodded. "Like a husband or wife, but with an unbreakable bond."

She tried a joke. "Sounds good. What's the catch?"

"You'd be stuck with me. Forever."

She bit her lip before it started to tremble. "That doesn't sound so bad. Is the castle part of the deal?"

She was joking, of course, and Liam laughed. "The castle. The butler." He frowned. "My whole crazy family."

She squeezed his hands. "You'd be stuck with my crazy family."

He flapped a hand. "Easy."

She tilted her head. "Is that it? Can mates just be mates, or is there a ceremony or something?"

He blushed, which only made him cuter. "Well, you...um... You take your mate somewhere private..." He motioned toward the bedroom. "Where you...uh... You know." He motioned vaguely.

Her pulse skipped. Oh, she got the gist, all right.

"Then, you — well...um..."

She furrowed her brow. "It doesn't involve sex toys, does it?"

"No. Just a bite."

"A bite?"

It was crazy, but her sweet, sexy, adorably tongue-twisted lion shifter managed to make biting sound good. Her neck tingled, and a hidden side of her soul cooed, *Oh, that would be nice.*

"It doesn't hurt. At least, so I'm told," Liam said. "You only do it once. I mean, you can do it lots of times, but only with that one woman you love."

"And then what?"

He shrugged. "Then you're mated. You love each other. Forever."

Liam's jittery voice made it perfectly clear that he'd hadn't thought through the details, but she hardly cared. Her heart thumped wildly, and she nearly said, *I'm all in.*

Still, she made herself take a deep breath, then joke it off. "Maybe we should save that for later. As appealing as it all sounds, I swear I'm not thinking clearly right now."

She *couldn't* have been thinking clearly, because she was ready to promise him everything. Her body. Her soul. Her future, whatever that might bring.

Liam's eyes glowed. "Wise woman."

She snorted. "Not so sure about that. But if destiny wants us together, then it will happen, right?"

His face clouded, but he didn't say no. And anyway, she was kissing him by then, making sure he knew how much she wanted him. At first, he held her tightly, as if worried something might rip them apart. Gradually, he relaxed his grip enough for her to run her hands over his rear.

"Mmm," she hummed, pulling him through the door.

The fire had died out, but her body temperature rose as Liam's kisses grew deeper.

"Now, where were we?" he murmured. "Oh yes..."

He skimmed the lower edge of her breasts, then untucked her shirt. Within minutes, they were both naked and toppling onto the bed.

"I call the top," she murmured, straddling him.

"Bossy little thing." He grinned.

"I'm not little."

He cocked an eyebrow. "No? Then prove it to me."

She grinned and made a show of looking him over. "Easy."

His chest seemed like a good place to start, so she ducked and kissed him an inch above one nipple, then kissed her way over to the other. And man, was that a lot of ground to cover.

The position was a little cramped, though, so she inched lower, tracing his centerline. She kissed her way over the ridge of one boxy muscle, then into a tiny valley. The man was built like the Welsh landscape. His belly button was the lake at the bottom of the valley, and she couldn't help but nuzzle her cheek there. Then she paused and glanced up.

He'd started with an easy smile, but he looked breathless now, and his eyes had started to glow.

She took a deep breath. It was only logical to continue downward, though she'd never been big on that kind of fore-play. Still, something deep inside her bubbled up, begging her to try.

Just one little taste, that inner voice begged. The voice of her inner dragon?

She dragged her chin down the lowest part of his belly, watching Liam's eyes go wide, then drop to half-mast.

A rush of power surged through her along with the insa-tiable urge to take him in. Which was a challenge, given the size of his rapidly swelling shaft. In the end, it was easy to go from little licks and pecks to sliding her whole mouth over him. And, wow. The tip was velvety soft, the rest of him rock hard. Liam didn't make a sound, but she swore he bit back a groan. That became her next challenge — to make him cry out the way he'd made her come undone.

His hands fisted the sheets, and she moved faster, bringing him closer and closer to the edge.

"Gemma..." he whispered.

She smiled, continuing her relentless slide.

"Gemma..." His voice was hoarse.

It's good for me too, she would have said if she hadn't been otherwise occupied.

His fingers furrowed through her hair while she bobbed up and down. But then he muttered and raised his head.

"Gemma."

She glanced up, lips poised over the silky tip of his cock. "Yes?"

His abs stood up in one mountainous ridge, and his eyes shone.

"Point proven," he rasped.

She grinned, tempted to keep going. Instead, she crawled back up until her breasts were within nipping distance and her legs straddling his waist.

"Just getting started. Now, where were those condoms?"

Liam pointed to the bedside table, letting her do all the — ahem — handling. She unrolled the condom over him with a few unnecessary squeezes, just for the pleasure of making him groan.

"Woman, you kill me."

"Now you know how I feel."

Moving slowly, she dragged her hips along his body until his cock lined up with her core. Then she sat back, hissing as she took him in, one achingly good inch at a time. When she paused, catching her breath, he jackknifed up, kissing her breast.

A shudder went through her. The man could probably make her explode in two or three licks. She clenched her teeth, determined not to shatter in pleasure — yet.

"A little closer," Liam whispered.

She dipped a shoulder, offering him one pink, pert nipple, then the other, grinding her hips at the same time.

And dammit, she started making noises too. But it felt so good. Liam was a master with his lips, tongue, and teeth, teasing her along the threshold between pleasure and pain. And as for what was going on below...

She reared back — way back — taking him deeper.

"Oh..." She mumbled, swaying.

Liam gripped her hips and ran a thumb along the crease of her leg. The moment he touched down on her hidden, aching bud, she cried out. Then she threw back her head and began to ride him in earnest, succumbing to the pressure building inside her. Coaxing it higher and higher until she thought she would explode.

Fated mates... like soul mates. The one person in the entire universe that destiny sends your way.

She'd never felt as connected to anyone as she did to Liam. But somehow, she wasn't quite ready to come. She groaned, partly in frustration, partly in delight. Then she realized what she needed to send both of them over the edge. Gradually, she leaned forward, panting.

Liam looked up, watching. Waiting.

"I have a new plan," she mumbled. "Do lions like doggy style?"

He broke into a huge grin. "Lions invented doggy style. Damn canines just stole the term."

She laughed then eased her hips up.

No, her body cried. *Don't let him go.*

But she wasn't letting go. She was just shuffling to all fours. Liam took his time getting into position behind her, running his hands over every inch of her body.

She groaned, practically waggling her ass. Didn't he know she was dying for more?

"Can't help it. You're too beautiful," he said.

Then he gripped her hips, and the sudden quiet told her he was concentrating... Lining up...

She lowered her head to the mattress, aching in anticipation. Would Liam thrust in with a powerful burst, or would he take it slow?

In the end, the combination he used left her howling. A gradual push, an equally slow withdrawal, followed by a piercing thrust. If the pillow hadn't muffled her cry, the sound would have carried through the castle walls.

"Okay?" Liam panted, checking in.

Was he kidding? She mumbled unintelligibly, but Liam got the gist, because he repeated the move.

Jamming her arms over her head, Gemma anchored herself. When she pushed back, meeting his third thrust, Liam hissed. On the fourth, she squeezed her inner muscles, making him groan outright. And on the fifth—

"Yes," she cried.

Blood rushed in her ears, and her heart hammered. Her body was on fire.

Liam paused, making her want to scream. She wanted to come, and come now.

But he bent over her, combing her hair to one side, then kissing her neck. No, wait. He was nipping her neck, sending a series of shock waves through her nerves. She held perfectly still, ready to beg him to bite. He'd only explained the basics, but she sensed exactly how it would go and how excruciatingly good it would feel. She just knew, deep in her soul.

A mating bite... with the woman you love...

Yes, she wanted to cry out. *Please.*

She turned, exposing more of her neck. To hell with thinking things through.

Yes, yes, yes, the animal inside her begged.

But then, with one ragged breath, Liam jerked back. He held her for a moment, panting like a man who'd wrestled with demons and barely made it out alive. Gemma drooped against the mattress. Did he not feel the way she did?

"Believe me, I want you. I want you so much," he whispered. "But I have to explain first. Everything." His tone was so grim, she wondered what he meant.

For the next few heartbeats, they remained still, sensing the moment slip away. But then the fire inside her flared all over again, and she wiggled her ass. Maybe the bite could wait, but she couldn't.

"You've got unfinished business, sailor."

Liam chuckled, running his hands over her back. "You really are amazing."

Then he tensed, took firm hold of her hips, and started pumping again. Gently, then harder. Faster too, bringing them back to the cusp of a screaming high. Every muscle in Gemma's body tensed, and she clamped down around him. Then she cried out, shuddering at exactly the same moment Liam came.

Her body blazed, and her head spun. Visions flooded her mind, moving in such quick succession, she couldn't make out any details. She was flying over London with Liam — or was she trotting beside him on all fours? Then he spat fire, and she saw a pair of massive wings beat. But none of it made sense, and every image was overlaid with a thousand shooting stars. She squeezed her eyes shut, wallowing in ecstasy.

Gradually, her panting breaths turned into satisfied sighs. Liam kissed her cheek, then slowly withdrew, making her moan.

"Believe me, I'd rather stay too," he murmured. "But soon..."

Soon was a promise she would hold him to, for sure.

Liam shuffled around, disposing of the condom. Then he lay on his side, spooning her tightly, caressing her shoulder. Outside, birds chirped, and a beam of light sliced into the room.

Gemma's mind galloped away with wild plans, and she didn't have the willpower to stop herself. She and Liam could talk things out. When the time was right, they would follow through with that bite. Then he would be hers forever, and she would be his. They could divide their time between pulsing, lively London and the peaceful timelessness of Wales.

And as for the scheming Guardians — not to mention the lurking Lombardis — she and Liam would find a way to solve those problems, too. Problems that felt light-years away in her current state of mind. Yes, evil was lurking out there. But right now...

She crossed her arms over Liam's, patting him. Right now, all she wanted was to bask in his warmth.

Outside, a cloud dimmed the golden sunlight, but she turned away. Nothing was going to ruin this moment for her. Nothing.

Chapter Fifteen

Gemma, I really have to talk to you.

Liam tried out the words a thousand times in his mind, but actually saying them was hard. Excuse after excuse filtered through his head, but none really held up. Finally, he took a deep breath and forced the words out.

"Gemma, we need to talk."

It came out half hidden in a kiss to her shoulder. But, hey. It was a start.

Gemma burrowed closer to his side. "Soon. Just let me enjoy this little bit of peace."

And, hell. Every soldier knew not to disturb something as precious as that. So, he held her for a good, long while, biding his time. Then her stomach rumbled, and he laughed.

"We need to get lunch before Gareth accuses me of starving you."

Gemma sighed, staring at the ceiling, then nodded. "All right. Back to the real world." She rolled toward the edge of the bed, then rolled back, groaning. "One more minute..."

That feeling, he could relate to all too well. Still, he dragged himself away and stood. "I'll get lunch ready. You can meet me there in a few minutes."

"You don't mind?"

No, especially since it bought him some time to figure out exactly what to say and how.

Gemma, I'm part dragon, and loving you has nothing to do with the Guardians ordering me to.

He stuck out his jaw. Yeah, that would go over well.

"See you soon," he called from the door after getting dressed.

"See you soon," Gemma mumbled, turning back to the pillow.

He strode down the hallway, rehearsing a different version of what to say. But, damn, those empty suits of armor silently judged him the whole way. Gareth's sharp look did the same once Liam entered the cavernous kitchen on the ground floor.

"Lunch, sir?"

Liam sighed. "Lunch. Please."

Gareth raised one thin eyebrow but didn't say a word.

Liam moved around, pulling out cold cuts and condiments, all the time wishing one of his buddies were there. Someone to talk to — anyone. Sergio, Tristan — even taciturn Marco would do. But Sergio was in London, tracking the Lombardis. Tristan was living the good life in Paris with Natalie, his mate. Marco had withdrawn to Lisbon, avoiding women like the plague. And the other guys were... Well, spread out all over the world.

He glanced at Gareth, considered, then shook his head. The raven shifter was not the type a guy could spill his guts to.

And yet, a minute later, he found himself saying, "Gareth?"

"Sir," the raven shifter said in his usual monotone.

Liam nearly substituted *Do we have any olives?* for what he really had to say, but somehow, he forced it out.

"I have a problem."

Gareth shot him a loaded look that said, *Lad, you have more than you know.*

"I mean, a question," Liam said in a rush.

Gareth took out a serrated knife and a loaf of peasant bread — one he'd baked early that morning, judging by the heavenly scent — and started cutting thick slices.

"A question."

Gareth's tone didn't exactly beg Liam to go on, but he did anyway. "About my parents..."

The sawing motion of Gareth's knife halted, then resumed in a slower, more deliberate way.

"I see."

Liam kept busy arranging a platter of cold cuts and cheese. "I think I remember some things, but they don't match what I know."

"Aha. And how do you know you know?"

"From what my relatives explained."

Gareth snorted. "What exactly did they explain?"

He frowned, looking out the window. "What a mistake my mother made, falling for my father. How much she hated it here."

So far, every slice Gareth cut was perfectly even, but the next one was a torn, ragged mess. "And you believe that?"

Liam thought about the rubber boots Gemma had used. A pair that scuffed and worn spoke of countless walks over the moors. Long, pleasurable walks, he decided, not walks to get away.

He stared out the window. "I don't know what to believe any more. About my mother or my father. . ."

"What do you remember about him?"

"My aunt says—"

Gareth cut in sharply. "I didn't ask what that woman told you. I asked what you remember."

The raven shifter's eyes flashed, and Liam stared for a moment. Then he closed his eyes and searched his memories.

"I remember his voice. It was all deep and rumbly. . ."

"Like your grandfather's," Gareth interjected softly.

"I remember him carrying me on his shoulders and how high it felt up there." Liam smiled faintly. "I remember that he would hug my mother while she hugged me, all three of us all wrapped up." Then he sighed. "That's what I see in my mind. But maybe I just created a little fantasy world for myself."

For the first time ever, Gareth's face was softer, more forgiving. "Not a fantasy, sir. That's how it was." His voice went all scratchy, as if it had been his loss as much as Liam's.

"But it doesn't make sense. I thought my father made a mess of things, and that my grandfather cast him out."

"Doesn't every young man make mistakes?"

Liam's eyes hit the floor.

"Your grandfather did indeed cast out your father in hopes that he would reform."

Liam scuffed the stone floor. "But he never did."

Gareth shook his head. "On the contrary. When he met your mother. When you were born."

"That's not what my aunt said."

"May I suggest your lion relatives had their own agenda?"

Liam stared at his feet. Yeah, that rang true. "But my father went off in a rage and got himself killed."

"On good grounds. The Lombardi clan was staging a coup—"

Liam snapped his head up. "Lombardi?"

Gareth nodded. "That led to their banishment from Europe. At least, at the time. Word has it, they have recently returned."

Liam's mind spun. It was all connected. His life, his father's. Gemma's and his mother's. The Lombardis. . .

"And as for getting himself killed. . ." Gareth's voice shook with anger. "Your father flew off to stop the Lombardis before they seized power. Your mother went to beg the Guardians for help. But the lions refused to heed her warnings, so she rushed to help your father. We arrived just in time to see him fall."

Gareth's voice wavered, shocking Liam. The old man had emotions? And, wow. He'd been so loyal as to follow Liam's parents into battle?

"We did what we could, but it was too late. The enemy was repelled, but your father paid the ultimate price. And your mother. . ." Gareth's voice drifted off sadly.

"She died of sorrow, mourning her mate," Liam whispered.

The wrinkles on Gareth's aged face deepened. "I see the lions told you one truth among all the lies."

A bang sounded, and Liam realized it was his own fist, thumping the table. "But why? Why would everyone lie?"

Gareth studied the knife wordlessly, then started sharpening it against a stone. Back and forth, back and forth, every slow pull scraping through Liam's ears.

"The days of a true alliance between lions and dragons are past, I fear," Gareth murmured between long strokes of the blade. "Lions always respected the power of dragons, but that turned to fear in time. Fear leads to mistrust, and mistrust leads to..."

"Lies. So many lies," Liam filled in.

Gareth took him by the shoulders. "Your father saw beyond the tribalism and took a stand. He was open-minded enough to love a lion. He laid down his life for the greater good — of everyone." He shook his head sadly. "Lions like to think they have a monopoly on courage and honor. But your father — and mother — possessed more courage and honor than all the lions of London combined."

Seconds ticked by as ponderously as the beat of Liam's heart. Gareth wasn't just a cranky old man. And Liam's parents weren't what his aunt had made them out to be. Not even close.

Gareth turned abruptly, rearranging the bread slices as if that mattered in some way. Then he snapped his fingers and motioned toward the pantry. "Get the mustard."

Back to the old — cold — relationship? Liam sighed. "Isn't there something like rank around here?"

Gareth shot him a side-eyed glance. "Indeed, there is, Mr. Bennett. You just have to earn it...sir."

Liam chewed on that for the next few minutes. He'd had the vague hope that the respect he'd earned in the Foreign Legion would carry over, but that wasn't how it worked. A man had to prove himself again and again to judges — like Gareth — who were notoriously hard to please.

Then soft steps sounded on the staircase, and they both looked up as Gemma approached.

As always, Liam burst into a smile, but it quickly faded, and he muttered, "Something tells me this is bound for disaster, like my parents."

He hadn't meant for Gareth to catch that, but the old man's senses were keen. "Your parents acted out of love. Pure, undying love. Have you resided among lions so long that you've forgotten that?"

Liam hung his head.

Gareth glanced at the doorway, then whispered sternly. "A man will never fail if he is guided by love — and if he abides by the truth."

Liam pursed his lips. Gareth had picked up on more than he'd thought.

Gemma came bounding down the stairs, peppy and bright as...as... Well, a gem.

"Hi." She thumped Liam on the shoulder then smiled at Gareth. "Hello to you too."

Gareth gave a little bow. "Good day to you, miss."

Gemma looked between Liam and Gareth, gradually sensing the tension in the air. "Can I help?"

Gareth shot Liam a sharp look. *The ball's in your court, lad.*

Liam swallowed hard, then took Gemma by the hand. "Care for a breath of fresh air?"

Her eyes studied his, but she followed silently. Liam pushed through the kitchen door and then the heavy outer door that led to a small garden with huge views over the landscape. There, he ran his hand over the sun-warmed rock wall, wondering whether his father had ever done the same, or his grandfather and great-grandfather before that. Then he paused, touching the rough surface again. Yes, they had. He could feel it deep inside. He could hear it in the whisper of the wind over the hills. This remote, rocky place had a history, and that history was his own.

He looked around, taking it all in. This place was home in a way the sprawling manor house in Richmond had never been.

The next breath he took ended up being a deep one, because it hit him for the first time. Who he was, and where he had come from. He wasn't Liam Bennett, lesser cousin of the Blackwood pride. He was Liam Bennett, son of a loving mother and a devoted father, whose life stories amounted to much more than a reckless, tragic end.

He sniffed the clean, crisp air the way he was sure his mother had done, then squeezed Gemma's hand.

"Everything okay?" Gemma whispered.

He nodded, collecting himself, then took her by both hands. "I have to tell you who I am. Who I really am, and what this is all about."

Puzzlement showed in her eyes, then trust. "You're the not-so-crazy man who keeps saving me. The one I tried so hard not to fall in love with and failed."

Her words were music to his ears, but he forced himself to go on.

"I love you, Gemma. I knew that the minute I met you, and I fall harder for you every minute we spend together."

Her lips curled into a bright smile.

"But there's so much I have to tell you. Things you need to know."

"Like what?"

"I come from a family of mixed blood..."

Gemma rolled her eyes. "Boy, do you Brits need to get with the times."

"Mixed shifter blood, I mean. My mother was a lion. My father was a dragon."

She froze. "Dragon?"

"Not one of the bad guys," he said quickly. "He loved my mother. He died for a good cause. He...he was so much more than my relatives ever admitted."

Gemma looked perplexed, but he went on. "That's one thing. There's another."

Now she really looked wary, and he wished he'd told her everything from the start.

"The Guardians... They ordered me to...to..."

She crossed her arms. "To what?"

He grimaced. "To find you. To seduce you. To mate with you."

"What?"

Roosting birds fluttered away as her screech carried over the stone walls.

Liam stuck up his hands. "But I already knew you're the one. My mate. My destiny. I only walked into that meeting afterward."

As if to clear her ears, Gemma shook her head. "Why would they order you to do that?"

"Because a Fire Maiden mated to a shifter with lion blood would make her easier to control."

Her face turned crimson. "To control?"

Oh God. He was getting it all wrong. "I didn't want any part of that."

Her eyes flashed. "You didn't? Then why did you bring me here? Why did you sleep with me?" Her voice rose.

He threw up a hand in a stop sign in case she tried to shove him into the moat. "I wanted you because I love you. I didn't want the Guardians to use you. Don't you see?"

"No, I don't see. I don't see at all." She waved her hands as if a nest of hornets had surrounded her. "The Guardians want to control me? What gives them the right?"

She spun on her heel and race-walked inside. Liam jogged after her, but when he touched her shoulder, she smacked his hand aside.

"Don't touch me."

"Gemma..."

"Don't talk to me. I need to think. No, I need to kill someone. Who do those assholes think they are?"

And on she went, racing through the house. Heading to the...pantry?

She opened the door, grimaced at the dead end, and slammed it shut. "How the hell do I get out of here?"

Liam hesitated. He could send her in circles around the maze of the castle until she cooled down, but that wasn't exactly fair. Instead, he pointed. What else could he do?

She strode through the correct door, almost kicked down several others, and burst into the forecourt. Her step faltered as she scanned the barren hills, and he could read her mind. No bus. No taxi. No way to leave.

Then her eyes narrowed on the garage, and she snapped her fingers. "Keys."

"Keys?"

"I'm borrowing your car."

"You can't leave," he said. But, bugger. That came out wrong, too.

She folded her arms and stuck up her chin. "Are you going to force me? *Control* me?"

He pointed to the sky in warning. "There are dragons after you."

"Which dragons? You? Or do you mean lions, like the ones who want to use me? Oh, wait. That could be you, too."

She was on a roll, and nothing short of flinging her over his shoulder would stop her. But that was out of the question.

"I control my life." She fumed. "Not you, not the Guardians. No one, you got that?"

"Believe me, I get it. They want to control me too. But we won't let them."

She whirled. "No? You've done pretty much everything they ordered, didn't you?" She covered her face with her hands. "How could you? How dare they?"

Liam touched her shoulder. "I mean it, Gemma. I love you in spite of them, not because anyone ordered me to. Please. Just think this through."

"That's exactly what I intend to do." She held out her hand, looking frighteningly resolute.

His gut folded, and his heart sank. Was it possible to make a bigger mess of things? No matter how fast his mind spun, he couldn't find a way out of the pit he'd dug himself into. Eventually, he motioned to the car, totally at a loss. "The keys are in the ignition."

She eyed him suspiciously.

He shook his head. No, it wasn't a trick. "I love you, Gemma. I'd do anything for you."

Her eyes flickered, and he could see her inner battle. But Gemma wouldn't be Gemma if she didn't have a stubborn streak.

"Then you'll let me go."

He opened his mouth. *I don't want to let you go. I want you to stay. Please.*

But then he sealed his lips, utterly defeated. What was it Gareth had said? *A man will never fail if he is guided by love — and if he abides by the truth.*

But, shit. Was he really going to let the woman he loved slip away?

He gulped, and the words he forced out came in a gritty whisper. "I love you, Gemma. I will always love you. But if you need to go..." He choked up, then pushed on. "Then you have to go."

Her lips trembled, and her hands tightened in an *I mean it, buster* move.

Well, he meant what he'd said, too. So, he repeated the words, praying she would believe him. "I love you enough to let you go. Even if I hate it. Even if it kills me."

Her jaw went all tight, and her eyes glistened with tears. But then she whirled, slid into the car, and backed it out of the barn.

No! Gemma, please, his lion roared.

Then, with one last look back, Gemma gunned the engine and shot down the road.

Chapter Sixteen

Gemma wiped the tears from her eyes and cursed for the tenth time. Why had she been so gullible? Why hadn't she learned more about supernaturals before getting involved with Liam?

And dammit, why couldn't she hate him?

She drove and drove, not sure what she wanted other than to gain some space. Did she really want to leave him? Hell no. But she couldn't stay. Not after discovering how she'd been used.

Cursing herself for leaving her phone on Valhalla in her rushed escape, she pulled into a small village and hurried into a phone booth — one of those traditional red ones. Haltingly, she fumbled with some coins she'd found in the car, punched in the number she'd memorized long before the era of cell phones, and muttered while the phone rang. "Come on...come on..."

She craned her neck, peering out each red rectangle of glass for any sign of trouble.

"Hello?"

"Dad?" she all but yelped. "I need to see you, right away."

"Of course. Do you want to come over?"

She snorted. If only she were just a few Tube stops away. "I'm in Wales. Dammit, why didn't you ever tell me about Fire Maidens?"

The line went quiet for a moment before he replied. "What's happened? Are you all right?"

It took five minutes to summarize and another few to decide on a meeting point on the outskirts of Bristol — a longer drive for her father than for her, but far enough from London to feel safe.

"See you there, then. The Fox and the Hounds."

"See you there." She hung up, jumped back in the car, and drove on — and on and on.

What seemed like hours later, she found the country road her father had described, and pulled into the parking area of the pub. There, she cut the engine, looking at the swinging sign above the door. In it, a fox peeked around the edge of a beer barrel while a dozen hounds downed frothy drinks.

Gemma snorted. The Fox and the Hounds — a fitting place for a woman on the run.

She peered around, then darted inside, taking a seat near a window and the back door. If any lion or dragon shifter appeared, she was out of there.

The problem would be recognizing shifters in human form. Every unfamiliar face spelled trouble, especially in her current frame of mind. The tall, balding bartender — was he an eagle shifter? The tireless waitress — a fox? And that group of men huddled by the fireplace — could they be a pack of wolves?

For the first half hour, she fumed, hating everyone — above all, herself. Liam and her father had tried telling her the truth, but she hadn't listened until it was too late. Then for the next hour, she dissected everything that had happened over the past few days, wondering where she'd gone wrong. Eventually, she moved on to sheer depression, because what the heck would she do next?

Finally, the pub door opened, and her father stepped in, along with his panting bulldog.

She nearly jumped out of her chair. "Dad! Winston!"

When they hugged, she held her father longer than she had in years. Then she sank into her chair, trying to decide where to start.

"Dragons... Lions... Fire Maiden..."

Once she started, she couldn't stop talking — babbling, almost, trying to explain everything that had happened from the time she'd spotted the stalker in the subway all the way through Liam's confession. How sorry she was for not believing her father, how upset she was about being used, and so much more. It all came out in a river of words — and tears — she

158

couldn't hold back. Then she blinked, waiting for her father's sage advice. He would know what to do, right?

But dammit, his eyes were wide with excitement, not terror.

"You saw one? You really saw a dragon?"

"Dad!"

"Sorry, sweetheart. I'm glad you're all right. But — a dragon! Just think."

Oh, she'd thought plenty. "That dragon was hunting me. I could have died. Liam or Sergio could have died, and they're shifters. I'm just me."

Her voice cracked when she uttered Liam's name, and her father's ears perked. "I thought you hated this Liam person."

"I do." Then she slumped. "No, I don't. They were using him as much as they were using me. But it scares me. Who can I trust — really trust? Liam is part dragon — just like the ones after me."

"Just like them? Did he attack you? Breathe fire? Hunt you down?"

"Well, no. But you should see his family's castle. It's full of armor — probably from victims roasted by generations of dragons."

"Wait. Do you mean Liam or the Lombardis?"

She thumped a fist on the table. "Liam." Why couldn't her father understand?

"But you said he helped you escape."

"He did, but then he... he..."

She hesitated there, not ready to share intimate details with her dad. Plus, Liam hadn't exactly seduced her, had he? She'd been the one turning up the heat the first time... And, oops. The second time too.

Memories played through her mind, and for a moment, she drifted along with them. She'd felt so *right* in Liam's arms. So at peace.

So at home, a mournful voice whispered in her mind.

"What can I get you, sir?"

The waiter leaned over to take her father's order, giving Gemma too much time to languish in her thoughts. When her father tapped her hand a moment later, she gulped her tea, trying to banish her steamiest memories.

"He what, sweetheart?"

He tricked me jumped to the tip of her tongue, but that wasn't true either. She'd assumed both of Liam's parents were lion shifters, but he'd never actually said so. And he hadn't forced her to flee London with him. On the contrary, he had offered to protect her in spite of the risks to him.

She frowned. Liam would probably lose his job for helping her. His family was likely to ostracize him, and then where would he be?

The waiter poured her a fresh tea, and she stirred it, desperately trying to get back on track.

"The Guardians want me—"

Her father nearly knocked over his drink in delight. "So, it's all true. The Guardians do exist."

She grimaced. "They're a bunch of barbarians, Dad. They're so desperate for a Fire Maiden, they'll do anything to control her." She took a deep breath. "To control me."

To control Liam too, she realized. He was just as much a victim of the Guardians as she was.

Her father's eyes shone, and he took her hands. "Fire Maiden. I guessed as much. I thought it might be your mother, but I see you are the one."

She wanted to screech, *So why didn't you tell me?* But he had — or he'd tried. She was the one who hadn't listened.

"It makes perfect sense," her father continued. "Our dragon bloodlines — mine and your mother's — combine in you. Each of those strands is insignificant in isolation — the Welsh on my side, the French and Chinese on your mother's. But wrapped together as one...they can be powerful, indeed."

Gemma gulped. That fit what Liam had said. But, wow. He had mentioned Welsh dragons and his friend Tristan in Paris. But, China? Were there dragons all over the world?

She'd heard the stories, of course — how her mother's grandfather had met his wife in the 1920s while working in the foreign service in China. But no one had ever mentioned shifters.

"Mom's grandmother had dragon blood, too?"

Her father nodded. "She begged your great-grandfather to take her to the States. From what my research suggests, she came from a powerful Chinese dragon bloodline."

Gemma bit her lip. He'd mentioned that before, but she'd never believed him.

"And as for this Liam chap..." her father went on.

Gemma covered her face with her hands. God, what had she done? Liam was the best thing that had ever happened to her, but she'd taken out her stubborn fury on him instead of the Guardians.

"He helped you get away from the Guardians *and* the Lombardis, correct?"

She nodded. "But you always said to watch out for dragons. You said they're cunning. Evil. Greedy."

Her father bit his lip. "Oh dear."

Gemma sat back. *Oh dear* was never a good start.

"I might have oversimplified," he finished.

"Oversimplified?" she screeched.

"Like humans, shifters run the gamut, and dragons are no exception. There are good dragons, and there are bad dragons. I believe your Mr. Bennett might be the good type."

My Mr. Bennett. God, she loved the sound of that. But had she lost him forever?

That inner voice whispered once again. *He's yours and you're his. It's destiny.*

She rubbed her eyes. "So, what do I do?"

Her father tapped his lips. "I have a book at home..."

"A book?" she half yelled. Everyone in the pub looked up, and she turned pink. "I don't need a book, Dad. I need help." Then a thought hit her. "Is it a book about magic?"

He shook his head.

No, of course it wasn't. Her father had never been a practical man.

"Believe me, I wish I knew more," he said. "But I only had the word of my great-grandfather to go on. No one else listened to him, and he died before I truly came to believe

161

him. Everything else I've managed to gather is hard to judge. I could never be sure which source to trust."

Gemma made a face. Exactly her problem.

"The only lesson I can draw — the one thing all my sources agree on — is the power of destiny."

She slumped. Was it her destiny to die young and tragically? Worse, would she live to a ripe old age in the clutches of the Lombardis or the Guardians?

"Alas, the foes you face are formidable. But you have allies as well."

"Like who?"

"This Mr. Bennett, to begin with. Half lion, half dragon could be a powerful combination, indeed. And the other one — that wolf shifter..."

"Sergio."

Her father nodded. "Destiny led you to them, and they have helped you many times. Selflessly, from what I understand."

She gulped. Well, yes. They had. "But what can they possibly do against dragons?"

Her father scratched his chin, and she was sure he'd say something useless like *Where there's a will, there's a way.*

But a car pulled up outside, and Gemma whipped around, afraid to find an entire motorcade pulling in. Would it be a contingent of Guardians in Rolls-Royces, ready to whisk her away? Or was it a handful of Lombardi gangsters on motorcycles, zooming in to abduct her to their lair?

Luckily, it was just a Mini Cooper, and she exhaled. But then the door swung open, and a tall man unfolded himself from the cab. The leg he swung out of the door looked half as long as the chassis, and when he stood, the car looked like a toy.

Her heart swelled, and she whispered, "Lancelot."

Her father blinked. "Who?"

The fresh breeze ruffled Liam's hair, and boy, did he look tired. Sad and hurt, too. So much so, she wanted to run over and give him a hug.

"Good gracious. Is that a dragon?" her father whispered in awe.

She was about to say, *No, silly. He's a lion. Can't you tell?* Liam's tawny hair seemed like a dead giveaway, as did the casual grace with which he moved.

But now that her father mentioned it, she could see the dragon in Liam as well. The powerful shoulders. The sharp eyes. And above all, the intensity.

Then she frowned. How could she be sure? It wasn't as though she knew dozens of shifters to compare Liam to.

I know my mate, the inner voice insisted. *And he is both of those things. Tenacious as a lion, mighty as a dragon. Above all, he is true — true to his heart and to us.*

Liam looked the building over and checked the sky. When he seemed satisfied, he closed his eyes, tipped his head back, and sniffed the air. The pub door was closed, but a tiny finger of fresh air drifted in and meandered around. Gemma could sense it winding between the chairs like a curious cat. When it reached her feet, the draft swirled upward, gently enveloping her. The air tugged ever so slightly at her sleeves, then swirled in excitement, and a smile played over Liam's lips. A teensy, tiny one, as if he was reliving everything they'd shared.

When he opened his eyes, they were aimed directly at her. Her whole body warmed, and she found a goofy smile tugging at her lips.

Hey, she could have sworn he called, ever so quietly.

Her heart thumped wildly as he stepped toward the pub door. Should she run in shame? Hide? Beg him for forgiveness? Tears welled up inside her, and it was a battle to hold them back.

When Liam entered, her father beckoned him over.

"Dad!" she hissed, turning crimson.

Hours ago, she'd ridden Liam's hard body like a cowgirl. Then she'd flipped out when he tried to explain the full truth. She slid down in her seat, not so much to avoid Liam as to avoid confronting her own mishmash of feelings. She loved Liam terribly, and she wanted him. On the other hand, she hated the idea of those manipulative Guardians getting exactly what they'd wanted. But, hell. Was she going to let sheer stubbornness keep her from the man she loved?

Liam hesitated, but her father waved again.

"No! Dad, no."

"Sweetheart, you need to talk to him."

She needed to melt into the floor was more like it. How could she ever explain to Liam how ashamed she felt?

"Tell him I'm not here," she tried.

Her father gave her a stern look. "If your mother and I taught you one thing, it's to stand up for what you believe in. To fight for what's right." Then his face softened. "You ask so many people to listen to your causes. Maybe it's time you listened to his."

"But... But..."

It was too late. Her father stood up, and even Winston lurched to his feet and sniffed Liam's shoes.

"You must be Mr. Bennett." Her father shook Liam's hand. "Archer here."

"Mr. Archer," Liam said, sounding a little hoarse.

"Why don't you join us?" Gemma's father pulled out a chair.

Liam looked at her, waiting... watching... Melting her heart all over again because he was waiting for her permission, not just her father's.

A man strode by, and Liam sidestepped, putting himself between the man and Gemma. It was just an ordinary pub customer, but Liam was as protective as ever. Maybe a little possessive too, because the man hurried along, looking meek.

"Gemma," her father prompted. *Are you really going to keep this nice man waiting?* his eyes asked.

Actually, yes. Yes, she was. Because her stubborn side insisted on one last test. Was Liam really the kind, generous man she'd fallen in love with, or was he a manipulative power-monger?

An awkward minute ticked by, and then another — long enough for a manipulative jerk to grow impatient and show his true colors. But Liam just stood with his hands shoved deep into his pockets, his eyes shining with... hope? Sorrow?

Gemma, her father's stern look warned.

Liam, meanwhile, didn't demand anything. He didn't break into complicated excuses, and he didn't try to change her mind. He just waited, leaving his fate in her hands.

Gemma took a deep breath, wishing she could think of something to say.

How about "Sorry" or "I missed you"? that inner voice snipped.

She wanted to casually pat the chair beside her and coolly invite Liam to have a seat. But her mind skipped into overdrive, replaying all their highlights, from the moment they'd first met to the last time they'd made love. That awkward first breakfast together in *Valhalla's* cramped kitchen. Their steamy night in Richmond, and the beautiful, chatty walk in Wales. It all flashed by like a movie montage, and before she knew it, she was on her feet and hugging Liam.

"You found me," she whispered.

Liam locked his arms around her. "I will always find you. I will always love you. That's how it is with mates."

A tear rolled down her cheek, then another, and for a little while, the world receded until it was just her and him.

Mates, that voice whispered in her mind.

She nodded in the snug universe of Liam's hug. The man was a keeper, for sure.

"I wasn't mad at you. I was mad at the Guardians," she mumbled. "But I took it out on you. I'm so sorry."

He held her tighter. "We'll never let them control us, Gemma. Never."

She nodded, rocking in his arms. Eventually, it struck her that half the pub was watching, as was her father. Even Winston looked up, trailing a long line of slobber.

"Um...yes." She backed away, wiping her cheeks. "Good to see you again."

Liam's laugh was a gentle roar, but she didn't mind.

Her father grinned and motioned to the table. "Let's talk things through, shall we?"

Gemma nodded without letting go of Liam's hand, but before she could sink to the chair he held out, a black Maserati screeched into the car park outside. Everyone looked up, and the bartender muttered something under his breath.

Gemma clutched Liam's arm. "Is it them?"

By *them*, she meant any of her enemies, but Liam shook his head.

"It's Sergio."

Gemma exhaled, recognizing that familiar black hair and powerful shoulders. The Italian jumped out of the low-slung car and trotted to the pub, his dark eyes shining intensely. Liam waved him over, but when Sergio joined them, he didn't sit down.

"Trouble. We have to go. Now."

"What is it?" Gemma asked.

"The Lombardis are on the move. They left London a few hours ago." Sergio's eyes darted outside. "We need to get Gemma to a secure location. *Andiamo*."

If Gemma had wanted further proof that Liam and Sergio were trustworthy, there it was. Their top priority was her, their own safety never even mentioned.

Her heart thumped wildly as she looked from face to face. Sergio was dead earnest. Liam was nodding, already calculating options, no doubt. Her father looked bewildered and excited at the same time, and Winston drew lines of saliva on the floor as he looked around.

"Back to your place?" She touched Liam's arm.

He took her hand, nodding. "It's our best bet."

"What about Dad?"

"I'll be fine," her father said.

A dozen ugly scenarios rushed through her mind. Shifters could kill her father. He was a bookworm, not a warrior. He could be roasted alive or held for ransom...

Then it hit her. God, was that how he felt every time she stepped outside?

Sergio and Liam locked eyes then nodded, coming to a silent agreement. Then Liam turned to her father.

"Stay here. Take a room and watch the skies. There, in the east. That's where they're likely to approach from. If you see anything — even a shadow or a cloud that doesn't match the others — call us. All right?"

Her father noted the phone number, and Gemma hugged him. She squeezed her eyes shut, praying he would be all right. Then Liam tapped on her hand, and she gulped away the lump in her throat. It was time to go.

"Take care, Dad. I mean it. Winston, too."

Her father smiled. "You, too. I'll see you soon."

Gemma could sense everyone in the pub wondering what was going on as Liam pulled her to the door with Sergio right on their heels. Not a soul could help, and she knew it — but, whew. With Liam and Sergio on her side, things didn't seem so hopeless. Still, she pulled Liam to a halt outside.

"We have to go," he protested.

"One thing," she insisted. "Are there any other details you need to share with me? I don't deal well with surprises, in case you didn't notice."

He studied her, and when his eyes hit the ground, her stomach sank. Shit. What now?

He motioned bashfully toward the Mini. "I stole Gareth's car."

She cackled in relief. "I think I can forgive that. Anything else?"

Beside them, Sergio stirred the air with his hands, hurrying them along.

Liam shook his head. "No secrets. No missing details. Never again."

She nodded, making a vow never to doubt him again. "Thanks. I guess that just leaves one thing."

He waited expectantly. Then his eyes widened as she flung herself into a hug and an insistent kiss. A kiss she hung on to for ages, just in case. When she eventually eased away, Liam remained puckered up for a moment, and his eyes only fluttered open a few seconds later.

"What was that for? And why so short?"

She smiled. "That's sorry and thank you and I love you. All of it kind of summarized, because. . . Well, incoming dragons."

She motioned upward. "But I promise to make it up to you later."

"I'll hold you to that." He grinned.

Sergio looked between them. "*Finito?* Can we go now?"

Gemma gulped, then looked at the Mini and the Aston Martin parked side by side.

Liam pointed to his sports car. "Definitely my car. If you're done borrowing it, I mean."

She flashed a tight smile and held out the key. "All done. Thank you."

"*Andiamo,*" Sergio urged.

"After you," Liam murmured, waving Gemma on.

She slid into the car and clipped on her seat belt just in time for Liam to peel out of the parking lot, scattering more gravel.

"Ready or not," he murmured as the tires screeched. "Here we go."

Chapter Seventeen

Driving wasn't normally a pulse-raising experience for Liam, but his heart hammered all the way home. It had started to rain, and the swishing wipers added to his sense of urgency. He kept checking the sky and the mirrors. No one followed — except Sergio, who was tailgating, as usual.

Can't you get any more speed out of that thing? Sergio muttered into his mind.

Liam shot a dirty look into the rearview mirror. *It beats the Mini.*

Sergio sighed and muttered something about Italy, real men, and real cars.

The sense of urgency was only one reason Liam's pulse was through the roof. The other was having Gemma back, which made his heart race in a good way. He reached for her hand and kissed her knuckles. What a fool he'd been. A lucky fool.

"I'm the lucky fool," she murmured, caressing his cheek.

He glanced over in surprise. She'd read his thoughts — a sure sign they were destined mates.

Of course she's my mate, his inner lion sniffed.

Gemma just smiled. Apparently, she hadn't noticed he hadn't actually spoken aloud.

"I did tell you about mates, didn't I?" he asked. The last thing he wanted was to miss one of those details she had a right to know.

She squeezed his hand. "I'd love to hear more, but right now, I'm more worried about the Lombardis. What do we do if they find us?"

Exactly what he'd been trying to figure out, but his mind was still spinning.

So, think, his lion growled. *Think.*

"Still working on it," he admitted. "The castle has its defenses, though."

The problem was, he wasn't sure how well they'd held up over the years, nor how many dragons to expect. He mulled that over all the way back home. So many unknowns, so little time to prepare, and too little intel on what was coming their way. Being with Gemma helped calm him, but her presence reminded him how much was at stake too.

Sergio revved the Maserati, reminding Liam he didn't have to face the enemy alone. The brooding mountains of Wales offered some comfort as well. It was as if the ghosts of his ancestors were out there, telling him he would make his stand on home turf. His last stand?

He pushed the thought away, as any good soldier would, and concentrated on factors within his control. Gemma gnawed her fingernails, and he wished he could reassure her. He knew that feeling all too well from his early days in the Legion — the agony of waiting out the calm before the storm.

"Almost there," he murmured as they swung around the last few turns.

Finally, they raced into the castle's forecourt. Gemma jumped out and threw open the barn doors, and both he and Sergio pulled their vehicles in.

"Coming?" Liam called over his shoulder.

Sergio stopped to touch the roof of his car, cursing the Lombardis if they dared damage his beloved Maserati.

Liam ought to have laughed, but all he felt was sorrow. He had a mate to fight for. All Sergio had was a car. Well, and pride and honor, but those went without saying. Just one more reminder of how lucky he was.

Then he ran to the main door, prepared for Gareth to bellow about his Mini Cooper being left behind. But when the old man appeared, he simply hurried everyone in.

"The Lombardis. I know."

Liam stared. Most of the time, Gareth took pains to demonstrate how blind, deaf, and achy he was. But there he was, bounding along like a man half his age.

"I have my spies, you know." Gareth pointed to the ravens circling overhead. "I've already started to prepare the defenses."

Liam could have hugged the man, but of course, that wouldn't do.

"Hurry along. You there."

"Sergio," the wolf shifter filled in, thumping his chest.

"Come along. Help me with the drawbridge."

Sergio stepped forward, but Gemma waved him ahead. "You and Liam go on. How can I miss my chance to raise a drawbridge?"

She flashed a thin smile, and Liam fell in love with her all over again. He would have stopped to kiss her if Sergio hadn't groaned.

"Enough kissing," the wolf shifter huffed. "Concentrate."

Liam nodded to Gareth. "We'll check the defenses and rendezvous in the dining room." Then he glanced at Gemma and sent the last part directly into Gareth's mind. *If the Lombardis strike before that, keep her safe. Promise me you will.*

Gareth pursed his lips in a stiff expression that said, *Do you have to ask?* But for the first time ever, his eyes sparkled with something bordering on respect.

Gemma turned and apologized to the raven shifter. "I'm sorry I left. I panicked."

Gareth put on his best sour face. "Mr. Bennett does have that effect on people, miss."

Liam forced himself to run ahead. The next three hours passed in a flurry of activity as they battened down the hatches, so to speak. The problem was, a castle had a hell of a lot of hatches to see to. That, and the niggling question of what exactly to expect.

Still, rushing through last-minute preparations was the easy part. Sealing entrances, removing loose kindling, closing fireproof shutters — all that kept a man's hands and mind busy. But then the waiting began. Everyone met in the dining room, feigning interest in the tea Gareth had served or the pattern of the stone floor. Hardly a word was spoken, though Gemma's touch spoke volumes.

171

I love you. I trust you. I know we can get through this.

Liam flashed her a thin smile. *I love you. I trust you. I...*

He couldn't bring himself to say, *I know we can get through this,* because that would be a lie. No one could promise that, not even a man ready to fight to the death for the woman he loved.

Instead, he added, *I love you,* and gave her hand another squeeze.

Gareth turned to Sergio. "What exactly do you know about the Lombardis?"

He made a face. "We have identified two. Petro, the older brother, recently returned from America..."

Gemma's brow folded into lines.

"...to join Lorenzo, the younger brother, in London," Sergio continued.

"Is he the one I saw on the subway?" Gemma asked.

Liam gave a grim nod. "Sounds like."

Gareth didn't look impressed. "The question is whether those young guns are working independently or under a seasoned commander."

"Like who?" Sergio asked.

Gareth frowned. "Enzo Lombardi. One of the old guard. We can only hope he won't stray this far from his lair."

Liam thought that over. The name sounded familiar, but why?

Silence set in again, and he stared out the window, listening to the tick of the grandfather clock. When the silence stretched, he looked around, waiting for someone to utter a few last-minute words. But then it hit him that he wasn't in the Legion any more, and the only commander present was... Well, him.

Gareth's eyes lingered on him. *You're the man of the house, lad.*

Liam took a deep breath and gulped down that stark reality. All right, fine. The question was, what to say? There was no need for a pep talk, not with a group as determined as this.

172

At first, all that came to mind were the guaranteed-to-work jokes everyone loved. *A lion, an Englishman, and a clergyman go to a pub...*

He scowled. That might do for a foot soldier who wanted to keep the mood light, but not for the position he found himself in.

Finally, he glanced around and spoke straight from the heart. "Funny how things circle around."

Everyone looked at him, waiting for more.

He studied the ornate wooden ceiling, then the heavy mantelpiece. "One generation lives in a place... They love the place, really, and turn cold stone walls into a home." His throat felt dry and scratchy, but he pressed on. "Then a child is born, and the home fills up more than it would with a hundred suits of armor." He looked into the fire as memories drifted through his mind. "Then everything changes, and the child becomes a man. Or so he thinks." He sighed. "He moves to a place as far from home as possible. To explore. Discover. To fight battles dictated by his commanders. But eventually, something pulls him back." He flashed Gemma a smile. "And that empty place feels like home all over again."

Sergio stared off into the distance. "Not everyone can go home."

Liam looked at his friend. The Foreign Legion wasn't big on digging through any soldier's past, so he'd never heard Sergio's full story. But, hell. If they made it through the next few hours, maybe he should ask.

He hunched his shoulders. "I thought I couldn't, but here I am. Maybe we end up where we started, no matter how far we wander in between. In a good way, I mean. And if—"

Cold air sliced through his nerves, and he broke off in midsentence, holding up a hand. Everyone froze. He listened, then pointed. Did they sense what he did? That feeling of a cold front sweeping in from the sea — except it was speeding in from the east.

At first, everyone looked at him strangely. But a moment later, Gemma paled, and Sergio's ears perked. Gareth looked

up exactly at the same moment the ravens outside started cawing wildly.

"They're coming," Gareth murmured without a trace of
emotion.

Liam's eyes locked with Sergio's. *Battle stations.*

Battle stations. Sergio nodded.

Liam's station was the roof, but he pulled Gemma into a
hug first. She slid her arms around his waist and pressed her
cheek against his shoulder.

"Be careful. Please."

"You too. Stay with Gareth. Stay safe."

She grimaced, making his heart ache. He hated relegating
her to hiding away, but there was no other way. Not with
deadly shifters closing in.

Then he kissed her — all too briefly — and glanced at
Gareth.

I promise to keep her safe. Gareth nodded, waving to the
stairs.

Which left Liam with no choice but to shoot Gemma one
last, heartrending look before charging away. Sergio was ten
steps ahead, and that wouldn't do. Around and around, Liam
went, following the spiral stairs to the roof. Then he thrust
aside the heavy metal door and burst outside.

Gemma... his lion mourned.

He forced himself to focus. In the past, he'd fought hard,
and sometimes, even fought smart. But if he wanted to see his
mate again, he would have to do both.

So he dead-bolted the door behind him, using the hidden
mechanism that slid steel bars into place from the inside. Then
he scanned the sky through the increasing drizzle. Somewhere
behind the clouds, the sun was setting, casting everything in
weak, yellow-gray light.

"Over there." Sergio pointed to the east.

Liam tapped the sky with a finger, counting shadows that
didn't fit among the clouds. "One... two... three... four."

His gut tightened. Four dragons against two land-bound
shifters? Not good.

Sergio shook his head. "Three dragons and something else."

Liam stripped out of his shirt. Whatever that was, he would challenge it in lion form.

A rhythmic, chopping sound reached his ears, and Sergio shot him a grim look. "Three dragons and a helicopter."

Liam frowned. What the hell?

A long plume of fire lit up the sky, and the first dragon cackled. *Ready or not, here we come.*

Liam nodded to Sergio. Oh, they were ready, all right.

He split off to the left, while Sergio went right, hunched over so as not to be spotted behind the ramparts. Within a few steps, they shifted and trotted to opposite points of the roof. The central area was as big as two volleyball courts and ringed by watchtowers and ramparts. Narrow, walled walkways radiated to the outer defenses, but for now, he and Sergio stuck to the central roof as they had agreed.

Liam crouched, peeking through a slit in the wall. One dragon led the way, with two flanking its wingtips and a helicopter not far behind. How on earth were he and Sergio going to stop so many at once?

But the first dragon swooped upward and started circling, letting the other two race ahead. The commander, from what Liam could tell — Enzo Lombardi, watching his young guns, Lorenzo and Petro, at work.

Fine. Let him watch, his lion growled.

He made eye contact with Sergio. *I'll take the first one. You take the second.*

Sergio nodded grimly. Liam slowed his breathing, though his heart hammered away. The air above him rushed, and the incoming dragon roared.

He coiled every muscle, ready to strike.

The dragon roared a second time, spitting a line of fire that scoured the roof. A moment later, the beast's head and long neck zoomed into view.

Now!

Liam jumped out, claws bared. For one thrilling moment, he was sailing through the air. Then, *smack!* — he crash-landed on the dragon's neck and dug in with everything he had. Claws. Teeth. Even his long, tufted tail whipped the dragon's side. When the enemy roared and twisted, Liam ditched, rolling to one side.

By then, the second dragon had swept in, ready to fire-blast Liam. But Sergio attacked it from the other side, and the dragon's spray of fire sliced wildly through the air. When Sergio jumped clear, the dragon shot onward, screaming in fury.

Liam watched as the dragons wheeled and regrouped. Well, fine. He and Sergio would regroup, too.

Incoming, Sergio murmured.

Liam watched as the helicopter hovered over one of the outer towers. One...two...three...four shadowy figures sprang out, and the helicopter flew off into the intensifying rain.

Mercenaries, Sergio muttered. *Three wolves and a lion.*

Liam stared. Fighting three dragons was a tall enough order. He and Sergio had to take on four-footed shifters too?

The newcomers split up and circled the outer walls, creeping along the narrow walkways to the central keep. With a hellish howl, they all closed in. Behind them, the dragons roared.

Liam charged through the rain, roaring in defiance. The first wolf, he batted aside with one huge paw. Then he lunged for the neck of the second wolf before rolling away. Sergio fought the third wolf, and behind them, something growled.

We meet again, a familiar voice rumbled.

Rutland, Liam spat, recognizing the scarred lion. Apparently, the mercenary had switched from Archie's payroll to the Lombardis'. That figured.

Mr. Bennett, Rutland chuckled.

Liam fumed — so much he nearly overlooked a sweeping shadow. He rolled clear at the last moment, and a dragon zoomed past, clicking its claws an inch over his head.

Coward, Liam cursed through his next roar.

Now he saw the dragons' plan. They would let their merce-naries do the dirty work, while they darted in and out oppor-tunistically. How long could he and Sergio possibly hold out against that?

Not long, Sergio grunted as the enemy split into two groups for their next attack.

Anger bubbled within Liam, threatening to slip over into sheer fury. Not the best way to keep a clear head in battle, but hey. The next time the mercenaries closed in, he parried quickly and leaped at the oncoming dragon. Lorenzo? Petro?

For one brief, glorious moment, the dragon's eyes went wide with surprise. *You, a mere lion, dare attack me?*

But with a flick of its long tail and two beats of its mighty wings, the beast moved out of reach. Liam extended his paws as far as he could, barely nicking the dragon's wing. Then he landed with a lurch and roared in frustration. How was he supposed to beat an enemy who refused to fight fair?

Keep cool, Sergio barked in the brief calm before the next assault.

Liam didn't want to keep cool. He wanted to tear those bastards out of the sky.

So, do it. Get them, something inside him growled.

Briefly, he registered that the *something* wasn't his lion. But his focus was trained on Rutland, who was rallying the wolves into another attack.

Behind them, three pairs of dragon eyes glittered, saying, *The sooner you fall, the sooner we get our Fire Maiden. The sooner London will be ours.*

The mud-brown dragon had to be Lorenzo — the scents matched. That meant the other was his brother, Petro, and the copper-colored old-timer watching from the sidelines was Enzo.

Liam roared in fury. *Gemma will never be yours, and neither will London.*

He was in lion form, but it felt as if there were another beast inside him, growling and prowling around, demanding to be let out.

You're already out, Liam wanted to scream.

A flock of ravens appeared out of the clouds, cawing loudly. Liam nodded. Reinforcements were always welcome.

Look out, Sergio barked.

Liam spun just in time to fend off Rutland and a wolf, while Sergio took on the other two. They met with a jumble of snarls and roars. A flurry of raven's wings surrounded them, pecking wildly. Meanwhile, Rutland feinted forward then hung back, letting Lorenzo rush in from overhead.

Now we've got you, Rutland laughed as the dragon opened fire. Fire so intense, it cut right through the rain.

Liam dove, rolled, and came up behind Lorenzo. The dragon chuckled and beat its wings, ready to shoot out of reach.

Not so fast, asshole, Liam roared, jumping.

It was the highest jump of his life. The longest, too, taking him awfully close to the roof's edge. Part of his mind registered the long drop, but somehow, he didn't care. He reached out, straining to claw the enemy.

And somehow, that jump — and the stretching sensation — went on and on, making him feel as if there was no need to land.

Watch it! Sergio yelled as Liam sailed over the edge of the roof.

Several stories below, the cobblestone courtyard loomed, ready to shatter every one of his bones — an injury not even a quick-healing shifter could recover from.

Liam! Sergio cried.

But Liam kept roaring in an ever-deeper voice. He kept stretching too. Something ripped at his shoulders, and at first, he thought that was Petro, clawing him from behind. But it wasn't. His body was morphing.

Stop resisting. Let me out, that inner voice snarled.

His neck ached. His tail caught on something and pulled. What the hell was happening?

If you care about Gemma, let me out, the voice roared.

He wasn't about to trust a mystery voice, even if it sounded a lot like his own. But then it hit him. That was a dragon's voice. *His* dragon's voice.

At first, he resisted, as he'd been taught to since his childhood. Whatever dragon blood he carried was rogue blood. It would be unruly. Uncontrollable. No-good.

And you believe that? Gareth's words echoed in his mind.

Liam bared his teeth at his conflicting memories. He thought of Tristan, too. His Parisian friend was one of the most honorable men — and dragons — he knew, and Tristan didn't have an ounce of nobility in his blood.

To hell with the lies you were told, that inner voice snarled.

And just like that, he embraced the transformation. Wind whistled in his ears — long, spiky ears, totally unlike his lion's. Heat built in his throat, and the next time he roared, sparks spurted from his mouth. He wanted to backpedal with his front paws, but instead, he found himself flapping wings.

Merde, Sergio breathed. *Liam.*

Shit was right. He'd had dragon dreams and visions in the past, but he'd only ever shifted into lion form.

At first, it was scary as hell, because every shifter knew the importance of taming his animal side, lest the animal seize control. But a nanosecond later, Liam realized he couldn't care less. What better time to call upon the fury of a marauding dragon?

He took a deep breath, did his best to steady out on his wings, and exhaled with everything he had. An angry plume of fire lit the air in front of his snout, giving him a rush of power.

Leave this to me, that inner voice said.

And just like that, Liam became the hunter, not the hunted. A streamlined dragon, not a landlocked lion.

And boy, was he pissed off.

Chapter Eighteen

Gemma stood gripping the mantelpiece in the dining room, listening to the chaos overhead. The windows were covered by fireproof shutters, but the fight was all too easy to imagine.

Gareth tuned in to the battle with his keen raven senses. "They've come with three dragons... a few wolves..."

Every time a roar sounded or a burst of fire ripped through the air, Gemma winced. She paced two steps, then snapped her head up at an agonized yelp.

"Was that Sergio?"

"No, that is one of the others." Gareth's voice was dry as ever, but his clouded eyes said everything.

The battle wasn't going well, and how could it? Liam and Sergio were badly outnumbered.

"We have to do something."

"Mr. Bennett's orders were clear, miss."

Her hands shook in frustration. "But they need help!"

A snarl sounded, and they both looked up. A moment later, Gareth shook his head. "I believe Mr. Bennett's military training will stand him in good stead."

Gemma paused. What she wouldn't give for Liam to hear Gareth acknowledge one of his qualities. Still, the battle seemed doomed.

"Please. We have to do something."

Gareth opened his mouth, no doubt to remind her there was nothing a mere human could do. But then his eyes flickered, and he gazed upward.

"What?" she whispered a moment later.

The lines on Gareth's brow deepened. "Enzo Lombardi is leading the attack."

181

Gemma wanted to shake him. So?

"The clan leader," he said in a frighteningly cold voice. Had Gareth and Enzo tangled before?

On the roof, a lion roared, and Gemma wrung her hands. "We have to help!"

Gareth looked at the stairs, considering. "I'll go. You stay here. Stay safe."

She shook her head, but Gareth motioned to the stairs that led to the cellar. "You remember what to do in the worst case?"

She scowled. Yes, Liam had already shown her the escape tunnel. Except she didn't plan to escape, dammit. She wanted to help.

But Gareth had already whirled to go, moving faster than she would have guessed him capable of. His footsteps hammered up the staircase, and a blast of cold air whooshed in. Then a door slammed and a bolt ground into place. Moments later, the caw of a fierce raven joined the melee on the roof.

Gemma stared. *Stay here.* Was he kidding?

She glanced at the pair of broadswords hanging over the fireplace. Stay safe? Like hell she would.

She pulled a chair up, then stopped. Those swords were too heavy for her, but there were dozens more in the hallways. Rushing to the suit of armor in the nearest alcove, she studied the sword. Too long. The next one was too wide, and the next...

Her arm tingled with a memory, and it hit her. That sword she'd tried out the very first day in the castle...

Careful with that, Liam had said. *The blade is spelled against shifters.*

She sprinted upstairs and murmured to the empty suit of armor.

"I need to borrow this."

The minute she pulled the saber from the scabbard, the blade flashed, and a surge of power zipped through her arm. She hurried through a few warm-up moves and, wow. It was as if the sword knew the same moves, cutting in a given direction at the very moment she thought of it. The weapon was perfectly balanced and light — far lighter than a weapon of that size ought to be.

When she spun, she caught sight of a shield. That might come in handy.

"Sorry. I could use this, too. Please tell me it's spelled against shifters."

Three quiet seconds ticked by as she stared into the visor of the empty helmet. Then a roar sounded, and she nearly took off running for the roof. But she froze, looking at the blade. Did she really dare take on a wolf, a lion, or even a dragon?

A split second later, she squared her shoulders. She was no damsel, letting the men do the fighting. She could sure as hell contribute to the fight.

Off she went, sprinting up the spiral stairs, making herself dizzy. The closer she got to the roof, the louder — and scarier — the sounds of battle grew. Dull, muffled sounds became fierce, life-or-death snarls. She hesitated at the metal door, then slid the bolt before her hands started shaking. Putting her shoulder to the metal, she took a deep breath and shoved the door open.

And, *whoosh!* Gemma ducked as a dragon swooped by, skimming the roof in pursuit of a wolf. The powerful shock of air set off by its wings nearly bowled her over.

"Liam," Gemma whispered, trying to get her bearings.

Raindrops splattered on her face as she pressed against a wall, staring at the chaos. Dozens of ravens wheeled and cawed, harrying wolves and dragons. Most of the ravens looked ordinary, but one was the size of a condor.

"Gareth," she whispered as he slashed a wolf's ears.

That wolf was one of three closing in on a lone canine at the far end of the roof — one with dark hair and shining, black eyes.

"Sergio!" she yelled through the rain. He was so intent on something behind her, he barely noticed the wolves. She spun, following his gaze—

—and nearly fell to her knees.

"Liam?" she breathed.

That had to be him — that lion leaping at a dragon. Her heart thumped in fear while soaring at his bravery. But it was all wrong. The dragon had lured him over the edge of the roof. Liam would fall to his death. She was sure of it.

But the scream that leaped to the tip of her tongue stuck there, because the lion's long body changed in midair. The whiplike tail thickened and extended. The fur receded, giving way to tough, leathery skin a shade darker than his lion hide. His shoulder blades warped, twisted, and extended into a massive pair of wings.

"Liam?" She stared.

He flew off in hot pursuit of the dragon. *Literally* hot, thanks to the giant plume of fire that exploded from his mouth and lit a sharp, sizzling line through the rain.

Caw! Caw! a raven scolded as it flew after the dragons.

Gemma stared. Liam could change into a dragon? Since when? And wait. Wasn't she supposed to hate dragons?

There are good dragons, and there are bad dragons. Her father's words ghosted through her mind.

And hell, there was no question which type Liam was. She stood marveling until something snarled behind her.

Whipping around, she sliced the air with her sword. "Hey!"

A lion — a goddamn lion! — had snuck up on her, and for a moment, it crouched, wary. Gemma stared. Gareth had mentioned dragons and wolves, but he hadn't mentioned any lions. Was this older, scarred feline working for the Lombardis?

The blade of her sword glinted, and for a moment, the lion looked concerned. Then he stalked forward, one deliberate step at a time.

The lion grinned. *Grinned*, dammit, as if he was amused.

"Watch it," she growled, swinging the sword.

But she was the one backing up, and the lion was advancing. Soon, he had her backed into a corner, where he stood out of reach. When a dragon roared from overhead, the lion's head bobbed, but he didn't move.

Rain streamed down Gemma's face, and her mouth swung open. The lion didn't want to kill her. He wanted her alive — a prize for his dragon master.

She gritted her teeth. She would no sooner cower in a corner than she would wait downstairs. She had made up her mind to help Liam and Sergio, and dammit, she would.

She flicked her wrist a few times. Liam said the sword was spelled against shifters, but what exactly did that mean? She sighted down the wickedly sharp blade, then took a deep breath. She was about to find out.

"Did I mention how sharp this blade is?" She took a step forward.

The lion bared three-inch-long teeth as if to say, *Get back in that corner where you belong.*

Gemma's cheeks heated. "Final warning."

The lion's eyes shone. *My final warning.*

Gemma shifted her weight from her front foot to the back. Coiling every muscle, she lunged. *Zing!* The sword struck stone when the lion rolled clear. When he jumped back to four feet, his eyes were red with fury.

You want to fight, I'll fight, the lion's gleaming eyes said.

Gemma hurried back to her starting position, on guard. The lion lunged, and Gemma found herself in a duel that broke every rule of fencing. The lion wandered all over the place, for one thing, instead of sticking to a narrow field of action. Her neat parries and thrusts quickly degenerated into rough slices and chops that would have horrified her coach. She shouted with every move, kicked at the lion, and even bashed him with the shield.

"I said, get back!" she screamed, thrusting one more time.

The lion sidestepped, and she only managed a glancing blow, but the beast screamed as if its heart had been pierced. It backed away, showing wide, wild eyes. Then it sank to its haunches with a low, mournful moan. A moment later, it fell over, motionless.

Gemma felt sick. She'd never killed anything, and she never wanted to. But this was no normal lion. It was a coldhearted man — a shifter — on a ruthless mission to make her little more than a slave. She shook away her disgust. She wasn't going to relish killing, but she wasn't about to regret it either.

A bird cried in warning, and Gemma ducked just in time to escape eight-inch claws that clicked over her back. *Whoosh!* A dragon zoomed by.

She gasped, rolled, and scrambled to her feet. The dragon twisted in midair, glaring.

I want you, Maiden. And I will have you, those fiery red eyes announced.

"Petro," she all but spat into the wind.

Somehow, she knew it was him, the bastard. The one who had caused all the recent upheaval in her life.

Scary as it was to face a dragon, fury won over. How dare he?

She blinked the rain out of her eyes and brandished the sword, daring Petro to come closer. But the coward climbed to a safe distance and circled toward Enzo, who had been hovering overhead, observing the scene.

The older dragon's eyes flashed. *Can you not subdue a lowly human?*

You try it, Petro's unhappy expression said.

Fire flared in the east, and Gemma prayed that was Liam, not Lorenzo. Ravens cawed and dive-bombed the wolves clustered around Sergio, who was slashing and jumping in a fight for his life. Meanwhile, Enzo roared at Petro, who flew off to the east.

"Liam!" she screamed in warning.

But he was too far to hear, and she watched helplessly as Petro rushed to assist his brother. Overhead, Enzo started circling again, watching her closely. Waiting.

Well, she wouldn't wait, dammit. Unfortunately, she couldn't reach Liam or Enzo, but she could help Sergio.

She ran toward the battling wolves, strangely unafraid. Possessed, almost, by some untapped power within her. The power of a Fire Maiden?

She'd had time to consider that notion over the past few days, though she hadn't been able to convince herself she could really be the one. But now, heat rushed through her veins, and her heart felt like it was pumping fire.

Then there were the bracelets, which warmed and surged with power. *Dragon treasure,* her father had once told her, back when she hadn't taken him seriously.

Well, she sure took him seriously now. If the sword was spelled, the bracelets could be spelled too.

"Back!" she yelled, running at the wolves.

The ravens scattered, and the wolf closest to her whirled. Enzo roared, egging her on.

Yes, my dear Fire Maiden. Show me how powerful you are.

She didn't mind latching on to fury and using it to her advantage. But when hate — and even worse, the cruel thrill of killing — crept closer to her heart, she looked up, aghast. Did Enzo Lombardi harbor enough power to manipulate her in some way?

She shook the sword and shield, yelling at the top of her lungs. "I will never, ever help you. Never!"

Oh, but you will, his red eyes said.

A raven screamed, drawing her attention back to the roof. The nearest wolf was lunging at her. Ravens swarmed in, clawing at its eyes. That left an opening Gemma rushed into, attacking the other wolves from behind.

She swung the sword again and again, cutting, slashing, and screaming. For a few minutes, everything was a blur, and it took all her concentration not to hit Sergio. A good thing his eyes shone with an intensity the others lacked, and his dark hair made him easy to recognize. Gemma hardly recognized herself, on the other hand, because she'd never wielded a sword with such determination or power.

When the last of the three wolves fell with an anguished cry, she stepped back, feeling her energy drain. Sergio panted as hard as she did as they both looked up.

Enzo glanced over his fallen mercenaries in disgust, then whipped around when a fireball exploded against the ground in the distance.

Boom!

Gemma gasped. Please, let that not be Liam.

But Enzo roared in protest, while Sergio barked in an *Attaboy* way. Gemma exhaled. Liam had killed one of the Lombardis. However, the other had wheeled around to rush back to the castle. Petro, she decided. Both he and Liam flew full tilt, directly at her.

Gemma's knees wobbled. They weren't just flying toward her. They were coming *for* her. She could see it in the cruel glow of Petro's eyes. Sergio growled and leaned against Gemma's legs, warning her to take cover.

Petro's voice rumbled faintly in her mind. *You will be mine.*

Yes, you will be ours, old Enzo echoed from above.

Gemma swung her sword. "Never!"

Petro's eyes flashed as he raced ever closer. *Then you will die.*

Liam was directly behind him, beating his wings in a desperate attempt to close the gap. But he was running out of space to catch up.

Run, Gemma! Run, he yelled into her mind.

Yes, run, Enzo cackled. *Entertain me.*

Petro opened his mouth, revealing a row of razor-edged teeth and a glowing point of light. Gemma gulped as he gathered his inner fire and aimed it at her.

Sergio rumbled, putting more weight against her legs. *Run, Gemma!*

She took a deep breath and tapped her shield, hoping to hell it could withstand fire. Then she braced her feet, making it clear she wasn't going anywhere.

Gemma! Liam shouted as Petro zeroed in.

She waved the sword in a *Come and get me* gesture, then muttered to Sergio, "Take cover by the walls or get behind me. Your choice. But hurry."

An offended growl told her Sergio wasn't going to flee any more than she would.

"Then get behind me. I mean it," she muttered. "On three. One..."

Petro's eyes narrowed to glowing points of fire.

"Two..." she barked, ordering her knees not to tremble.

The inferno in Petro's throat gushed forth, reaching for her.

"Three!" Gemma yelled, dropping to one knee with the shield thrust before her.

She had just enough time to gulp a lungful of air before the fire hit — really hit, nearly bowling her over. If Sergio hadn't been huddled behind her, she might have tumbled backward. But together, they withstood the force of that fiery onslaught, and the fire divided around either side of the shield, missing them both.

Gemma! Liam cried.

But everything was distant, even the sound of his voice, what with the roar of the fire all around her. Petro was zooming in at low altitude, and her moment to strike drew near.

Now! something in her yelled as Petro's pale underbelly zipped overhead. The huge span of his wings blocked the rain, and his tail coiled, ready to bash her to her death.

Gemma held her ground. She would strike first, dammit.

She lunged upward, burying the spelled blade in the dragon's underside. For a few heart-stopping moments, she was dragged along, bumping and bashing the flagstones of the roof.

Let go! Move over! Liam boomed into her mind.

With a sharp grunt, she released the sword, then slammed to the ground and rolled. At the very same instant, a river of fire erupted behind her, overtaking Petro. He clawed at the blade buried in his belly and screamed at the oncoming fire. The sword clattered to the roof, but Liam's fire closed around Petro, throwing him to the ground outside the castle walls.

The rest, Gemma didn't see, because Sergio huddled closely, protecting her. But then the earth shook and sizzled, cutting off Petro's anguished cry.

She wanted to sink to her knees, but she couldn't. Petro and Lorenzo were dead, but Enzo was still circling overhead.

Sergio lifted his muzzle and snarled. Liam swooped upward, roaring in defiance. Gemma collected her nerves and raised her shield, daring Enzo to come closer. Rain pelted her face, and the ravens chattered wildly. In the midst of the din, Gemma closed her eyes, soaking it all in — that feeling of united power. Of allies battling for a common cause. Of love giving her strength and courage.

Enzo roared at Liam, and Gemma's heart sank. But the next whip of the older dragon's tail propelled his body backward, and he twisted in midair. Then he beat his wings, fleeing for the horizon.

Sergio barked in triumph, but Gemma swayed, praying it was really over. She watched as Liam gave chase before finally breaking away. He circled twice, and Gemma could sense his dilemma. Should he finish Enzo off or fly back to her while his strength lasted?

"Come back," she whispered. "Please."

Liam circled once more. Then, with a final roar of warning, he turned for home.

As he drew closer, the ravens quieted down. Sergio sank to his haunches and licked an injured paw. Gemma blinked as the reality of it all hit her. She really was standing beside a wolf who could turn into a man. That oversized raven wheeling around was the butler, and that rapidly approaching dragon was her lionhearted lover.

Liam glided in, touched down, and folded his wings awkwardly, as if the instincts that had guided him through the fight had suddenly petered out. His eyes were wary, almost pleading.

It's me, Gemma. Good dragons, remember?

Gemma stepped forward without the slightest hesitation. Dragon... lion... human. Liam was Liam, no matter what shape he came in.

She stepped forward. It was still raining, and the wind whipped her hair, but she barely noticed. All she really saw was the man she loved. Sergio gave a low chuff and turned away. At Gareth's quiet caw, the ravens dispersed. And Liam—

His eyes shone brilliantly, so full of hope, she could have burst. The space around his wings shimmered, and a charged current filled the air. By the time Gemma reached him, he was human again, with arms that held her tighter than ever before.

"Gemma..." he croaked.

She squeezed her eyes shut and clutched at his shoulders. He smelled of ash and sweat. Burn marks crisscrossed his bare back. But he was alive, and so was she.

Slowly, Liam pulled away, taking her hands. "I'm sorry. So sorry."

"For what? Nearly getting killed? For saving me?"

He shook his head. "For turning into a dragon. I swear, that's never happened before. I would have told you if I'd known I could."

Her heart ached. The poor man had truly taken her *No secrets* policy to heart. She reeled him back into a hug. "You can turn into a warthog for all I care. I love you. You got that? I love you."

His lips curled the tiniest bit. "A warthog, huh?"

She made a face. "Don't take that too literally. But, yes. I loved you when I thought you were crazy. I loved you as a lion. I can love you as a dragon too. Correction — I'm *proud* to love you as a dragon." She cupped his cheeks. "Are you seeing the common denominator here? You, Liam. I love you."

His yellow-green eyes took on a golden hue as he drew her into another hug. Then he kissed her, long and deep, only breaking away to murmur, "You, Gemma. I love you."

Chapter Nineteen

Liam held his hands toward the massive fireplace in the study, where Gareth had stoked a raging fire. But Liam's eyes weren't on the dancing flames so much as on his own arms. Wow. Had he really shifted into dragon form?

Gemma set down her mug of hot chocolate and curled her elbow around his. "What are you thinking?"

He sighed. "How much my lion relatives are going to love hearing about this."

She snorted. "Don't tell me you're worried about what they think."

He thought it over. "Not worried. Just a little... tired of explaining things. Things I don't even understand properly."

"Like turning into a dragon?"

He nodded. "To begin with."

He looked at Sergio, who sat in a nearby chair, quietly nursing a brandy — and a badly mauled arm. Sergio had experienced far worse, but clearly, he wasn't in the mood to talk. Gareth stood to one side, staring absently into the fire. Grumpy, infuriating Gareth, who had always pretended not to care.

Liam hid a smile. Gareth cared, all right. The raven had fought as bravely as anyone and, with his flock of wild ravens, he'd tipped the tide of battle. He'd also organized blankets, hot drinks, and that fire without so much as a grumble. Meanwhile, his gray hair was still plastered to his scalp, and one arm hung stiffly at his side. The man was injured, for sure, though he refused to acknowledge any such thing.

"Gareth," Liam called softly.

193

The raven shifter turned with his usual guarded expression. "Sir?"

"What do you know about the Lombardis?"

Gareth grimaced and looked back into the fire. "What is it you'd like to know?"

Good old Gareth, keeping his cards close to his chest.

"Enzo Lombardi..." Liam's voice cracked, so he started again. "He killed my father, didn't he?"

Gareth glanced over sharply, and Liam could see him weighing up what to say. In the end, all he offered was a curt shake of the head. "No. That was his brother, who died of the injuries he sustained."

Liam exhaled a little. At least there was that. Allowing Enzo to flee would be harder to live with if that had been the case.

"You were right to let him go," Gemma said as if she'd read his mind.

Liam frowned. "Was I?"

At the time, he'd been too exhausted to go on — and too worried about an ambush from the rear that could have threatened his mate. But now, his mind replayed the decision a thousand times.

Gemma wove her fingers through his. "No regrets. Everyone did what they could. Petro and Lorenzo were the real threats anyway."

Gareth shook his head. "They were the foot soldiers and the heirs to a cruel dynasty. But Enzo is the mastermind, and he has many more nephews. They will continue plotting their clan's return to power."

"Plotting to return here?" Gemma's hand went cold around Liam's.

Gareth's eyes drifted to Liam, and though his voice was neutral, his eyes sparkled with pride. "I believe we have safely eliminated that possibility."

Liam hid a tiny smile. Maybe Gareth didn't despise him after all.

"They will only set their sights elsewhere," Sergio muttered.

Gemma didn't look comforted. "First, they attacked Paris. Now, here. What next?"

"Any of the great cities could attract their greed," Gareth said. "Dublin. Lisbon. Amsterdam."

"Rome." Sergio's dark eyes flashed as he stared into the fire.

Liam watched the embers glow. He'd been so focused on the immediate problem, he'd lost sight of the big picture. The Lombardis might have been vanquished in their most recent battle, but they wouldn't abandon their quest.

He groaned. "I can see it now. We'll have to roam all over Europe, hunting them down one by one."

Sergio shook his head. "You and your Fire Maiden must stay here and protect your home. It is up to the rest of us to finish what you and Tristan started."

"Lord knows there's enough to do here," Gareth agreed.

Liam's heart stuttered. Sergio and Gareth were assuming Gemma wanted to stay with him and take up the role of a Fire Maiden. But he'd learned not to assume anything when it came to his mate.

"Wait." He looked at her. "We were born into this. You have a choice."

She pulled the blanket tighter around her shoulders. "I was born into this too. I just didn't know it."

"You still have a choice." Liam gulped. "About me, I mean."

She chuckled and nestled closer. "Well, that's a no-brainer. Where you go, I go, Mr. Bennett." Then she turned to Gareth. "What do you think? A good choice?"

Liam paled, picturing what Gareth might say.

Gareth cleared his throat. "It isn't my place to judge, Miss."

But Gemma rolled her eyes. "Oh, come on, Gareth. Help me out here. What do you say?"

Liam fought the urge to shrink under Gareth's stern gaze, as he'd done as a child. But a tiny smile appeared on the butler's lined face. "I think, miss, you could do worse."

Sergio laughed outright, as did Gemma. Liam sank back, letting out a long, slow breath.

"I think I could not do better," Gemma announced with a huge smile. "In fact, I know it. So there, destiny."

Liam all but pulled her into his lap, and if it hadn't been for Gareth and Sergio — well, who knew how far he and Gemma might have taken things on that couch. He settled for kissing her — a long, loving kiss, but still far too brief for his liking. His lion was prowling around inside him, demanding to claim his mate. Hell, he had a dragon in there as well, clamoring for the same thing. And Gemma didn't make it any easier to resist, what with the way she pressed her body against his.

Not yet, he told himself. *But soon.*

Very soon, Gemma's needy hum said.

Finally, they broke apart. Gemma took a sip of her hot chocolate, then put the mug down with a jolt.

"Oops. Should we be keeping a lookout or something?"

Gareth shook his head. "All taken care of, miss."

A raven cawed outside, and Gareth lifted his chin like a general proud of his troops. With good reason, Liam decided. He had never thought much of ravens, but then again, he'd been wrong about lots of things.

"What about that lion?" Gemma asked. "Did the Guardians send him?"

"Rutland was a mercenary. No one will miss him," Liam growled.

For the next few minutes, everyone was silent. Then Gemma nodded toward the sword laid out on the table — the one she'd struck Petro with, which Gareth had retrieved and cleaned.

"What do you know about Excalibur there?"

Liam chuckled while Gareth waved a hand in one of those gestures that implied, *I know so much, and you know so little. Where on earth would I begin?*

All he said was, "It's been in the family for generations."

"A trophy taken when a dragon defeated a knight?" Gemma asked, tensing.

196

Liam sure as hell hoped not. Gemma might have said she was okay with his dragon ancestry, but he didn't want to push his luck.

"Not at all, miss. Legend says it came from a knight who fell in love with a she-dragon."

Liam did a double take. Hadn't his mother told him a bedtime story like that? She must have, because when Gareth went on, the tale was hauntingly familiar.

"The knight had been sent to slay her, and she was prepared to kill him. But one look, and they fell in love. The knight pledged himself to the she-dragon, and she took him as her mate." Gareth smiled faintly. "You have nothing to fear from that sword. It is a symbol of love and devotion, not hate or revenge."

Liam closed his eyes, listening to the faint echo of his mother's voice. Then he looked around sadly. His parents had died so young — too young to see him make something of himself.

The fire popped and crackled, and Liam imagined a pair of voices whispering, *We see. You do us proud, son.*

He bit his lip, hanging on to that thought. His parents were there in spirit, and yes, they would be proud. But he had a lot to accomplish before he could rest easy. He and Gemma had to face the Guardians, for one thing. They would have to establish their own ground rules, the way Natalie and Tristan had in Paris. London still held its fair share of threats, and he was far from finished protecting the city. He and Gemma would be busy, indeed.

The fire crackled merrily, and Liam found himself smiling. No matter what challenges lay ahead, he and Gemma could handle them together.

"Are all the swords spelled?" Gemma asked, peering around uncomfortably.

"I don't think so. But who knows what treasures your keen eye might uncover?" Gareth's eyes twinkled.

Gemma held up her bracelets. "Like these?"

Liam leaned closer. He'd been wondering that himself.

Gareth nodded. "Part of the great Rhiannon's treasure hoard — a Fire Maiden from the thirteenth century."

Gemma tilted her head. "And they have the power to...?"

Gareth smiled. "The power to empower, so to speak." Then he gave a little bow and backed toward the door. "Now, if you'll excuse me, it is time for this old man to retire for the night. Shall I show you to your room, sir?"

Sergio rubbed his eyes and stood wearily. "Please." He turned to Liam. "All right with you?"

Liam held his friend's gaze for an eternity, trying to pack all his gratitude into a few heartbeats. But Sergio shrugged in that *You would have done the same for me* gesture they'd developed in the military. Of course, Liam would. But he had the sneaking suspicion he wouldn't get the chance to. Whatever battles Sergio faced in the future, he would face alone.

Sergio shook his head ever so slightly and spoke into Liam's mind. *Whatever challenges I face, I face with allies, new and old. And you, my friend...* His eyes drifted to Gemma, and he winked. *You take good care of your mate.*

His words had a saucy edge, and Liam wanted to protest. He and Gemma were too tired for that kind of fun, their minds too full of what had transpired. But a minute after Sergio and Gareth left the room, calling their goodbyes...

Liam kissed Gemma's ear. Just a little kiss, really, along with what he loved most — finger-combing her long, silky hair. But one kiss followed another, and before he knew it, Gemma was lying back and tugging him with her. He followed eagerly, and the next few minutes were a heated blur. The fire crackled and sparked, just like the electricity between him and Gemma. The blanket slid to the floor, and soon, Gemma's clothes followed.

Gemma ran her hands over his rear. Shifting back to human form had left him naked, and he'd only been covered by the blanket since they'd come down from the roof.

"So convenient," she murmured. "I could get into this shifter thing."

He chuckled, letting the last corner of the blanket slip away. "You'll be the same way soon." Then he froze. Oops. Had he told her about that? "If I make you my mate, you'll be a shifter too."

Gemma didn't so much as blink. She just grinned and cupped his ass. "Lion or dragon?"

He stared. "You don't mind?"

"No, I don't mind. It's in my blood, isn't it?"

"What about the Guardians? This is just what they wanted, you know."

She shook her head. "No, they wanted a couple of puppets to control. And anyway, no one is part of this decision except us."

Liam liked the sound of that. No — he *loved* the sound of that. *Us.* Him and her, a team of two.

"And, hey," she went on. "I wouldn't mind having a second means of self-defense in case that sword isn't always handy."

He frowned, because she was right. Fire Maidens could develop great powers, but they had great responsibilities too. Enough that she might have to fight more battles.

"Come what may, I can handle it," she whispered, kissing him. "But only if you're my mate. Now, where were we?" Her voice became a purr, and her hands slid over his hip, moving from his rear to—

He hissed as she palmed his cock and murmured, "Oh, yes. We were right about here."

She fisted his shaft, and when she started to slide, his eyes rolled back.

"Poor little lion. Er, dragon," she whispered, stroking faster.

"Not little," he said through clenched teeth.

If she kept that up, he'd be a goner in no time. As it was, he was aching for release. Still, he lay there, enjoying his mate's touch for another few minutes of immeasurable pleasure while a plan formed in his mind. Then he jackknifed up, scooped her into his arms, and rolled.

"Oh!" she squeaked.

"My turn." His voice was a growly mixture of human, feline, and dragon desires.

199

"No, my turn," Gemma cooed as she lay back and closed her eyes.

His blood rushed at that sign of her surrender, and a wave of adrenaline swept through him, guiding him in a thorough exploration of her body. First, he claimed her mouth in a deep, searing kiss. Then he treasured her breasts, licking and nipping until she cried out. Finally, he slid to his knees beside the couch, spread her legs, and consumed her.

Gemma wove her fingers through his hair. "Yes..."

Her flavor acted on him like a drug, and he couldn't stop tasting... touching... exploring. Gemma started gyrating, and her moans grew louder.

"Yes..."

His hands, tongue, and fingers were all devoted to her pleasure, but his mind spun ahead, calculating. The two of them would never fit on that couch, and the bedroom was too far away. That left the floor — not exactly a classy place for the act of mating, but hell. He doubted Gemma would mind, and the fireplace did lend a certain ambiance...

When he eased away from Gemma, she whimpered, tugging him back.

"Don't stop. Please..."

"Just relocating. All right with you?"

Her eyes were hazy, and he was fairly sure she would agree to relocating to just about anywhere if that's what it took. The barn. Hell, on the roof in the rain. He wouldn't mind, except for the time it took to get there. So he lowered her to the floor and slid into place over her body.

"All right with me." She wrapped her legs around his waist. "Just promise me Gareth won't walk in, offering more hot chocolate."

Liam laughed. "I think he has a sixth sense for these things."

"That, or I'm loud enough to give us away." Gemma blushed.

Liam brushed a lock of hair behind her ear and grinned. "I'll take that as a challenge."

"Wait," she yelped, but only in jest. "Don't you dare... Oh!" She cried when he tugged her knees higher.

"Ready?" he asked through clenched teeth.

"Ready," she breathed, extending her arms over her head.

The moment he thrust into her, a heat wave rushed through his veins, steamrolling away any lingering inhibitions. Soon, Gemma was bucking against every thrust, taking him deeper and deeper. Best of all, it was skin-on-skin, without that barrier of a condom. But somehow, his inner beast wanted more.

"Liam..." Gemma rolled her head from side to side, exposing the creamy skin of her neck.

He kissed her collarbone, sniffing deeply.

So close, his lion growled.

Very close, his dragon side agreed.

Every shifter knew about mating bites, although the actual mechanics had always been a mystery to him. But instinct guided him, just as it had with flying. And now...

His heart hammered. Now, he was on the cusp of a whole new life as a mated shifter. A concept he would have scoffed at months earlier had suddenly become the guiding light of his existence.

When he nipped Gemma's neck, she tugged his head closer. Then she clenched her inner muscles, making his cock burn.

"Mate," he rumbled. It came out a little slurred as his canines extended.

Sealing his mouth over her neck, he drowned in heavenly sensations. Gemma's sweet, soft body, calling to his. The steady pump of her jugular just beneath the skin. The burning slide of his cock as he thrust inside her.

"Please..." Gemma begged.

When he bit down, she arched off the floor. Her cries could have meant anything, but her thoughts flooded his mind, and they spelled pure ecstasy.

Oh... Yes... So good...

He bit deeper, keeping a tight seal with his lips. In a distant, detached way, he registered the taste of her blood. More important was the sensation of her life essence mixing with his.

201

Something beyond flesh, blood, or even heat. An ephemeral force wove this way and that, bonding their souls forever.

With one final thrust, he exploded inside her. His lion roared in triumph, but his dragon side murmured, *One last thing.*

What else was there? They were as deeply connected as a couple could possibly be.

Then he found himself inhaling sharply. Heat flared in his chest, and—

The brand, he realized a heartbeat before he exhaled.

Most shifters mated with a bite, but dragons crowned the act by sending a searing breath through their mate's veins. He'd heard about it, but doing it—

Now, his dragon side demanded, and he exhaled.

For the briefest of instants, his mouth burned. Then the fire shot into Gemma, and they both shuddered. Brilliant lights went off in his mind, blinding him to everything but core-deep pleasure. His *and* hers. Both were clear in his mind yet foggy at the same time, because ecstasy that intense was overwhelming. It filled him. Buoyed him. Made him want to beat his chest and howl.

He held Gemma just as desperately as he held on to that high, refusing to let go. Then instinct tapped a distant corner of his mind, telling him to release her — slowly. His teeth receded, though he kept his lips tight and his tongue firmly against the wound until it sealed. Then, with a gasp, he broke away and collapsed over her.

Her chest heaved, lifting and lowering him like a wave. He gulped, inhaling the sticky-sweet scent of sex. Then he traced the outline of Gemma's pounding heart with one shaky finger. Their bodies were limp and slick with sweat, but he didn't mind.

Mate, he wanted to roar. *My amazing mate.*

Gemma sighed, slowly drawing her hands down his back. A log cracked and disintegrated in the fireplace, and gradually, the swirling sparks gave way to the quiet glow of embers.

"Now who's the crazy one?" Gemma chuckled weakly a moment later.

He propped his chin on her chest and met her eyes. "I don't know. Who?"

She laughed. "Me, because I want you to do that again. And again." She tipped her head back, making her breasts rise. "God, I can come just thinking about it."

A minute or two later, with a little help from him, she did, shuddering and crying a second time. Liam's cheeks ached from smiling, but he couldn't help it. Watching her come undone was fun. So was holding her and basking in the knowledge that she was his — and laughing out loud at what she said next.

"If I become a shifter, do I get to do that to you too?"

His cock twitched, and he broke into peals of laughter.

"What?" she demanded.

"My turn," he managed to mumble between chuckles.

"Your turn to what?"

"My turn to come just thinking about it."

Gemma laughed, then cuddled closer. "I've created a monster."

"No, I've created a monster."

When they finally stopped laughing, he pulled the blanket over them both and spooned her against his chest. Then he kissed her and gazed into the fire.

"Cut that out," Gemma murmured a moment later.

"Cut what out?"

"Thinking ahead."

She was right, and he knew it. Sooner or later, they would have to make their way to the bedroom. And sooner or later, they had to decide on their next steps. But for now...

She turned in his arms, purring like a kitten. "Tonight, nothing matters. Nothing but being together."

Then she kissed him, pushing every thought into the distance.

Chapter Twenty

Two weeks later...

Gemma swung Liam's hand as they walked along the Thames, looking left and right. It was one of those rare, not-a-cloud-on-the-horizon days in London, with crisp spring air and blue skies. So many iconic sights were hers to enjoy, from the Houses of Parliament to Big Ben and the London Eye — the futuristic Ferris wheel set along the Thames.

"It's kind of thrilling, being back in the city."

"Yeah, thrilling," Liam grumbled.

She squeezed his hand. "I'd call last night pretty thrilling."

He grinned, and heat ricocheted around her veins. "Thrilling, yes. Though cozy came to mind first."

She play-smacked his arm. They'd spent their first night back in London on good old *Valhalla* and stayed up late making love. Cozy was right, because Liam had kept bumping his head on the low ceiling of her bunk. In the end, she'd taken the top, cowgirl style, and, in the heat of the moment, she'd even returned the favor of a mating bite.

Yes, a mating bite. She'd shifted into dragon form for the first time in Wales and had spent the past ten days learning to control that amazing new body. Liam had taught her to fly and how to breathe fire.

I need a lot of practice myself, he'd admitted with a huge grin.

So far, she hadn't changed into lion form. And who knew? Maybe she never would. But one new body — and the skills that went with it — was enough to master for the time being.

She looked around. Flying over the remote, rocky landscape of Wales had been great, but she couldn't wait to fly over London. Still, first things first. It was their big day — the day she and Liam had decided to confront the Guardians.

When Liam caught her checking her watch, he frowned. "Damned lions."

She kissed his hand, helping him settle down. Still, he grumbled, pointing at the huge South Bank statue, then at the bronze heads decorating the riverbanks. "Lion. Lion, lion, lion. They really think they own the place, don't they?"

"They don't own us."

Liam flashed a smile and slid an arm over her shoulders. "True. But they will try to control us. All in the name of the city's best interests, of course."

She shrugged. "They can try, but they won't succeed. We'll show them there's more than one way to serve the city."

She had a long list of projects she couldn't wait to sink her teeth into. But it all started with meeting with the Guardians, so she reluctantly turned toward Westminster Abbey.

Liam scowled. "More lions."

Indeed, the column outside the abbey was flanked by growling feline statues. But when she craned her neck around...

"Ha. A dragon." She pointed to the gold figure atop a nearby building. "See? They're around, too. Just less in your face."

Liam sighed. "I guess so."

"It's like Gareth said — dragons have protected London all along. At least, they did until the lions started dominating things." She kissed his hand. "Besides, I'm not about to get down on lions. I fell in love with one, you know."

He grinned. "I guess you did. Funny how things work out, don't you think?"

She laughed outright. "Funny is my dad and Gareth."

Liam burst out laughing, and she did too. When they'd gone to pick up Garth's Mini after the dragon attack, Liam had invited her father to the castle, where her dad had gushed over every tapestry, every leather-bound volume, and every suit of armor.

Good gracious. Is this genuine Royal Almain Armour? he'd exclaimed.

Finally, Gareth had said, scowling at Liam. *Someone who appreciates history.*

The two had spent hours discussing shifter genealogies, politics, and traditions. Late one night, Gemma had even stumbled across Gareth sitting — actually sitting, not to mention sipping brandy — in the study with her father as they debated the merits of Norman versus Edwardian castles.

Finally, Gareth had someone to debate esoteric topics with. And finally, Gemma's father had someone to discuss shifters with. A match made in heaven, as Liam had said. When Gemma and Liam had headed back to London, her father had remained in Wales.

And as for her mother — well, Gemma hadn't broached the topic of shifters yet. Maybe someday, and in person, she would. But for the time being, she'd only shared key parts of recent events with her mom — like starting a relationship with a wonderful guy named Liam. A relationship Gemma knew would last a long, long time.

Liam's wistful look, however, told her he was still thinking about Wales.

"Do you wish we'd stayed there longer?" she asked.

He shook his head. "I love it there, but I'd go crazy if I stayed in the countryside too long — even with you there. Plus, if we don't save the Guardians from themselves, who will?" He sighed. "I really believe their hearts are in the right place. It's just how they go about things."

"I guess that can be our objective for today. Getting that message through."

He snorted. "Getting a sword through solid stone would be easier." Big Ben chimed three-quarters of an hour, and Liam frowned. "We're going to be late."

"Good. Let them wait. They need a little less pandering to and a little more... dragon attitude."

Liam laughed. "Dragon attitude?"

She nodded firmly. "Watch out, baby. Here we come. Not that I'm letting this Fire Maiden stuff go to my head," she

207

hurried to add.

"Not a chance." Liam pulled her closer to his side.

He'd briefed her on his understanding of the job, and a couple of phone calls to Natalie, the Fire Maiden of Paris, had given her an idea of how to get started. It was daunting but inspiring at the same time. Finally, she had a chance to raise critical issues with influential people. There was so much to be done in London and around the world. Social issues... climate change... human rights...

She took a deep breath. Even a Fire Maiden couldn't work miracles. But she sure as hell would do her best.

They turned right, cut through the Horse Guards archway, and skirted the edge of St. James Park. Buckingham Palace stood in the distance, its dozens of windows reflecting the sun.

Liam must have caught her looking, because he dismissed the palace with an unimpressed wave. "It might be big, but it's nowhere near as cozy as our place."

She bit her lip. Wow. She'd never considered that mating with Liam made his castle hers too. And, wait a minute. How did he know how the two buildings compared?

"Have you been inside Buckingham Palace?"

He shrugged. "Only a few times."

"Only a few?"

"The Queen is nice, but I'd hate to live in that place. Anyway..." He pointed. "We're nearly there. Should we detour? I have to admit, I'm dreading this."

She clasped his hand with both of hers. "Well, I can't wait to give them a piece of my mind."

And, as it transpired, she did. Focusing on recent history helped her stomp directly past the awe-inspiring trappings of the courtyard at Lionsgate. What right had they had to treat Liam's parents so unfairly? And how dare they keep the truth about his parents from him for so long?

She barely noticed Sergio waiting for them by the front gate. All she caught in her building fury was Liam's amused whisper.

"Watch out. She's on a roll," he warned his friend.

208

She *was* on a roll, dammit. The lions had seen fit to meddle in her private life in the most barbaric way. Worse, their long-range plan had been to manipulate her and her future children. *Her* children, dammit!

The more she thought about it, the more she fumed and the faster she walked. One moment, she was striding through sunshine, and the next, she was striding down a gloomy Tudor hallway, channeling her inner bitch. A pair of guards stood at the far end, their crossed axes closing off the Great Hall beyond.

"You have got to be kidding me," she muttered, powering ahead.

The guards' eyes went wide, and she glowered. No, she wasn't going to stop. They'd better move those axes, or else.

"Fire Maiden, coming through," Liam called cheerfully.

The guards broke apart with a clatter, and everyone in the Great Hall looked up.

Well, fine, she decided. Let them stare. The sooner they realized she was not to be messed with, the better.

She whisked down the length of the hall without a glance to either side. The room was filled with shifters — mostly men — all of them painfully silent. According to Liam, the Council of Elders would be at the far end, so that was where she headed.

An imposing, gray-haired woman looked down from the dais at the end of the hall in disdain. "Mr. Bennett. Miss Archer."

Gemma balled her hands into fists. That had to be Electra.

If ever an occasion called for an old-fashioned curtsy, this was one. But Gemma kept her chin high and her legs straight as she greeted the head Guardian.

"Mrs. Huxley," she ground out through clenched teeth.

"A pleasure to meet you at last." Electra's eyes shot daggers.

Gemma let a silent beat go by, then another. The hall was so quiet, you could have heard a pin drop. Everyone was waiting for her to lie back to Electra. Well, forget it. She wasn't going to claim it was any kind of pleasure to meet a merciless manipulator. Instead, Gemma stood tall, letting painful seconds tick away.

Electra's eyes narrowed. "You're late."

Gemma crossed her arms. "I'd say I'm just in time."

An older man stood beside Electra, and his shaggy eyebrows jumped up. That had to be Augustus, she supposed.

"Just in time for what?"

"Just in time to snatch my future back," Gemma announced, loud and clear. "Or were you going to consult with me about your plans?"

I consult with no one, Electra's haughty gaze said.

But Augustus spoke first, the good cop to Electra's bad cop. "My dear girl, you must have been misinformed. I can assure you—"

Gemma was tempted — so, so tempted — to thrust her hands on her hips and repeat everything Liam had told her. But she knew an opening when she saw one, so she leaped on it.

"Oh, good. No plans for meddling with my future? Perfect. Allow me to inform you of my intentions, then."

She looked around the room, catching a glimpse of Liam, whose awed expression said, *You go, girl.*

"Apparently, you were looking for a Fire Maiden. It so happens that I have been considering settling in London — if I so choose," she emphasized. "Of course, there are some points we must discuss if we are to form a collaborative relationship."

Electra's eyes blazed. *I give orders. I don't collaborate.*

Augustus frowned. "What points?"

"Number one: anything I do, I do of my own free will."

Augustus pretended to be baffled. "Naturally. We wouldn't want it any other way."

Liam made a gagging sound.

"I knew you would agree," Gemma replied.

Electra twisted her lips. Was that supposed to be a smile? "Of course, we agree. You may do anything you want. In fact, I have a number of suggestions."

I can't wait, Liam muttered.

Gemma arched an eyebrow. "Suggestions?"

"Of course. To begin with, I have taken the liberty of appointing you a personal secretary."

When Electra motioned a carefully coiffed woman forward, Liam started coughing. *I love her definition of suggesting.*

"Lady Miriam Burke-Smythe," Electra announced. "She'll go through all your correspondence—"

"She'll what?" Gemma screeched.

"Just to assist you, my dear. You know, weeding out unnecessary messages."

Gemma met Liam's skeptical gaze. Yeah, she figured as much. Lady Miriam Whatshername would ensure she stayed out of the loop on any important issues.

"What if I don't need help weeding?"

"Oh, but my dear. You're so young. So inexperienced."

"So uncorrupted," Gemma offered brightly. "I don't need help. I have Liam. My mate, in case you didn't know."

Electra flashed the first genuine smile of the meeting. "Oh, we know. And we're delighted."

A polite smattering of applause broke out, making Gemma grind her teeth.

I swear, if I didn't love you so much, I'd dump you just to piss them off, she whispered into Liam's mind.

Uh, thanks? he shot back, but his grin said he knew what she meant.

Gemma took a deep breath, reminding herself it didn't matter that Electra had wanted that from the beginning. The lion matriarch would soon realize she'd gotten more than she bargained for.

"Yes, yes. Such good news," Electra gushed. "In fact, I have a gift for the happy couple. A lovely little estate in Kent. It comes with staff. . . stables. . . forty-four rooms."

"Only forty-four?" Liam quipped.

"With an addition planned," Electra added quickly.

Liam stroked his chin. "That doesn't sound very cozy."

Electra's brow furrowed. "Cozy?"

Gemma nodded. "We prefer cozy."

Electra looked mystified, but she powered on. "You will be granted a regular allowance. Appointments with Britain's top fashion designers. . . "

Gemma held back her snort but not her words. "Very generous, but we already have a place to live. A nice little narrowboat on the canal."

Never mind that she and Liam had agreed to move into his penthouse as soon as *Valhalla's* owner returned. She couldn't resist the tease.

Electra's mouth wobbled in horror. "Good gracious. That will never do. Not for a Fire Maiden."

"Oh, but it will. I promise you." Gemma growled. "I will also manage my own finances."

"My dear, I am only trying to make things easier for you."

Gemma frowned. How gullible did the woman think she was?

Electra suddenly turned sweet as pie. "Being a Fire Maiden comes with great responsibility, you know."

"Oh, I know. Just having to meet all those fashion designers..."

Sergio snorted, but Electra didn't seem to catch the sarcasm.

"Exactly," Electra agreed. "We'll spare you the trouble of attending council meetings..."

She might as well have said, *No reason to worry your pretty little head about complex issues.*

"How considerate," Gemma muttered. She opened her mouth, tempted to bait Electra for a while longer. But it was time to establish her position once and for all. She took a deep breath, because this was it. The foundation for a life free of the Guardians' interference. Whatever control she gave away now, she might never regain.

You got this, Liam murmured.

"You're very generous, indeed. However, my understanding of a Fire Maiden's role is quite different."

How different? Electra's frozen features demanded.

"I have no need for a secretary, nor an estate." *And definitely no fashion designers,* she nearly added. "I will continue to work toward serious issues."

She winked at Liam. As it turned out, he had quite a fortune to draw from. Gareth had managed his father's estate

212

well. Not only that, but as a Fire Maiden, she was heiress to a vast fortune of her own. That meant she could devote herself to important causes full time. Like raising awareness of social injustices. Taking decisive action to stop the climate crisis. Bringing people together on a grassroots level to actually get things done.

"I will report to you regularly on my efforts..." Gemma continued.

Electra smiled that evil smile. *Of course you will.*

"...just as I expect you to report to me on shifter matters," Gemma finished.

Electra frowned. *I report to nobody.*

Gemma mimicked the woman's fake smile. "You know, to make some suggestions. We will be collaborating after all. There's the Say No to Racism campaign, the Clean Air initiative, the Safer Parks Panel..."

"Safer what?" Electra blinked.

Ignoring her, Gemma turned to Liam. "What else was there?"

At first, Liam looked at her, startled. But she nodded, encouraging him to speak. He needed this — a chance to finally make peace with the Guardians.

"What else is there? Where do I begin?" He prowled forward, and Electra scuttled back. "You will never meddle with our personal business. Ever. You will not attempt to manipulate my mate. If you do..."

His eyes glowed, and Gemma saw sheer dragon fury burning beneath the surface.

"Suffice to say, you will regret it. You will never malign my parents again. Any of you," he shouted, glaring at the entire hall.

Everyone shrank back as his words echoed from the oak rafters.

Gemma touched his arm. Whoa. Where had that come from?

Liam took her hand, and the angry glow turned to pure determination.

ANNA LOWE

"Are you finished, Mr. Bennett?" Electra said after an awed minute of silence.

His eyes flared, and he strode right up to Electra, showing his full height.

"No. There is one more thing. Any children my mate and I decide to have will be ours to raise, free of your influence. Do I make myself clear?" He paused, then turned to the others. "Do I make myself clear?"

His roar thundered through the hall, and dozens of dumbstruck shifters nodded. Gemma nearly did too. Liam the warrior, she'd seen plenty of. Liam the jokester, too. But this was a whole new Liam. A leader. A future Guardian.

And just like that, she glimpsed a future she'd never considered. A bright one, with a newer, fairer Council.

Electra's mouth opened and closed until she squeaked, "Of course. I would never dream of it."

Liam glowered. *You'd better not.*

A ripple went through the crowd as they nodded in respect or murmured to each another — words along the lines of *That Bennett boy came out all right, don't you think?*

"I think we're done here," Gemma said, reaching for Liam's hand.

His eyes locked on hers and warmed. "I'd say we are."

Gemma looked at Electra, then decided she didn't need anyone's permission to leave. Turning on her heel, she moved toward the door with Liam at her side. Sergio fell into step behind them, and everyone hurried out of their way. The moment Gemma frowned at the bear guards at the door, they uncrossed their axes and jumped aside. A minute later, she, Liam, and Sergio stepped into the fresh air.

She tipped her head back and took a deep breath, basking in the sunlight as they left Lionsgate Hall. Whew.

"You were brilliant," Liam whispered, pulling her into a hug.

"No, you were brilliant." Her voice was muffled by his shirt.

"Yes, I was." He chuckled. "But only because of you."

Beside them, Sergio sighed. *"Amore."*

Gemma smiled into Liam's shoulder. It really was *amore.* But, wait. Was there a note of longing in Sergio's voice?

By the time she looked, the wolf shifter's expression was inscrutable. Then he checked his watch, and she pulled away from Liam, remembering what else they had to face that day.

"How soon do you have to go?" she asked.

Too soon, Sergio's bittersweet expression said. "My flight departs in a few hours."

His eyes locked with Liam's, and though neither spoke a word, so much passed between them. Memories. . . regrets. . . gratitude. Enduring a decade in one of the roughest, toughest military corps in the world had bonded them as closely as brothers, as had the events of the past few weeks.

"Are you sure?" Gemma whispered.

Sergio flashed a tight smile. "Not so sure. But it is time to go. Lisbon first, then Rome. Liam is not the only one with an ancestral home he has been neglecting."

Gemma wondered what that might be. A villa in Tuscany? A palace in Venice?

"I hope their Guardians are a little friendlier than ours," she said.

He snorted. "You'll have to come visit and — how do you say it? Ah, yes. Whip their asses into shape."

Liam chuckled. "She's good at that."

Gemma shook her head. It had been an intense morning, and she needed a break from heavy thoughts. So she hooked one elbow through Liam's arm and the other through Sergio's and led them down the street.

"I know a nice pub where we can enjoy a quiet goodbye lunch. After that, we can have dessert in a beautiful spot right by a canal."

Sergio laughed. "No dragons this time?"

"Just the good kind," she assured him. Then she leaned her head on Liam's shoulder and murmured, "Just the good kind."

Epilogue

Gemma exhaled slowly and took in the view. "This is great."

Liam grinned at her over the remains of the candlelight dinner he'd set up on the penthouse terrace. "A little less stressed now?"

She laughed. Not only was she not stressed, she barely remembered what she'd done all day. That was the thing about coming home to Liam. The minute she saw him, her worries fell away, and her soul felt at peace. He'd bounded to the door the minute she'd walked in, too, looking like someone had turned on a light inside him.

He raised his wineglass. "To a successful day at the Towpath Task Force."

She grinned and clinked her glass against his, letting the clear sound ring.

"To the Task Force, a cleaner canal, and the kids."

She'd spent the afternoon working on one of the community projects she loved, and it had gone brilliantly. Organizing canal cleanups was easy, but she'd gone a step further by recruiting student volunteers from two schools that were worlds apart. Privileged kids from a prep school had worked side by side with immigrant children from a low-income area, tackling an environmental problem and breaking cultural barriers at the same time.

"It was so nice watching them get to know each other," she said.

"No one got pushed into the canal?"

"Thankfully, no. No younger version of Liam there today."

He chuckled. "I'm sure there are worse."

"Maybe I need to enlist the Guardians for the next canal cleanup," she joked. "Or not."

He burst out laughing. "They could use a little cross-species team building."

"That, they could."

She snuggled her foot against his. "Someday, I might actually try that, although I find it hard to picture Electra holding a garbage bag for, say, a unicorn. But for now..." She exhaled and leaned back. "I'll take it one step at a time."

For the next few minutes, they sat quietly, mulling over the view. Late spring was giving way to summer, which meant they could sit out on the terrace and enjoy the sunset. *Valhalla's* owner had returned to London, and Gemma was slowly settling into the penthouse. The place definitely had its pluses. Higher ceilings. More space. And the views... Hyde Park stretched before her like a green carpet, and the bustle of London felt far, far away.

"It's amazing how quiet it is up on the ninth floor."

Liam grinned. "Speaking of which, I have more planned for tonight."

"More than this?" She gestured over the plates, candles, and white tablecloth. Liam seemed to have a different little surprise for her every day.

He came around behind her and gestured at the view from over her shoulder. "That's next."

She tilted her head. "What's next?"

"Even better views and even quieter heights. You and I are going flying."

Her pulse skipped. When she'd first come home, all she'd wanted was to wind down after a busy day. But being with Liam had renewed her energy, and her dragon side was burning to be set loose.

Before she got carried away with the thought, though, she looked around warily. "Knowing my landing style, we'd better clean up first."

Liam squeezed her shoulders. "I'll clean up. You sit. And don't knock your landing technique. It's great."

"I land like an albatross."

She'd taken to flying from her first day as a dragon, and landing on the castle roof hadn't been a problem. Landing in confined spaces was another matter. It had been easy enough on the towpath by the canal. But the first time she'd tried landing at the penthouse, she'd knocked over everything on the terrace — the table, chairs, potted plants...

"It may not be elegant — yet," Liam called over his shoulder as he carried away the dishes. "But who cares? It's our house. We make the rules."

She closed her eyes, smiling. How lucky was she to have such a supportive mate? Liam had spent most of the day investigating leads on where the Lombardis might head next, as much for the Guardians as for his own peace of mind. Yet he had taken the time to treat her to a lovely dinner — and now, he was ready to see her through another flight.

She smiled. She needed the practice — and it would probably help Liam too. So she stood and helped clear away dinner then pushed aside that pesky table and the chairs, just in case. Finally, she stood at the edge of the terrace with Liam, looking down.

"It's funny. When I bought this place, I thought Hyde Park would make a good lion prowling ground," he mused. "But it's great for flying too."

"Maybe deep down, you knew about your dragon side."

He shrugged. "Maybe it's destiny. Either way, I'm ready. How about you?"

She nodded and slowly stripped. No sense in shredding perfectly good clothes. Her pulse skipped, partly in anticipation of flying and partly from the cheap thrill of checking out Liam in the buff. No matter how much time she spent in bed with her mate — and, yes, they had logged plenty of hours there, putting all that shifter energy to good use — her blood still heated at the sight of his perfect ass... shoulders... abs...

Liam cocked an eyebrow, and she blushed. Caught ogling yet again. But, heck. He was peeking at her in the same way.

219

ANNA LOWE

Liam chuckled. "This is always the hardest part."

"What is?"

"To go flying instead of taking you straight to bed."

She waggled a finger. "Mr. Bennett, you have a dirty mind."

"No, I have an irresistible mate. Let's get moving before I lose my resolve."

Gemma was tempted to suggest bed first and flying later, but Liam was right. She shuffled closer to the edge of the balcony, then took a deep breath and backed up, giving herself space to shift. *Ready?*

Ready, an inner voice growled.

She closed her eyes, focusing on the sensations her dragon side sent through her mind. How cramped the beast felt after a day on the ground, and how liberating it would feel to fly. Picturing cool wind flowing over her wings, she held her arms wide. Then she inhaled deeply, picturing the view changing to that from a bird's eye.

Dragon's-eye view. Her inner beast chuckled.

The more she wiggled her fingers, the more the webbing between them stretched. The more deeply she inhaled, the more her nostrils flared. Her skin rippled and twitched as leathery dragon hide emerged. Her toes curled, and the nails became sharp, pointy claws.

Slowly, she opened her eyes and, wow. She was a dragon. A huge, golden dragon — the color of royalty.

Of course, her dragon huffed.

She nearly rolled her eyes. She'd been ignorant of so much for so long. Now she was a dragon — and a pretty formidable one, at that.

Foot-long flames spouted from her nostrils as her dragon showed off.

Watch it, she muttered.

If there was one thing she'd learned about shifting, it was to conceal her animal side from the human world.

They'll just think we've turned the barbecue up high, Liam said.

She turned, and there he was, looking as dashing in dragon form as in his human body. His skin was a yellowish, mustard color — a darker shade of his lion hide — and his eyes were the same goldish-green hue, glowing and sparkling as he took her in.

Like I said, the world's most beautiful mate.

When she snorted, sparks crackled from her nostrils, and she chastised her dragon. *Would you cut that out?*

I will if you quit gawking and finally let me fly.

She steeled her nerves and snipped back. *I will gawk as long as I like, and you will do as you're told.*

Liam had emphasized the importance of controlling her animal side, and he was right. If she gave the beast an inch, it would take over, and she might find herself spitting fire over the London skyline. Fun as that sounded, it just wouldn't do.

Her dragon side muttered under its breath, but Gemma refused to give in.

Ready? Liam asked, spreading his wings.

With a nod, she mimicked him.

Set... Liam crouched, extending his tail.

Gemma bent her legs, relishing the power coursing through her body.

Go!

A tiny push was all it took to leave the terrace and — *wheee!* — she sailed through the air. The wind flowed under her wings, giving her lift, and she glided silently over Hyde Park. First, she swooped over the Rose Garden, taking in the neat, circular pattern. Then, with a slight tilt of her wings, she curved over the still waters of the Serpentine. When Liam beat his wings once and banked right, she followed.

Where are you heading?

Just a little detour, he murmured.

Gemma looked around, studying the network of streets and squares below. That dark patch was Regent's Park, and beyond it, the sweeping lawn of Primrose Hill. And over there...

Her heart squeezed a little when she realized where Liam was heading. To the canal, lined with narrowboats in neat

ANNA LOWE

rows. They both dipped and peered down until *Valhalla's* dark
hull came into view.

That one? Liam pointed with one claw.

That's her, Gemma sighed. She could tell by the flowerpots
on the deck.

A single light glowed from the cabin, and Gemma pictured
herself there a few weeks earlier, wondering about the cute,
crazy man who insisted on protecting her. Her life had changed
so much since then. And now that *Valhalla's* owner had returned, that chapter was behind her for good. Still, she would
cherish the memories forever.

Even that annoyingly low ceiling, Liam chuckled, reading
her mind.

Her mind filled with heated images of the time they'd spent
making love in the bunk.

It was cozy, she insisted.

Liam chuckled. In all honesty, she found the penthouse
cozy too, and even the castle in Wales. Cozy came from decor,
and above all, from good company. With Liam around, she
could call any place home.

She beat her wings, gaining altitude. Even with an ancient
spell in place, concealing them from human eyes, she felt a
little safer higher up.

That spell is stronger than ever, Liam said. *Thanks to you,
my dear Fire Maiden.*

She wanted to brush that off as just another sweet comment
from her mate, but even the Guardians had commented on an
increase in the protective spell. Apparently, they hadn't been
exaggerating the benefits of having a resident Fire Maiden.

Gemma gulped a little. Most of the time, she felt like
plain old Gemma, with more upscale accommodations and the
world's most amazing partner. But occasionally, the responsibilities of her role reared up in her consciousness — sometimes
like a ton of bricks, other times in smaller pinches that said,
Remember. Everything you do makes a difference.

Then she shook her head. Her parents had always insisted
that any average person could make a difference if they tried,

and they were right. But, hey. Having wings and a tail sure helped.

She grinned and flew on, ticking off landmarks. Over on the left was Buckingham Palace, and — *whoosh!* — St. James Park slid by under her belly. Rows of buildings flashed below, and then, the dark, inky ribbon of the Thames.

That way. No, that way, Liam called exuberantly, starting out in one direction, then turning to go the other.

Gemma beat her wings to follow, staying high above the level of the London Eye. One bridge after another spanned the river, their lights reflecting in the water. Vehicles crossed those spans in steady streams, and barges glided silently over the water. Following the curve of the river, she ticked off several more landmarks — the floodlit dome of St. Paul's, brightly lit Tower Bridge, and futuristic skyscrapers like the Shard and Walkie-Talkie.

Should we continue to Greenwich or turn around here? Liam asked.

Turn around. I'm still getting my bearings.

Me too. Liam laughed, leading her through a long, graceful arc.

Up to that point, they had been beating against the wind, but changing directions put them into a smooth, effortless glide. Gemma gulped down the lump forming in her throat in one of those *pinch me, I'm dreaming* moments. Was she really flying over London on her own power? Did she really get to spend her life with the man of her dreams?

Yes, you are. Yes, you do, a voice whispered on the wind. The voice of destiny?

She took a deep breath. The burdens of being a Fire Maiden certainly came with their rewards, and she vowed never to lose sight of that.

It's so beautiful, she breathed.

Double-decker buses crossed Westminster bridge, leaving a trail of red and white lights. To her right, neon lights flashed, marking the hive of activity at Piccadilly Circus. The Mall, in contrast, seemed to slumber, along with the occupants of

Buckingham Palace. Liam, on the other hand, was executing rolls and figure eights, enjoying every minute of the ride.

Bong... Bong... Big Ben hammered as they flew by.

Gemma wheeled at high altitude, listening to every stroke of the bell.

Look down. What do you see? she called when Liam joined her.

Um... London?

She laughed and gestured to Westminster Abbey with one wing. The motion nearly made her topple sideways, and she yelped, then steadied out.

When we walked down there, you complained about all the lions. But from up here...

Liam chuckled. *Not a lion in sight. What's the moral of the story?*

She smiled. *That it's all a matter of perspective. Lions don't rule London, but dragons don't either. We need to work together to keep the city safe.*

Spoken like a true Fire Maiden.

Gemma laughed and looked around. *We're so lucky. Flying in Wales was peaceful, but this is exciting.*

Liam nodded. *We get the best of both worlds. Like being a lion and a dragon.*

She smiled. Liam might pretend to resent lions, but he would never shake his love of prowling through tall grass at dusk. And who knew? Maybe someday she would get to experience that as well.

In the meantime, she gazed ahead, trying to match landmarks to her mental map of London. *What happens if we keep following the river?*

Liam snorted. *It loops around and leads to Richmond. We could visit my aunt. Yay?*

Liam drifted closer, and their wingtips brushed. A tingle traveled through Gemma's body, and a new set of thoughts filled her mind.

I have a better idea.

Oh yes? Liam's voice dropped as he read her mind.

Flying over London was thrilling, but now that she'd had a good look, all she could think of was going home and getting her hands on her mate.

Enough sight-seeing for one night? she asked.

Liam rumbled in approval, making her blood heat.

In truth, she would never get enough of flying over London by night, just as she would never get enough of her mate. But, hell. She would do her best, especially when it came to spending time with Liam.

A lifetime, he murmured as they glided home, wing on wing.

Sneak Peek – Fire Maidens: Rome

Ever since the time of Romulus and Remus, wolves have ruled Rome. And with the city under threat, the Guardians of Old have called in a new generation of shifter protectors. These warriors are sworn to their duty and absolutely, positively sworn off love. That is, until destiny brings in a woman one lone wolf just can't resist...

Book 3 in Anna's **Fire Maidens: Billionaires & Bodyguards** series is set in the Eternal City, where nothing is what it seems. Don't miss it!

Books by Anna Lowe

Fire Maidens - Billionaires & Bodyguards

Fire Maidens: Paris (Book 1)

Fire Maidens: London (Book 2)

Fire Maidens: Rome (Book 3)

Fire Maidens: Portugal (Book 4)

Fire Maidens: Ireland (Book 5)

Aloha Shifters - Jewels of the Heart

Lure of the Dragon (Book 1)

Lure of the Wolf (Book 2)

Lure of the Bear (Book 3)

Lure of the Tiger (Book 4)

Love of the Dragon (Book 5)

Lure of the Fox (Book 6)

Aloha Shifters - Pearls of Desire

Rebel Dragon (Book 1)

Rebel Bear (Book 2)

Rebel Lion (Book 3)

Rebel Wolf (Book 4)

Rebel Heart (A prequel to Book 5)

Rebel Alpha (Book 5)

The Wolves of Twin Moon Ranch

Desert Hunt (the Prequel)

Desert Moon (Book 1)

Desert Wolf: Complete Collection (Four short stories)

Desert Blood (Book 2)

Desert Fate (Book 3)

Desert Heart (Book 4)

Desert Yule (a short story)

Desert Rose (Book 5)

Desert Roots (Book 6)

Sasquatch Surprise (a Twin Moon spin-off story)

Blue Moon Saloon

Perfection (a short story prequel)

Damnation (Book 1)

Temptation (Book 2)

Redemption (Book 3)

Salvation (Book 4)

Deception (Book 5)

Celebration (a holiday treat)

Shifters in Vegas

Paranormal romance with a zany twist

Gambling on Trouble

Gambling on Her Dragon

Gambling on Her Bear

Serendipity Adventure Romance

Off the Charts

Uncharted

Entangled

Windswept

Adrift

Travel Romance

Veiled Fantasies

Island Fantasies

visit www.annalowebooks.com

About the Author

USA Today and Amazon bestselling author Anna Lowe loves putting the "hero" back into heroine and letting location ignite a passionate romance. She likes a heroine who is independent, intelligent, and imperfect – a woman who is doing just fine on her own. But give the heroine a good man – not to mention a chance to overcome her own inhibitions – and she'll never turn down the chance for adventure, nor shy away from danger.

Anna loves dogs, sports, and travel – and letting those inspire her fiction. On any given weekend, you might find her hiking in the mountains or hunched over her laptop, working on her latest story. Either way, the day will end with a chunk of dark chocolate and a good read.

Visit AnnaLoweBooks.com

Made in the USA
Coppell, TX
12 November 2021